D1500708

Book Cover Design by Brian Hickey

Summary: A narrator recounts the comical experiences of a 12 year old boy growing up on the small island of Bell Island, Newfoundland in 1985. Brian relates the many colloquialisms of this small community in the colourful ways he used to escape the many chores set by his father.

ISBN: (Print)
ISBN: (Online)

[1. Fiction – Newfoundland and Labrador. 2. Fathers and Sons – Newfoundland & Labrador. 3. Young men – Family Relationships - Newfoundland and Labrador. 4. Bell Island – Newfoundland & Labrador]

For Marilee ♥ ♥ ♥

July 19, 2023

Michelle,

Thank you for your support. All the best!

Brian H

CONTENTS

PROLOGUE

It's Friday night, July – 2015 and my girlfriend's two boys have been waiting since summer holidays began, for their Mother and I to camp out with them over night in the back yard. I've never enjoyed sleeping outside; I think that it's insane that people freely give up their comfy bed to sleep on the ground in a nylon tent. In fact, this is exactly why I went to school, got a job and work hard every day; so that I don't have to sleep outside. Some campsites even charge you money to sleep outside; can you imagine, charging you for the privilege of sleeping on the ground? I've often wondered how homeless people feel about that.

My 10 year old nephew Spencer is also staying with us for the summer. He gets along wonderfully with the boys as they all have a lot of similar interests, such as video games, Star Wars and tormenting the crap out of me. The boys have spent the better part of the day setting up their tent. They have packed themselves a snack and have their little hearts set on tonight's camp out. I guess I have no other choice than to take the puck-in-the-head for the team; grab a couple of bottles of wine for me and the missus, and freeze my ass off in a sleeping bag tonight. I'm not happy about it, but I guess you gotta do what you gotta do.

My spouses name is Marilee, the love of my life, and we live

together with her two sons, Zachary and Cole, who are 12 and 10 respectively. The four of us were all born and raised on Bell Island; a small Island 9 miles long and 3 miles wide, in the middle of Conception Bay, in the picturesque Province of Newfoundland & Labrador. We live about a 20 minute Ferry ride from the city of St. John's, the capital city of Newfoundland and Labrador. The boys
are really good kids, smart, kind and caring, but they can't seem to be away from their video games for more than five minutes. Especially the youngest Cole, I can honestly foresee a gathering of his family and friends in the near future, as we conduct some type of half-assed video game intervention.

We've promised the boys that we will camp out with them tonight under one condition; there are no video games allowed. All we will have is a flashlight and our imaginations to entertain us.

The boys reluctantly agree and so we all head out into the tent, with just a small camp fire burning outside to keep us company. As the boys finish up with their snacks and hot chocolate, Zachary asks me what kind of things I liked to do when I was his age. I assured him that there were no video games to play and we certainly didn't have the luxury of being escorted by our parents to our weekly soccer or softball games. We certainly were not afforded weekly trips to St. John's for swimming lessons or karate practice. We organized our own games and orchestrated our own fun. We created our own entertainment, which in turn shaped our identities and produced wonderful memories that would last a lifetime.

Zachary asked me to tell him more about the sorts of things we used to do. So I took him back to a simpler time, before computers and video games; a time when you could simply go outside and enjoy the sun, without your Mom drowning you in Sun-screen.

A time before baby seats in cars and kids being required to wear seatbelts because quite frankly, we weren't considered "too precious" to go flying through the windshield with the rest of

the family! A time when bicycle
helmets were not mandatory and you didn't have to lock your
door at night and your friends and neighbours would keep an
eye on you just as closely as your own parents. I took the boys
back to the summer of 1985 when I was 12 years old, full of life
and wonder, with the hopes of showing them how growing up
on Bell Island back then, was very different than it is today.

.

1

The Last Day of School

My name is Brian Hickey, better known to my friends as Hickey-Dickey or Gonzo from the Muppet Show, but I will get to that later. I am a scraggly, 12 year old boy from Bell Island, Newfoundland. I am currently in grade Seven and I attend the Catholic High School, St. Michael's. Our school has classrooms ranging from grades Seven through Twelve, so although I may only be 12, I share the halls and School bus with kids 18, 19 and even 20 years old.

I know what you're thinking and yes, you're right, this has been one rough and death-defying year for me. However, that's all about to change because today is the day that I have been dreaming about all year long. It is Friday, June 21^{st,} 1985, or more importantly............. The last day of School!

I eagerly jumped down from the top bunk of our bunk-beds that my younger brother and I shared, anticipating the final day of the school year. I glanced down at the bottom bunk and said, "Get up Jason, it's the last day of school", as I began riffling through my dresser for some clothes. My brother Jason was two and a half years younger than me. He was a very quiet kid, who followed orders and demanded little, but he appeared less excited this morning than I.

"Come on," I said, "hurry up and get dressed, we only have a half day at school and then we are off for the summer".

He got out of bed and stood there sleepily, showing no sign of emotion or exuberance.

I asked, "Well….. aren't you excited?

He just yawned, scratched his arse and farted, all the while sporting a morning boner. He was obviously excited about something, so I quickly finished getting dressed, got the hell out of there and made my way to the kitchen for some breakfast.

"Good morning Family", I shouted, as I met my Dad and older brother who were already sitting at the table, eating breakfast.

I reached for the giant, plastic bag of Puff Wheat cereal. You remember the ones; the industrial size bag of plain white oat cereal that took two full grown men to help pour one bowl, and when you added milk, they shrunk and shrivelled up to nothing and cost about a dollar fifty for a 20 pound sack! "You would think that since this is the last day of school that we could celebrate with Honey Combs or Fruit loops or something good?" I said sarcastically. "Eat them or eat nothing", Dad snapped, "And be thankful there's breakfast here for you at all." "I'm only kidding", I said.

I knew that Honey Combs and Fruit Loops were too extravagant for our finances. Every once and while, if they were on sale and there was extra money, we might get them, but for the most part it was Puff Wheats or Corn Flakes. Sometimes, on rare occasions during Tax-Return Season, Mom and Dad would go to the grocery store and bring back those mini, multipacks of cereal and we would lose our minds. Remember those; there were 8 different types of cereal to choose from and each box would fill one bowl. When these were brought home, we would all fight over who was going to get what box the next morning. I wouldn't be left out, so I would drink 3-5 glasses of water before I went to bed, that way when I woke up 4 O'clock in the morning to use the bathroom, I could pick out what cereal I wanted and sit and eat it in peace in the early hours of the morning.

My Mom was standing at the counter with a pair of underwear on her head, which of course meant she was preparing to bake her delicious homemade bread. I never fully understood the correlation between baking bread and wearing underwear on your head, I guess it had something to do with baking hygiene. Still, pretty ridiculous looking if you asked me.

I remember one morning when Mom was baking bread, and

it was Provincial Election time in Newfoundland and Labrador. Our local Member of the House of Assembly came knocking on the door looking for votes and Mom stood there in the porch talking to him with a pair of her underwear on her head. She even poured him up a cup of tea and her and Dad chatted with him for over 15 minutes and she didn't realize her mistake until after he left our house. Of course, once Dad pointed out her little error, she was embarrassed to tears.

"Don't worry about it", Dad told her, trying to comfort her.

"It could have been worse, imagine if you had been wearing a pair of my ragged, crap-stained drawers on your head"!

All I knew was that there were two reasons to look forward to Fridays; first there was the fact that it was the last day of the school week and the weekend was just around the corner. Secondly, was because every Friday morning Mom was elbow deep in dough, magically creating fresh toutons and warm, buttery bread. That woman religiously baked 8 loaves of homemade bread every single Friday morning. That adds up to an amazing 416 loaves of yummy, homemade goodness every year. Dad used to joke that we ate so much bread that we were going to crap doughboys.

Before I go any further, let me try to impress upon you how important Mom is to our family. Her name is Mary and she is not only our wonderful Mother but our maid, cook, nurse and perhaps most importantly; peace-keeper. She is the only person standing in the way of Dad killing us- especially me. I witnessed my Mom mop more floors, clean more dishes, wash more dirty laundry and wipe away more tears than any one person should ever be asked to do. On several occasions, I've even called upon her to perform the Heimlich maneuver on me, after I got a chicken bone lodged in my throat from wolfing down one of her many delicious dinners.

Mom gave a lot and asked for very little in return. She was a church going lady who never drank or smoked or gossiped. She never liked to hear people talk negatively about others and there wasn't a bad bone in her body. The only time she really left the house was to go to the Community Bingo every Thursday night with some of her lady friends. She would never lay a finger on us, as she left the disciplining to Dad, but whenever we disobeyed her or pissed her off, she would simply say, "Just wait until your father get's home from work"!

The moment Mom threatened to tell the old man on us, we knew we had pushed her too far and had to do some tremendous back-paddling and sucking up to win Mom back over. Overall, Mom is a Saintly woman and we all loved her very much.

"What are you so chipper about this morning", Dad asked me, as he buttered his toast?

"Oh nothing", I replied, "I'm just looking forward to this beautiful day".

Dad's eyes glanced at the rain beating off the window and then he started in on one of his rants.

"What in the name of God, are you talkin' about my Son", he yelled, "It's pissin' down rain outside? Not hard to tell it's the last day of school; I usually need the jaws-of-life to pry you out of bed, but this morning you come prancing out of your bedroom, you wouldn't know be-Jesus if you were Gene Kelly."

"But that will all end after today because school is finished for the year and now the real work begins," he said with a gleam in his eye.

"There are 15 cords of wood outside and I need it all sawed up and packed in the shed for the winter. We have tonnes of hay to cut over the next two months and plenty of vegetables to harvest. The cows need to be milked, the eggs need to collected, the pigs need to be fed and watered everyday and I want that barn kept spotless!"

I just sat there quietly, eating my breakfast and as Dad rambled on, I simply drifted away to my Happy Place. Now, before I go any further, I think it is crucial that I tell you about my Happy Place, especially since I spent so much of my young life there. Whenever I felt bored, threatened, stressed or alone I would drift off to my mystical, magical perfect world that I had created inside my head, known as my Happy Place.

In essence, it was my way of turning off my brain and escaping from reality to a place where no one could bother me and I was in charge. It was a place filled with wonderful times and memories, where I was God's gift to women. In my Happy Place, I was always the underdog hero and there were no chores to do and Elvis tunes were constantly playing in the background. It's how I coped with life and it made the mundane and monotonous; bearable. I've always been a bit of a dreamer and my Happy Place provided me with an escape to live out my wildest fantasies in my undisturbed Utopia.

But like everything else, all good things must eventually come to an end.

"Are you listening to me"? Dad shouted, as I drifted back to reality.

"Get your head out of your arse My Son and pay attention," he shouted louder.

Ah my Dad. George Hickey; I think he was at his happiest whenever he was roaring at someone. He loved to yell and shout, but already at the age of 12, I was smart enough to know that his bark was much worse than his bite.

I affectionately called him Georgio and this nickname was catching on because some of my friends were starting to call him Georgio as well. He also had a knack for making up words and phrases such as 'windsucker', 'funsil of a knobgobbler' and perhaps my favourite, 'that cursed-jingles rogue is on the whore-racket'. We referred to these made-up phrases as *Georgeyisms* and although they made little sense, you still managed to get the gist of what he was trying to say.

Nevertheless, his comical word usage aside, if I had learned anything over the years it was to never interrupt or backtalk the old man. So I just let him bellow on until he ran out of steam.

Dad was an extremely hard worker. Not only did he work 40 hours a week as a janitor at the local hospital, but he also raised his own livestock, grew his own vegetables and cut his own firewood. He was no stranger to working an eighteen hour day and now with summer holidays looming, he was looking forward to getting a lot of free labour out of his sons.

I didn't really worry about it however, for sitting next to me was my older brother Paul. He was 14 years old and quite literally, a work horse. As long as I'd known him, Paul was never one for watching TV, goofing around or slacking off, he actually enjoyed working.

I can remember him changing the tires on Dad's old, brown Dodge at age 9 and using Dad's chainsaw as early as the age of 10. Here I am 12 years old and I can barely lift the chainsaw. How many times have I seen the worst kind of winter storm, with the wind howling and snow blowing to the point where you couldn't see 10 feet in front of you? It was during these storms that Paul would pace back and forth the house like a caged animal because he couldn't get outside. To make matters worse, in the middle of the storm, he would say, "Brian we should go outside and dig a path from the house to the wood-shed." Dad of course would overhear this and look at me with a smile as I glanced at him with panic in my face. "That sounds like a good idea", Dad would say, "Get on your snowsuit Brian and help Paul dig a path to the wood-shed. You might as well shovel out the driveway while you're at it." Damn, Damn, Damn, what the hell was wrong with Paul? Here I was on a cold, stormy winters night, all snug and comfortable in my pajamas, happily watching "The A-Team" and now I have to get dressed up and shovel snow, all because Paul can't sit still for a couple of hours. Normally I would protest but Paul handles so many chores that Dad might retaliate by making me go outside and do it all myself.   Yes Sir, Paul was the oldest; the most relied upon and would undoubtedly handle the lion's share of the chores during our summer holidays.

Of course, any duties that were assigned to me, I could always reassign to my younger brother, Jason. You see, Dad worked from Monday to Friday at the hospital, so although he assigned each of us particular duties, he never really knew who was doing what. For about the past 2 years I have been blackmailing Jason into doing most of my chores.

It all started one day when I was supposed to be babysitting him, but I couldn't find him anywhere in the house. Jason was only 7 years old at the time and as I looked around for him, I yelled out his name, until finally I could hear him giggling in Mom's and Dad's bedroom. I assumed he was just playing hide and seek, but when I snuck into the bedroom, I was shocked to find him going through one of Dad's adult magazines, or Skin-books, as we used to call them.

I yelled at him, and made it seem like it was a much bigger deal than it really was. By the time I was finished with him, poor ole Jason thought he was going to be in more trouble than he could possibly imagine. However, I promised him that I would never tell Mom or Dad, just as long as he did a few of my chores for me.

Here we are, two years later and I am still holding it over Jason's head, and as soon as he refuses one of my many commands, all I have to do is to say the word 'skin-book' and he reluctantly agrees.

I keep telling myself that blackmail is an awesome power, but I must try to use it sparingly.......(*yeah right*). Therefore, with regards to my share of this summer's workload, I felt as though I had all my ducks in a row and was quite satisfied that between Paul the work horse, and Jason the pervert, I should be able to keep my summer duties to the bare minimum.

We all gathered at the bus stop waiting for the bus, just as we have done every morning. Today however, was a little different. Although it was raining, everyone seemed a lot happier, friendlier and much more energetic. For some of the older kids, it was the last day of grade 12, which meant the last day they would ever step foot inside St. Michael's School. For others who maybe struggled with this year's curriculum, there was a real concerned look in their faces.

Some prayed out loud, "Oh God, I hope I passed that exam," while others stood there quietly, knowing that they would have their test scores soon enough. There was no sense in worrying about the inevitable.

I immediately sought out my best buddy Al Rees, just as I

have done every day for as long as I could remember. Since the age of three, I have been hanging around with Al. We were not only neighbours, but also have been in the same class since kindergarten, and got into a lot of mischief together. If I trusted anyone on God's green earth it was Al. We were partners in crime, thick as thieves and I was more than happy to be the Robin to his Batman.

Al was as foolish as an odd sock and you never knew what he was going to say next. He had a certain way about him; very likable and funny, nothing ever seemed to bother him and he never got upset about anything. Al was also very hairy. In fact back in Grade 4, he was the only kid in our class photo with a moustache. Now in grade 7, Al was even hairier, sporting sideburns and a full chest of hair protruding out from beneath his shirt collar. The older boys would tease him by saying his mother must have had sex with a Sasquatch, but Al just laughed it off, as if somehow he was impervious to their insults. He was also extremely skinny for a kid his age and unfortunately this only made his body hair even more evident. It was due to his hairy and skinny physique that the older boys had nicknamed him Super Grover.

"How's it going Al? I asked, "Are you all ready for the summer holidays"?

"You know it, buddy," he responded. "I'm looking forward to staying up late and sleeping in like crazy".

That was another thing about Al, as long as I'd known him he had always been a night owl, which in turn made him lazy and sleepy during the day. A couple of weeks ago he came to the bus stop one morning, and I noticed some weird yellow gunk all over his ear. It looked like he had a bad ear infection and when I pointed it out to him, he rubbed his ear only to discover it was covered in egg yolk. Apparently, he had fallen asleep, face down in his breakfast that morning.

Al was also known for pulling off power naps on the bus ride to and from our school. About two months ago he fell asleep on the bus ride home from school and we managed to get every student on the bus to quiet down and let him sleep. The poor guy missed his stop and rode the bus all around Bell Island and was the last person left on the bus.   When he didn't come home that evening, his parents frantically called the school looking for him, until finally around 8:00 that night he was found, still sleeping like a baby in the back of the bus. The bus driver thought the bus was empty and didn't notice Al sleeping in the back seat. So he just parked the bus and locked it up for the evening.

When Al Rees says he is looking forward to sleeping in, he isn't kidding. Anyone who knew Al understood that during the school year, if you wanted to talk to him on the weekend, it was useless to even phone him before 3pm, because most likely he was still in bed.

As the bus pulled up, I hesitantly boarded, but quickly scouted around for a safe seat. The bus can be a breathing ground for bullies and this past year alone, I have been beaten up, thrown under a seat, had my head sat on and stabbed in the ribs with a hair brush.

Back in October, on the bus ride home after school, a poor kid from the eighth grade had his pants totally torn off by some older kids and thrown out the bus window, forcing him to ride all the way home in his tidy-whitey underwear. Unfortunately, all the commotion of tearing the pants off this kid must have upset his stomach and made him have an accident because now the back of his underwear looked like a Picasso painting. Poor kid, from that day on he would forever be known as Skidmarks.

Today the kids on the bus were particularly aggressive and energetic. The atmosphere was extremely loud, people were throwing things and you could tell that the bus driver was losing his patience. Al and I were lucky enough to get a seat near the front of the bus, just behind Skidmarks. He wasn't the most popular kid on the bus, but at least he wasn't a psycho, like some of these other big idiots.

"Did you watch Johnny Carson last night?" Al asked me as the bus pulled ahead.

Now keep in mind, *The Tonight Show*, starring Johnny Carson did not air on television until 1:00 AM, and because it was a school night, Dad made me go to bed at 9:30 - just as he did every school night.

"Nah", I replied, "I fell asleep after *Magnum P.I.*".
We both knew I was lying and that I wasn't allowed to stay up that late, but as always, Al was satisfied with my answer and passed on the opportunity to make fun of my early bed curfew.

"Oh man, Carson was awesome last night." He continued, "He had Springsteen on, singing a tune from his *Born in the USA* album. Then he had Michael J. Fox on, talking about his new movie, *Back To The Future*".

I never fully understood how someone, who was my age and lived only 2 houses away, had such a grasp on, and was light-years ahead of me, when it came to music, movies and television. It must have been due to the fact that he had three older siblings who, undoubtedly, had an influence on what he watched and listened to. Also, when you consider the fact that he was awake and watching television every morning until 2 AM, he was really exposed to a different pop culture, not normally experienced by the average 12 year old. I mean; here I am still watching Circle-Square Ranch and the only songs I knew were Elvis songs that Mom would play on her record player. Al, on the other hand, could write a biography on The E-Street Band, and was watching late night documentaries about Hitler and the Second World War. How I envied him for being permitted to stay up so late.

"That *Back to the Future* movie should be good," I responded.
"The trailer looks amazing and Michael J. Fox is pretty funny."

As the bus pulled into the school parking lot, I could see the other buses dropping off the rest of the students from other parts of our community. This was always a little frightening and overwhelming to me. Sure, there were big kids and hoodlums on my bus, but I could recognize who they are. They are from my neighbourhood, the East End of Bell Island. Some of the kids on my bus may be hard cases, but at the end of the day, you knew them and more importantly, you knew their parents, and you could take a certain amount of comfort in that.

At least the idiots on our bus were OUR idiots from OUR neighbourhood. We may sometimes fight amongst ourselves and call each other names but that's ok, because we are East Enders. Let someone from another part of the Island try that same crap and you could rest assured that a fellow East Ender would have your back.

Growing up on Bell Island was an interesting dichotomy to observe from a distance. The main and perhaps biggest divide, pitted kids from our Catholic school, (St. Michael's) against kids from the Protestant school (St. Boniface), as we competed against each other in an annual all-out-war soccer and hockey rivalry.

Besides the school rivalries, you also had your territorial contentions as East Enders would quarrel with kids from The Green, who fought with kids from West Mines, who disliked kids on The Ridge. All were very territorial and yet if someone from St. John's or some other community talked trash about Bell Island, all Bell Islanders would get their backs up and come together as one.

As I've mentioned, the older kids from the other buses were all anonymous to me and they used their unfamiliarity to harass and intimidate you because they realized that, for the most part, they were unidentifiable to a scared 12 year old.

I tried not to make eye contact with them as I made my way to the school and I whispered to Al, "Thank God some of these big arseholes will be graduating this year so we won't have to deal with them again in September."

The chaos continued into the classroom, so much so that our homeroom teacher, Mr. Miller, had difficulty maintaining order. At least in our classroom, we understood each other, we were all the same age, and we had all known each other for the past 7 years. Most of us were good friends and we realized that after today, we wouldn't see each other again until September. I think we all really enjoyed being together but we were entering our teens and everything was changing. The influences and peer pressures from the older students were forcing us to grow up much faster than many of us had wanted.

But for right now, as long as we were all together, we could still hang on to our childhood and our innocence for just a little while longer. At our age and amongst each other, there was some, but not too much pressure to be cool and the thought of drugs or sex were still foreign to the majority of us. We didn't have to pretend to be something we weren't, and we could still enjoy the fact that we were kids.

Again, Miller called for order but we continuously ignored his requests to settle down, until finally he slammed a stack of report cards down on his desk and shouted.
"If you all don't sit down and shut up, I won't be giving out these friggin' report cards and I swear to God and Sunny Jesus that we will all stay here until six o'clock this evening".

He wasn't joking, not only was he known for wearing the same old, ugly brown suit every day, he was also heralded as the king of detention and last day of school be damned, he would relish the opportunity of making the whole class stay late and walk home - just for the hell of it.

He also wasn't opposed to giving you a good crack upside the head, if the mood struck him. In fact, several times this year he had given me a few shots for interrupting his class with "smart ass" remarks. He was also a deadly shot with a piece of chalk. He would catch you not paying attention in class and snipe your ass with a piece of chalk from 30 feet away. After more than 20 years of teaching, Mr. Miller was like John Wayne with a piece of chalk.

It's true what they used to say; only in the Catholic School system do the Nuns and teachers have the God-given right to smack the crap out of their students. And if there was any indication that God wasn't present on a particular day at St. Michael's School, you could always count on one of the Nuns or Mr. Miller to deliver God's wrath for him, in his absence.

Miller himself was a God fearing Catholic who was

also known to enjoy the occasional alcoholic beverage. Consequently, during lunch period it wasn't uncommon to find his car parked outside of one of Bell Island's many local taverns, as he enjoyed a liquid-lunch, undoubtedly unwinding from a hectic morning of throwing chalk and flinging disparagements at his students.

I can only assume that it was for this very reason that our beloved teacher was aptly nicknamed Miller Lite. It was often said about Miller that he had so much alcohol in his system, that if he was ever to be cremated, he would burn for at least six weeks.

"Okay, good morning and listen up people", he started.

"As you all know, today is the last day and I am left with the task of handing out your report cards. But before I do that, I wanted to say what a pleasure it has been to teach you all this past year. I know the transition from the elementary school to the high school can be a difficult one, but I have to say, you guys have grown a lot throughout the year."

What was this; a piece of civility from old Miller Lite? Could it be I had been wrong about him and in reality he was just a misunderstood, educating genius? His uncharacteristic, pleasant disposition left him vulnerable and I was having difficulty restraining my exuberance. I knew it was only a matter of time before I would once again take a comedic jab at old man Miller.

"Anyway", he continued, "I just wanted to remind everyone that right about now, Sister Grace is making her rounds from class to class to say a final prayer to keep you all safe this summer. Before she gets here, I wanted to tell everyone to please be careful this summer, be smart and think before you do anything stupid."

"I've been a teacher on Bell Island for the past 22 years and have witnessed entirely too many serious accidents and fatalities of students over summer holidays. God knows we don't need to suffer any tragedies over our summer break."

"Also, as you all enter adolescence, life will get a lot more complicated, so before this happens, I have asked God to grant me one wish. Would anyone like to venture a guess as to what that wish might be?" He looked expectantly at the students.

I could no longer contain myself and without thinking I shouted out, "A new suit and a case of beer"?

The class erupted into hysterical laughter. I knew that with every single giggle and snicker, Mr. Miller's blood pressure would only climb higher and higher.

The only question now was, did I push him too far, or will he simply laugh it off?

"No Smartass," he yelled, as he ripped a piece of chalk off my chest.

"I wish that you guys spend your summer playing and hanging out and doing the things that kids your age are supposed to do. You guys are quickly becoming young men and young women so you'd better enjoy your youth while you still can."

Hmmm, that was pretty cool, I thought to myself, as I contemplated for a moment what Miller had said. Suddenly I felt a sharp, searing sting in my shoulder and the class again erupted into laughter as I realized that he had hurled another piece of chalk at me from the front of the class.

"Anything else you want to say Hickey?" Miller asked.

"No Sir," I responded. "I only hope that you and your family have a wonderful summer." We both grinned at each other as I sat there rubbing my chest and shoulder.

After a sequence of delicate knockings on our classroom door, in walked 82 year old Sister Grace. She was a wonderful Nun, an outstanding teacher and the whole school seemed to love her. She was different from the rest of the Nuns. She would never smack you or embarrass you in front of your friends. She was a very kind lady and in my opinion, she was the quintessential Nun who represented what all Nuns were supposed to be like.

Unfortunately the other Nuns were nothing like Sister Grace. The other Nuns would take the strap to you or beat your knuckles with a wooden ruler just to put the fear of God in you.

In my Happy Place, I would often daydream that these Nuns were actually Ninjas and not really Nuns at all. They were hired assassins, sent down by Jesus to kick the crap out of any student participating in blasphemous or sacrilegious activities. They crept around the school in their long, black ninja attire, using stealth and lethal cunning to catch some poor oblivious student who may have inadvertently taken the Lord's name in vain. They were professionally trained in hand to hand combat and were well skilled, highly educated poetic warriors. With cat-like reflexes, they would pull out a wooden ruler from inside their sleeve and wielded it like a ninja sword. With uncanny precision and accuracy, the unaware student would feel the sting of the wooden ruler upon his knuckles or ass. The Nuns all wore a set of Rosary prayer beads around their necks and hanging from the beads was a crucifix. I imagined that the beads were also a weapon in disguise, as it allowed a Nun to sneak up on an ignorant student, slip the prayer beads around his neck and choke him out; quietly and efficiently. If a student ever tried to make a run for it, the pursuing Nun would simply detach the crucifix from her prayer beads, fling it like a ninja-star and take that escaping student down.

Ah, but Sister Grace was different and I knew her personally, as I am an Altar-Boy and I would see her in Church every Saturday Night. She looked after the School's library and taught grade 11 and 12 English courses. I had spoken to her several times and she was extremely intelligent and sprightly for someone her age. In fact, her only flaw was that she was incredibly hard of hearing and whenever you had a conversation with her, you were forced to literally yell at her.

I even heard the older kids say that, while in the classroom, it wasn't uncommon for her to keep on teaching, even after the bell rang to end class. She simply didn't hear that well and that of course left the door wide open for some kids to have a bit of fun with her.

There was this one kid, Brad from grade 10, who really enjoyed tormenting her. Earlier this year, I got sent to the Library as punishment for misbehaving in class. Being sent to the Library was for an offence not deemed serious enough to be sent to the Principal's office. It was similar to being sent to a juvenile detention center instead of prison, where as a substitute for doing hard-time, you would be sentenced to help Sister Grace organize the library, or sit and read quietly.

There were a few older kids there for basically the same reasons as me and Brad was one them. There were about 7 of us in total and Sister Grace told everyone to sit quietly and read a book and reflect on why we were being punished. After a short while, Brad raised his hand and when Sister Grace finally acknowledged him he shouted,

"Sister, may I please be excused to play with my penis in the washroom"? Everyone in the library burst out laughing.

"Pardon" she said softly, "Please speak up".

Brad just smiled and said even louder, "May I leave to spank my monkey in the washroom"?

Again the entire library broke out into a fit of laughter. She looked around at everyone, getting a little annoyed, wondering why we were all laughing.

Finally she walked right up to Brad, face to face and asked, "what is it you want Brad?"

Brad just smiled and politely asked if he could go to the washroom.

"Of course," responded Sister Grace, "go right ahead."

As Brad was leaving the library, he turned to Sister Grace and shouted, "If you'd like to join me Sister, I'll be in the second stall".

Once again, laughter sounded throughout the library and Sister Grace approached me wondering what Brad had said before he left.

"Oh nothing Sister", I shouted to her, "Brad just said he will be back in 2 minutes". She just smiled and returned back to her seat.

"Alright, everyone listen up and give Sister Grace your full attention", shouted Mr. Miller. "She would like to have a short prayer with you before we start our summer holidays."

Mr. Miller rolled his eyes and folded his arms as he let Sister Grace take over his class. He was fully aware that with Sister Grace, there was no such thing as a short prayer; in fact it was widely thought that she could out-preach anyone. She loved to tell stories from the Bible and quote scripture. Every now and then I would ask her a religious question, just to keep her on her toes.

One day, just before Christmas holidays, I asked her, "How many different animals Moses took with him, when he built his Ark?"

She insisted that he took a male and female of every species on his Ark. I told her I didn't think that she was right, but she was very adamant that Moses took two of every type of animal in the world, as it is contained in the Bible in chapters 6–9 of the book of Genesis.

"That's odd." I said, quite pleased with myself. "I always thought that it was NOAH who took animals on the Ark."

She found this very cute and amusing and as a result, I now had Sister Grace on my side, which was very important, since she carried so much weight in everyday School decisions.

"Good morning everyone", she said in her little voice, "Is everyone excited to be going on summer holidays"?

"Yes Sister", the whole class responded.

"Well", she continued, "I just wanted to remind everyone that I fully expect to see you at Church either Saturday night or Sunday morning throughout the summer. Just because we are on vacation from School, does not mean that we are on vacation from the Lord".

Everyone laughed along as Sister Grace chuckled to herself over her little joke.

"Now", she continued, "I would like everyone to stand as we will say the *Our Father* and a *Hail Mary*, to look after us, to protect us and to keep us safe over our Holidays".

As we began to stand, I noticed my buddy Paddy, who sits

directly in front of me, already had a snicker on his face. Paddy was a very shy and quiet guy, but for some strange reason he always fell into a fit of laughter at the most inappropriate times. He was one of those guys who would laugh during a funeral and the harder he tried to make himself stop laughing, the worst he got.

As we stood by our desks and prepared to start our prayers, I whispered to Paddy, "Hey buddy you'd better be careful, I heard Sister Grace has been eyeing you and wants to take a ride on your baloney-pony".

While the rest of us were reciting the *Our Father,* Paddy was busy biting his bottom lip, turning blood red, trying with all of his might not to laugh. A few giggles managed to slip through his tightly clasped lips and as the prayer continued, the whole class was looking in Paddy's direction, just waiting for him to burst. By now, Sister Grace could see the silly smirk on Paddy's face and as everyone continued with the prayer, she walked across the classroom and positioned herself directly in front of Paddy, giving him the evil-eye as he continued to struggle.

As we finished with the Lord's Prayer, we were about to start on the *Hail Mary* and I could see that Paddy was already regaining his composure.

This was no good, I thought to myself, it's the last day of school and I won't get to mess with Paddy anymore until September. I needed something funny, perhaps sexual in nature, to push him over the edge. I could see that a few of our classmates who were standing closest to us were all counting on me to make something happen.

God Bless them all, they worked so hard this year and deserved a final laugh to bring this school year to a close. So as the prayer began, I leaned slightly towards Paddy and whispered to him an improvised, poetic version of the Hail Mary Prayer:

Hail Mary, Sister Grace
pulled up her dress
and sat on my face.

Only a few kids could hear my verse change, but it was enough to send Paddy into hysterics. His outburst of spit and laughter resembled a bursting pipe as he very nearly drowned Sister Grace. It was a scandalous site indeed, Sister Grace just stood there mortified and shocked as she pulled some tissue from her sleeve to wipe Paddy's spit from her face.

The classroom fell deathly quiet, the prayer came to an abrupt halt and both Miller and Sister Grace just glared at Paddy in disbelief as he stood there wiping his mouth, still unable to stop sniggering.

Not accustomed to this level of insolence and sacrilegious behaviour, Sister Grace grabbed Paddy by the ear and dragged him out of the classroom and slammed the door behind them, but you could still hear Paddy laughing his ass off, all the way down the hall to the Principal's Office.

"What the Hell got into Paddy?" Miller screamed.

"Hickey, did you have anything to do with that outburst"?

"No Sir", I insisted, "I have no idea why he was laughing". I knew Miller didn't believe me, but since he couldn't prove anything, I felt I was in the clear. I did, however, feel bad for Paddy. Poor guy, it's a hard lesson to learn but as in nature, high school lived by the golden rule; survival of the fittest, and poor Paddy was just another innocent causality. As unfair as it may seem, in order for chaos, anarchy and overall juvenile behaviour to exist in the classroom; someone must always take the puck-in-the-head for the team, and for once, I was just glad that I wasn't part of the collateral damage.

"Well, it doesn't look like Sister Grace is coming back." Miller announced.

"I guess it's time I give out these report cards. To prevent any further anxiety, I will tell you that out of a class of 28 students, nobody failed this year, however there were a few students who just barely scraped by. I tried to keep in mind that this year was your first experience at the High School and that you are all small fish in a big pond, when I was correcting your exams. I went easy on some of you, but I will warn you that next year, your grade 8 teacher will not be as generous with their marks as I have been. "Many of you are capable of doing much better than what you have done this year and I urge you to work harder next year."

I was starting to lose interest in what Miller was saying. I gazed out the classroom window and I could see that the rain had stopped and the sun was starting to shine. Once again I started daydreaming about sleeping in, ball games, barbeques, and enjoying the warm weather. Miller was rambling on about academic achievement, while I was fantasizing about the great outdoors and how much fun I was going to have over the next ten weeks.

My daydreaming came to an abrupt end when a piece of chalk ricocheted off Al's desk and Miller yelled, "Wake up Sleeping Beauty; this is the last time you will fall asleep in my class".

The entire class laughed as Al sat up after being awakened from his midmorning nap.

"As I call out your name, please come forward to receive your report cards and then go quietly to the hall and clean out your lockers, class is dismissed".

Mr. Miller began calling out his students names in alphabetical order and the volume level in the hall was increasing tremendously, as students from all grades were making their way out of class. When Miller called my name, I walked towards him and shook his hand.

He grinned and said, "your marks are very good Hickey, but you are somewhat of a disruption in class. Just to let you know, you didn't get away with as much as you think you did this past year. I let a lot of your foolishness and silly comments slide because of your age and the fact that you have a playful, well-meaning manner about you, as opposed to a defying or insolent one. And I also know, God-damned well, that you said something questionable to get poor ole Paddy into trouble this morning. Keep in mind, your behaviour doesn't interfere with your test scores, but it does affect those students around you, who have to work harder than you. You may want to think about that throughout the summer".

As he handed me my report card I thanked him and responded, "I will certainly consider that in the future Sir". I walked out of the classroom, I quickly cleaned out my locker and headed out to the school parking lot.

As I took my seat at the front of the bus, I couldn't help but think about what Miller Lite had told me. Could it be that I was responsible for some kids not doing as well as they could have in class? I always knew that goofing off and shit-disturbing inevitably led to someone getting into trouble, but I had never considered the kids who had a harder time learning and catching on. I certainly didn't want to be responsible for one of my friends having to repeat a grade because of my shenanigans. This was very disconcerting to me indeed and I knew I would give it a lot of consideration over the summer and ultimately throughout my entire High School tenure.

This life changing epiphany would have to be further explored at another time because a Grade 12 student, Lenny, just cracked me on the head with one of his books.

"How's it going Hickey-Dickey", he asked, "Did you pass"?

I hadn't even opened my report card yet out of fear of one of these Neanderthals grabbing it from me, discovering my scores and labelling me some kind of nerd. The truth of the matter was, I never had a problem with school, it came pretty easy to me and when I applied myself I could Ace any exam. "Yep", I responded, "I passed, how about you"?

"My exams were all Publics." Lenny said, "I won't get my marks until later this summer. Are you going down to Lahey's this evening?" I was amazed that Lenny was even speaking to me.

"Yeah," I said, "I'll be there."

As Lenny took his seat in the back of the bus, Al sat in the seat next to me, "How'd you do Buddy?" He asked.

I opened my report card took a quick glance and said, "I passed everything, but Miller commented that I am too much of a disruption in class. How did you do?"

Al checked his report card and said, "I passed everything too, but Miller commented that I am too tired in class and I need more energy". We both laughed at the comments as our bus pulled away from the school parking lot.

I couldn't help but notice that this particular bus ride home was completely opposite from every other bus ride home this past year. As I looked around I could see that the kids, who were normally quiet on the bus and had done well on their report cards, were now the kids that were making the most noise. They were celebrating and excited for their summer holidays and rightfully so. On the other hand, the usually loud-mouth kids and the trouble makers were uncharacteristically quiet. They seemed to be lamenting over their report cards as they had come to the realization that, while some of them would have to go to summer school, others would have to repeat their school year. You could see the sadness and disbelief in their eyes.

It was hard for me to feel sorry for them, as these were the same hooligans who made travelling on the bus for this past year a living hell for us younger students. But now, revenge is sweet as they are forced to make their way home to their parents and tell them the bad news and suffer whatever punishment may be delivered.

Meanwhile for me, as long as I can escape most of my chores and stay out of Georgio's way, I should be in for a pretty fun-filled summer.

2

The Players

Later that afternoon, I was enjoying a ride on Lahey's swing with Krissy, the youngest of the 6 Lahey children. The sun was now fully shining, and although you needed a summer jacket, the rain had dried up and it was a beautiful day.

Krissy was a year older than me and we had been next door neighbours and good friends for all my life. We liked to swing together and sing songs and it felt like the higher and faster you would swing, the louder and wilder the songs would get. It seemed like the entire East End of Bell Island liked to avail of the many resources in Lahey's yard.

Like ourselves and most families in our neighbourhood, the Lahey's were not rich folks, or at least not rich in the sense of monetary possessions. But they were certainly rich in generosity, patience and good-heartedness. Their Dad had built a swing set out of 5 inch steel pipe, which was anchored about 30 inches into the ground with cement. There were 4 swings hanging from the set and this acted as a gathering place and East End community playground for all the neighbouring kids. You could also find 3 or 4 bicycles standing neatly against their back porch, which too were used by many, as communal and public transportation.

If swinging or bike riding wasn't your thing, you only had to open their porch door and find the greatest collection of baseballs, bats, catching mitts, Frisbees, jumping ropes, footballs, soccer balls and other sports paraphernalia that one could possibly imagine. As I said, the Laheys were not a rich family, but each of them took great care in preserving and maintaining what little they had. It wasn't uncommon to find Gerald, the oldest son, busy stitching up the covers of old softballs and baseballs or re-sewing the threads on catching mitts with fishing line, just trying to prolong the life of their sporting equipment.

What amazed me the most was how they never seemed to mind whenever someone borrowed their stuff. As long as you returned it without damaging or destroying it, you could borrow whatever, and whenever you wanted, without even asking.

Often times, I tried to imagine some poor kid coming to my house, opening the door without knocking and taking my baseball glove or Jason's Frisbee, without asking. Dad would have chased them out of the yard with one of his hay prongs or sent our German Sheppard dog after them.

But the Lahey's were different, their yard was our hangout and I have witnessed, on many a warm summer's evening, 20-30 kids and teenagers all gathered in that yard, laughing and joking and being very loud. My God, the patience and restraint shown by Mr. And Mrs. Lahey was nothing short of outstanding. They must have patched up more cuts and scrapes, and iced down more bumps and black eyes than a General Practitioner. They were two of the easiest going, calm and pleasant people, you could ever hope to meet. I consider myself very lucky to have such great neighbours as the Laheys, a kinder, friendlier family, you will never find!

"How did you do on your report card today?" Krissy asked, breaking the silence.

"Good", I replied, "how about you"? "Oh, I did well," she responded. "Do you think any of the crowd will be coming around this evening"?

We both looked at each other and smiled. "I hope so." I replied. "Remember how much fun we all had last summer"?

Our conversation was disrupted by a crashing sound just outside the fence, on the lane. From my swing, I could see that

Krissy's brother Sam had toppled over on his bike.

Sam was a year and a half older than Krissy, and although very quiet and harmless, he proved to be a little awkward and clumsy. The fact that he was 14 and a half years old and had just fallen off his pedal bike, did not surprise me in the least. In fact, it was quite predictable.

"Are you alright Sam?" I shouted from the swing. "No problem Hickey," he replied as he laughed at loud.

Suddenly, I could see Dad's old brown Dodge coming up the lane. I knew it must be 4 O'Clock, since Dad was coming home from work and I also knew I would be called into supper very shortly. Dad stopped the car in front of Laheys and waited for Sam to get himself and his bike out of his way. After about 20 seconds, Dad could wait no longer, as he blew his horn and roared out through his car window.

"Hurry up and get off the road Sam, for Christ's sake, I'm trying to get home!"

As Sam limped his bike back to the yard, Dad drove past us, still shouting in displeasure. Krissy just looked at me and shook her head disapprovingly as Sam muttered, "There's something mentally wrong with your father Brian, that man has some serious issues." I couldn't help but laugh as I retorted, "You may be right Sam, he's not what you would call a patient man". A few minutes later, just as I had predicted, Mom was yelling out to her kids to come home for supper.

The family had gathered at the supper table to enjoy a hot meal, prepared with love by our Mom, just as we did every evening. For some strange reason, the men in the house all ate like it was our last meal. It always looked like we were starving to death and periodically Mom would say,   "Slow down boys, you're eating like a bunch of savages, no one is going to steal it from you".

It's not like we didn't have enough food in the house. Dad grew his own vegetables and raised his own farm animals, so there was always an abundance of beef, pork, chicken, eggs and of course milk. Dad would milk the cows early every morning before work and bring home two small buckets of milk. Can you imagine two beef-buckets of milk everyday for a family of six? I drank so much milk that I was afraid that when I hit my teens, I was going to start lactating.

There may not have been money to burn in our family, but I can't ever remember being hungry. So Mom had a valid point, why were we eating like a pack of wolves? Whatever the reason, I wasn't putting my fork down for a split second. You never knew when someone may try to nab your last chicken wing or even worse, steal your Sunday dessert.

Jason was the little culprit you had to keep an eye on; he would grab something off your plate, as quick as a flash, and stuff it in his mouth before you even knew what happened. In our house, Jason was known as "The Pork Chop Bandit" and although only 10, he was quick and elusive like a martial artist with a black-belt in food-snatching.

You know how some people have a 5-second rule when it comes to dropping food on the floor? Well in our house, we had a 2-second rule, which meant that if you dropped food on the floor, you had about 2 seconds to reclaim it before Jason swooped in and stole it away from you. I swear that boy kept an extra fork and knife in his back pocket at all times. And for a skinny 10 year old boy, he could eat as much as any full grown man. You had no worries about anyone in our family leaving the supper table for a few minutes, because we all knew that upon your return, the only thing left remaining on your plate would be a few bones. Jason was like a human garbage can; I would give him the grizzle off my pork and the skin off my chicken, anything just to try to appease him and keep him away from my plate.

I can remember the phone ringing supper time and everyone in the house being afraid to leave the table to answer it, out of fear of Jason emptying your plate. On several occasions, I actually took my Sunday dessert to the bathroom with me while I was peeing, just to prevent the Pork-chop-bandit from stealing my jelly and custard.

Dad was closely looking over everyone's report cards while we ate. Everyone had passed including our baby sister Jennifer who had just completed kindergarten. She was very excited and told anyone who would listen, that she was going to Grade One next year. Dad was reading the teachers comments at the end of my report card. It read pretty well the same as it had read every year. *Brian's scores are satisfactory but his disruptive behaviour wastes valuable teaching time.*

"I see you still haven't learned to keep quiet in class", in a stern voice. "My Son, you got to pay better attention and stop acting like a class clown".

That was all Dad had to say about that. He was pleased everyone was doing well in school, and if one of his son's had a bit of a smart mouth, I guess he would learn to live with it. After all, it was partially his fault. Had he not stood up for me as often as he did, I may have learned to stop tormenting people.

I can't even count the number of times Dad came to my rescue and saved my ass from being kicked by someone that I had irreconcilably upset. It was no secret that my mouth had gotten me into trouble in the past, and many a times, without question, Dad was there to back me. He didn't mind letting you know that if you mess with one of his children, you are messing with him and he had the temper and disposition to back it up.

On many occasions, he was even forced to protect me from my older brother Paul, who although quiet and easily embarrassed, had a monster temper just as fierce as Dads. I knew how to push Paul's buttons too and there were many times I tormented him to the point where he could no longer take it and quite literally, attempted to kill me.

Just a few months ago, on our way home from school, he was sitting on the bus with a girl from his class, that he had a tremendous crush on and for no reason at all I decided to mess with him.

I walked up to the both of them and said, "Now Paul, don't forget when we get home from school today that you are grounded and you have to go straight to your room, because last night Mom caught you playing with your wang".

Of course this wasn't true and hadn't really happened, but the girl burst out laughing and Paul just sat there turning blood red. You could actually see the hate growing in his eyes.

When the bus pulled up to our stop, I knew my only chance to get home in one piece, was to make a run for it. I jumped off the bus and ran for my life but it was no use, Paul had caught up with me just outside Lahey's house.

He threw me up against the fence, pulled back his fist and punched me in the belly so hard that the contents of my stomach came shooting out of my arse.

You know that old expression; *I'll knock the shit out of you*? Well, Paul hit me so hard that he did just that. I guess all those years of sawing wood and carrying buckets of water and lifting hay had made him as strong as an ox and with one mighty smack he had literally made me crap my pants.

As I stood there, hunched over with the wind knocked out of me, trying to catch my breath, he hauled off and kicked me in the ass so hard that I still have the word *Kodiak* permanently imprinted on my arse. Not only did this swift kick in the arse hurt tremendously, but it also made the crap in my pants splatter down my leg.

Unfortunately, I also had my shirt tucked into my pants so the crap actually splattered up my shirt and on to my back and neck. He should have been a professional soccer player because his kick actually lifted me off the ground. While airborne, I remember relapsing back to my Happy Place and thinking to myself how peaceful and nice it was up there.

When I finally hit the ground, I remember rolling around in severe pain, praying he would show some compassion and that perhaps the worst was over. Sadly though, there was no sympathy to be found that day; I had simply pushed him too far. The next thing I knew, Paul climbed on top of me with a look in his eyes that told me he wasn't finished yet and that all the begging in the world wouldn't save me.

I was exhausted and couldn't defend myself, I had nothing

left and I knew the end was near.

As he pulled back his fist I remember screaming, "Get ready for me oh merciful Jesus, I'm coming home".

All of a sudden, to my relief, Dad appeared out of nowhere, pulled Paul off me and yelled at him to go home and calm down. I just lay there on the ground, rolling around in my own shit, scared as a kitten and crying like a schoolgirl. Dad helped me up and walked me home.

"I don't know what the hell happened," he shouted at me, "but just as sure as you're covered in your own shit, I know damned well, you started it. What's wrong with you my son, do you have a death wish? One of these days I'm not going to be around to save your arse. There'll come a time when I won't have enough strength to hold Paul back from pounding the living daylights out of you. Smarten up for Christ's sake and think before you grab a tiger by the tail."

When we reached the house Dad instructed me to stay outside on the step and he yelled out to Mom to bring me out a roll of "shit-tickets" because I had crapped my pants.

Shit-tickets: that's what Dad called toilet paper and when Mom came outside and saw the condition that her son was in, she just shook her head at me in disapproval. Dad was right of course, it was all my doing, but as usual he was there to the rescue. Throughout it all, Dad had bailed me out of more trouble then he would like to remember. Who knows, maybe he would have been better off letting me take a couple of beatings. If that's what it takes to learn a lesson, perhaps a couple of hard, shit-knockings would have smartened me up.

No sooner had Mom cleared away the supper dishes, when a knock came on the door. It was our cousin Rod Butler, undoubtedly looking for Paul to hang out with at Lahey's.

"Come in and close the door, we're not heating up the East End!" Dad yelled with a smile. "How did you do in school today?"

"I did well Georgio." Rod answered. "Is Paul home?"

Dad roared out to Paul and then turned his attention back

to Rod. "Me and the boys have a lot of work ahead of us this summer Rod, I hope I can count on you to give the boys a hand?"

"No problem Georgio," Rod retorted, "Anytime you need me just give me a call."

Rod was impressively smart and a very hard worker. His mom and my grandmother were sisters, which made us second cousins. He was the same age as Paul but much more athletic and obsessed with sports. Although only 14, he was already a star player for the St. Michael's hockey, soccer and basketball teams. He was very likable and a bit of a hero to me. I tried to hang out with him as much as I could, but often times this proved difficult since he and Paul were such good friends and of course, Paul didn't like me hanging out with them all the time. Nevertheless, this was one time Paul didn't object to me coming with them and as we put on our jackets, the three of us headed down to Lahey's.

As we approached Lahey's yard, we could already hear the laughing and commotion spilling out into the neighbourhood. The yard was already filling up with people as the insults and sexual innuendoes echoed throughout the evening air.

Seated on two of the Lahey's bikes were Lenny and Rick Kavanagh. Lenny was 18 and his brother Rick was 17. Lenny, usually the oldest kid present, was sort of the ring leader and orchestrated many of the activities. He was very funny, had a fast mouth, and could cut you in half with an insult or zinger. He had a nickname for everyone, as he liked to call me Gonzo, from *The Muppet Show*, and he referred to Paul as Farmer Hickey. Although funny and insulting, he was overall a good guy, who wouldn't physically hurt you, unlike his buddy Howie who was pure evil.

Howie Nolan was 17 and loved to dish out the pain to us younger kids. He was the type of guy who liked showing off and tried to look cool in front of his friends by beating up and putting the fear of God into us. He wasn't happy unless he was putting the hurt on someone and I have even witnessed him during past summers, chasing girls in their shorts and whipping them on the back of their bare legs with those sharp stinging nettles.

He had a mean streak in him that ran pretty deep and he could be a real heartless bastard. Last summer he got into trouble for drowning Seagulls down at the beach. It all started one morning when Paul, Rod and I had gone down to the beach, fishing off the wharf. Much to our dismay, Howie was there as well. We wanted to avoid him so we decided to help out a local fisherman unload his catch. I climbed down into his fishing boat and loaded his gray fish tubs with big, beautiful, fresh Atlantic Cod. Paul and Rod would hoist the tubs of fish up to the old Skipper and he would quickly fillet the fish and toss the guts to the awaiting Sea Gulls.

"Thanks for the help," the old fisherman said, "I'm only interested in the fillets, so you young Lads can help yourselves to the napes and the tongues."

Once we finished unloading the small fishing boat, Paul and Rod started in cutting the tongues from the Cod heads. The fisherman rinsed out his fish tubs, tied up his boat and loaded his tub of fresh fillet in the back of his pickup truck. "Thanks again for the help boys," he said as he waved goodbye and drove away.

Meanwhile, Howie had picked up part of a fish carcass, attached it to the hook of his fishing rod and cast it off from the wharf. The carcass would float and bob around in the waves until a hungry seagull swooped down and snatched it up. Once the carcass was swallowed, Howie would then reel it in, Seagull and all. The seagull would struggle, but Howie would eventually win the battle and capture the bird. What he did next was not only sick and disturbing, but extremely sad. He would tie a heavy beach rock around the Seagull's legs and throw it off the wharf. I remember watching in horror as the poor bird frantically flapped his wings and tried to stay above water, but eventually he would become exhausted and the weight of the rock would pull him down to his watery grave.

Thankfully, a concerned citizen saw what Howie was doing and reported it to the police. The police drove by but unfortunately, because they couldn't prove anything, they simply gave him a warning and drove him home to chat with his parents.

Once we had cut out all the cod tongues, cheeks and napes, I called Dad from the payphone at the Ferry Terminal and asked him to bring us down a clean garbage bag. Dad eventually came down to the beach and he drove Rod, Paul and I home with a garbage bag full of Cod tongues, cheeks and napes.

On our ride home, I told Dad what Howie had done to the seagulls and Dad just sighed in disgust and said, "Maybe someone needs to take that arsehole, tie a rock around his feet and throw him off the wharf"!

Yes Sir, it was safe to say that I disliked Howie, and on several occasions, Dad was forced to confront him for bullying and picking on me. Dad actually worked with Howie's Dad at the hospital and coincidently, Dad didn't like him, anymore than I liked Howie. I can recall last summer when Dad banished Howie from Lahey's Yard for two full weeks because Howie had tried to burn one of the younger kids with his cigarette. Howie protested and said that Dad didn't have any authority over him.

Dad responded by grabbing him by the front of the jacket, shaking the hell out of him and telling him if he catches him anywhere near Lahey's yard over the next two weeks that he would bury him somewhere in the woods.

Howie stayed away for the full two weeks too, I mean, he was crazy, but he wasn't stupid and he knew Dad meant business. Since then, Howie pretty much left me alone; however I still avoided him whenever possible.

Over in the swings chatting, were Krissy, her older sister Shirley and their friend Karen. Shirley, 16, was the oldest of the Lahey daughters and a bit of a tomboy. She loved to hang out with the boys and took a lot of criticism for doing so. Lenny like to tease her by saying she was the most masculine of all the Lahey kids. She could play baseball, football and wrestle just as well as any of the other older boys.

Karen however was entirely different. She was 14 years old and Al's older sister. She was as feminine as you could get with her perfect hair, pretty outfits and she always smelled so good. When it came to playing sports or horsing around, she preferred to watch and cheer, rather than play and risk getting dirty or breaking a nail. She always had a thing for the older boys, which didn't sit well with me, seeing as I was harbouring a huge crush on her since I was 6 years old. Quite often, I resorted to getting my buddy Al to put in a good word for me with his sister Karen. But it was no use - she liked older men - and she simply looked at me as a pest and a nuisance. I however was not discouraged and tried to kiss her as often as I could.

The majority of the kids were over sitting on the hood of the Lahey's blue family station wagon. Once again, I was amazed at how Mr. and Mrs. Lahey could abide by a bunch of kids sitting on the hood, and leaning up against, their fairly new car. They certainly did subscribe to the notion of live and let live and advocated tolerance, patience and acceptance. Sitting on the hood was Gerald, Don, Randy and Morris. Gerald was 18 and the oldest of the Lahey children. He was often responsible for looking after his siblings and was a very serious, no-nonsense type of guy. Gerald was very intelligent and had just completed his last year of high school. He looked forward to moving to the big city of St. John's in the Fall, to learn a Trade and get a job.

Don was one year younger than his brother Gerald; however, the two couldn't possibly be any more different. Don loved to laugh at himself and was always fun to be around. He was more like their younger brother Sam, a little clumsy, the type of fellow who would trip over his own shadow. Don was a little smaller than Gerald and like many of us brothers, they often shared the same clothes. As a result, many of Don's outfits were too big for him. His pants were always hanging down around his arse and his friends would often call him droopy-drawers. I had learned a lot from Don over the years, as he had taught me how to ride a bike, how to catch a baseball and how to build a kite. Many of us younger kids looked up to Don, as he was like everyone's big brother.

Randy and Morris were cousins and best friends. They were both 17, they loved drinking beer and they both enjoyed the company of larger women. It was common knowledge on the East End that these two often had competitions regarding who could romance the most unattractive girl. Randy was a muscular guy with rosy cheeks which could be attributed to the fact that he had been drinking beer since he was about 10 years old and although only 17, he had no problem polishing off a case of 24 beers before making that shameless, late-night, intoxicated phone call to one of his many hideous lady friends in waiting.

Randy was a very likable guy and rumour had it that he was hung like a Shetland pony. In fact, Randy himself could often be heard telling the ladies, "You don't always have to go to a hotdog stand, if you want a foot-long!" He proudly sported a tattoo of a rooster on his calf muscle, just so he could tell the ladies that he had a cock below his knee. There must have been some validity to this rumour because stories of Randy's conquests over undesirable women were the stuff of legends. One cold afternoon this past February, Randy was spotted taking an intoxicated pee in a snow-bank. Apparently, his wang cast such an enormous shadow, that the nearby neighbors predicted six more weeks of winter!

It was also rumored that last summer Randy and a lady friend were skinny dipping in a local trout pond. While Randy was swimming naked across the pond, he accidentally caught a large-mouth Bass!

Morris Noseworthy was Randy's cousin and best friend and he was even worse when it came to beer and women. Although Morris wasn't known for being as well endowed as Randy, he still had his own claim to fame when it came to his wang. Apparently, Morris was the proud owner of a much longer-than-normal foreskin. Some of the boys caught a glimpse of it in the locker room after Gym class and the story quickly spread that Morris had so much foreskin that they called it five-skin! This however, never bothered Morris, he would just laugh it off and say that it was like a turtleneck sweater for his wang and if he was to ever get caught in a snowstorm, he could simply pull down his zipper and stretch his foreskin up over his head, like a hood!

Morris's nickname was Butterballs because a couple of years ago he was trying to have sex with a woman in his uncle's hay barn. Without getting into too much detail, let me just say that all the parched and dusty air from the hay made things kind of dry for Morris and his lady friend and so lubrication was needed. When no lubrication was available, Morris decided to improvise and ran into his uncle's house and returned with a block of butter. I don't really want to say anymore about it, however if you use your imagination, I'm sure you can figure out how he got the nick-name Butterballs!

About 3 summers ago, Morris and Randy built themselves a shed or "Skin-Hut," as they named it. The weekly Friday and Saturday night, alcohol-fuelled, bone-a-thons held in that shed by Morris, Randy and several of Bell Island's monstrous females would make any normal man toss his cookies.   They actually revised their own adaptation of the popular children's game "Red-Rover." They would line up a couple of ladies in the Skin-Hut, make them hold hands and say, "Red-Rover, Red-Rover bend Maggie right over!" The boys thought that they were Bell Island's version of Don Juan; only instead of being suave and charming with beautiful women, the boy's would invite gruesome girls back to their Skin-Hut with the promise of beer, cigarettes and sexual ecstasy.

I can't even begin to describe how many times Dad warned my friends and I to stay away from that shed. He threatened us with bodily harm if he ever found out that we came within one hundred feet of that place. He used to say that some of the sexual acts that transpired in that shed were unhealthy, ungodly and indescribably grotesque. "Keep away from that shed." Dad would say, "Morris and Randy are nice enough young fellows, but they drink too much and would service a shitty arse sheep."

You should have seen this shed, it was about 12 feet long and 10 feet wide, windowless, and the walls and ceiling were painted jet black. It had ugly, grey shag carpeting and one entire wall was lined off with cases of empty beer bottles. It had a table with four chairs, a radio, a strobe light and homemade bunk beds which housed two of the dirtiest, jizz-soaked, mystery-stained mattresses imaginable.

The whole place reeked of beer, cigarettes, cheap perfume and sex, and on the door hung a wooden painted sign that simply read, "Skin-Hut." There was a nude calendar dated 1980 proudly displayed on the wall above the table and next to it was a handwritten sign that read, *The Skin-Hut: where the men are men, the beers are cold and the women are hot.* I've always felt that the sign should have read, *The Skin-Hut: where the men are men and the sheep are nervous!* Believe me when I say that the type of women that sauntered out of that shed every Sunday morning were definitely not supermodels. I'm talking about 300 pound greasy creatures with straight hair and curly teeth; if in fact, they had any teeth at all. With these girls, you didn't wonder if you could pinch an inch; you wondered if you could flap a foot! It's been said that *Love Is Blind*; and apparently, so were Morris and Randy!

However, the boys loved it and they would often joke and say, "Gotham City might have a Bat-signal but the Skin-hut has its own Fat-signal". Morris even kept an old box of souvenir bras and panties as a memento of the wonderful pleasures provided by some of these beauties. He referred to this box of undergarments as his "tickle-trunk" and I guess that was accurate; had Mr. Dress-up been an alcoholic pervert with a sick fetish for taking toothless skanks to Pound-Town. On occasion, Morris would take his prized box of undergarments outside in a sad attempt to impress us and if you were unlucky enough to be down-wind and catch a whiff of these unmentionables, you would swear to God that you were standing next to a Caplin pit. "Love 'em and leave 'em," the boys used to say. It can be argued that Morris and Randy ruined the lives of more fat women than chocolate cheesecake!

I remember one day asking my Dad why Morris and Randy chose to live the way that they do. I mean, the Catholic Church preached against sex before marriage and it certainly looked down on multiple partners and this kind of sexual deviant behaviour. I'll never forget Dad's response, he just put his hand on my shoulder, looked down into my eyes and said, "Brian, there are two types of men in this world. First, there are guys like me that get married, settle down, buy a house, raise a family and grow old with their wife and hopefully die peacefully, surrounded by their children and grandchildren. Then you have guys like Morris and Randy who wake up most mornings hung-over, in some married skank's home, washing their pecker in the bathroom sink and trying to get the hell out of there before her husband gets home, or her kids wake up in the next room. All the while, she is still buck naked on the couch enjoying her whore's breakfast; a cigarette and a glass of Pepsi!" Yes Sir, that's one thing I can say about my Dad; he could always paint a lovely picture. He was like Picasso with words.

Last summer Morris and Randy got together and had themselves a little beauty pageant at the Skin-Hut. They filled the shed with beer and cigarettes and invited five of their weekend regulars over for a no-holds-barred beauty pageant entitled, "Ms. Bell Island". Now folks, I wish I could tell you that the pageant was a success but from what I understand, during the swimsuit contest, Ms. Lance Cove got into a racket with Ms. Main Street and tore the triple-extra-large, one-piece bathing suit off her and pushed her out the door of the Skin-Hut in the nude and locked her outside. Apparently, any innocent bystanders who happened to be walking by the Skin-Hut that day got a glimpse of a 300 pound naked woman wearing nothing but a sash that read Ms. Main Street. To make matters worse, I was eleven years old when this happened and sadly, I was one of those unfortunate bystanders, riding my bike along the road in front of the Skin-Hut when my eyes fell upon this indescribable spectacle.

My very first time seeing an actual naked lady and this is what my young mind had to try to process. I stopped my bike and just stood there in shock as this very large woman with the big flabby boobies and a hippo-ass stood there banging on the shed door, screaming obscenities. It would take decades before I could come to terms with what I had witnessed on that day. For several years later, it was not uncommon for me to wake up screaming in the middle of the night in a cold sweat. Yes folks, I can honestly say, I had my Vietnam and if it wasn't for my Happy Place, I don't think I would have ever been able to get past it. I have never told a single soul about that life changing event until right now, and as I relive it while I type this; it still sends shivers down my spine.

The cops were eventually called to the scene and all these contending beauties were eventually carted off home; most of them in a paddy-wagon, for obvious reasons. So the first and only Skin-Hut Beauty Pageant "Ms. Bell Island," had come to an abrupt end and sadly, but not surprisingly, on that fateful day, no winner was crowned!

Standing next to the family car, chatting and laughing were Mark Barnes, Andy Bennett, Howie and Mickey Foley. All four of the boys were 17 and just finished Grade 11. Mark was the Casanova of the group. He was good looking and very athletic and never had any problem with the ladies. He had the full attention of Karen and for this reason, I disliked him.

Andy was a really nice fellow as well. Out of everyone in the yard, Andy was the only one who came from a well-to-do family. He already had his own car and always had a pocket full of cash. What I liked about Andy was the fact that he never tried to impress anyone. He was always himself, and no matter who was near, he treated everyone with respect. If I happened to be at the corner store and Andy walked in with his friends, he would always say hello and many times, buy me an ice cream. If you were walking down the road and he drove by, he would always stop and offer you a ride or if he was going in the opposite direction, he would always blow his horn at you. Let's face it, when you are 12, it's just nice to be acknowledged and Andy never failed to make you feel accepted.

Last summer, Dad brought Paul and I a set of lawn darts for passing in school. First of all, what genius invented this game for kids; an eight inch long, steel spike that you hurled through the air? How many kids, I wondered, ended up in Special Ed after playing with this death trap? I remember, we set it up and before long, everyone started to come around and the next thing I knew there was a lawn dart tournament happening in the Hickey yard. Oh, how great it felt to be co-owner of this wonderful outdoor game. It may have only cost around 10 bucks, but it was just as good as if we had installed a backyard pool.

Things were going great with the tournament. There were eight teams, consisting of two players per team and the winner would be crowned champions of the world. Mom was keeping the crowd refreshed with jugs of Tang and Dad was flipping out and yelling at anyone who was trampling his lawn. Shirley and I were partners and we had advanced to the quarter finals. It was our turn and we were facing a much bigger and older team in Lenny and Andy.

The boys were beating us by 2 points and as I let my dart fly, I noticed Andy wasn't really paying much attention until my lawn dart went straight through his sneaker and pieced his foot. He dropped to the ground in agony and blood was squirting everywhere. Dad threw him in the Dodge and rushed him to the hospital. He walked with a limp for the rest of the summer but the weird thing about it was he didn't even get mad at me. Of course it was an accident, but when you cripple someone on their summer vacation, at the very least, you expect them to be upset with you. Dad immediately boxed up the lawn dart set and sent it back to the store. Three things happened after that day; we never played lawn darts again, no one would ever be allowed to congregate in the Hickey yard and Andy would forever be ridiculed for suffering agony of "da-feet"!

Al and I were standing around chatting with Paul, Rod and our friend Greg Bartlett. Greg was a year older than me but was a bit smaller than the rest of us. He was quick as a cat and although small in stature, would face anyone who stood in his way. He refused to back down from anyone or anything. He was smart and funny and had a good sense of humour. He was also very athletic and competitive and was always one of the guys I could count on to help out with the chores.

Our chatting and laughing was interrupted by the high-pitched, nasally voice of Carl Power, another East Ender that lived just up the road in a small house in the woods with his Mom. Carl was a bit of a wild-card, as he didn't really have a best friend and he would just show up. No one really seemed to mind. He was 14 years old and very immature for his age. He was one of those guys with bad allergies and who seemed to have a head-cold 365 days a year. His nose was constantly running, so we all called him Snots. He pretty much came and went as he pleased, but he certainly wasn't a regular amongst our group, probably because he was so accident prone and clumsy. He would usually hang out with us for a day or so, get hurt, go home crying and we wouldn't see him anymore for a couple of weeks.

Snots was a little slow for his age and although he attended our school, he mostly hung out in the challenging needs class. Snots was one of those kids who was still wearing diapers by the time he was 5 years old. No matter how hard his Mom tried to toilet-train him, he refused to pee in the toilet. Finally, a local nurse told her to put something in the toilet and try to get Snots to pee on it. Make a game out of it until he finally learns to pee in the toilet. At that time, Snot's favorite breakfast cereal was Honeycombs. He ate honeycombs every morning when he was a small boy so his Mom would throw a few honeycombs in the toilet and get Snots to pee on them. Believe it or not, it actually worked and Snots started peeing in the toilet, just as long as there were two or three honeycombs to pee on. One morning however, the plan backfired.

Snots' Mom served up a bowl of honeycombs for his breakfast, but I guess Snots got confused because when she turned her back, he stood up on the kitchen table, whipped out his wang and pissed into his bowl of cereal!

He was different for sure; remember how all the cool kids had those sleeveless jean-jackets with the name of their favorite Heavy Metal band such as AC/DC, Metallica or Iron Maiden written in black marker on their backs? Well Snots, not to be outdone, took his old yellow raincoat, cut the sleeves off it and wrote the name Harry Hibbs on the back, with a red crayon. He would wear his Harry Hibbs raincoat to school and people would say to him, "Rock on Harry", and Snot's would reply, "Right on buddy, Harry Hibbs is a musical genius, I loves *Between Two Trees*".

God love him, as hard as he tried, he just couldn't seem to fit in. As I've said, Snots lived with his Mom and he had never met his father. According to popular opinion, Snot's Dad could have been any one of a hundred different guys, as his Mom was anything but a virgin. Her name was Tonya and she was a heavy, somewhat attractive lady in her mid-thirties and we simply called her Two-Tummy Tonya. Everyone from the East End of Bell Island knew about her sexual escapades. As Dad would so delicately say, "She's out on the whore-racket and she'll squat for anyone!" Many a young man made that long trot into manhood at the very capable hands of Snot's Mom. The woman simply made no bones about it; she loved the baloney-pony. In fact, the older boys like Lenny would often tease Snots about his Mom's sex life by saying things like, "Hey Snots, your Mom has taken more loads than a dishwasher". Comments like this were often enough to send Snots home crying.

Snots was standing next to his cousin and only friend Calvin Power. Calvin was the same age as Snots, but he was a tad bit smarter. He was one of these guys that you could only tolerate for so long and if he had a little knowledge on a particular topic, it made him a real authority. He was a real know-it-all type of fellow, when in reality, he knew very little. Calvin was also probably the biggest dirt-bag that I had ever met. His Dad and Snot's Mom were brother and sister. His Dad also had a reputation of being a bad drunk and never worked a day in his life. I can only assume that it was due to the fact that his Dad was always drunk, that Calvin was as dirty as what he was. His clothes were ragged and smelly and he had ugly, black teeth. His breath was so bad that you could smell him entering a room. He rarely smiled due to his crooked, rotten teeth and he always carried around chewing gum to try to mask the fact that his breath was so rancid. We all called him Snaggletooth, because of his awful teeth and believe me, he didn't like it.

One time Dad and I stopped and picked up Calvin in the old Dodge, while he was walking home in the rain. He was only in the car for a minute or two before the smell of his breath began to take over the car.   "What in Heavenly Jesus is that God awful smell?" Dad shouted as he looked at me?

I immediately noticed Calvin reaching for a piece of gum in his pocket. Finally Dad couldn't take it anymore and he pulled the car over to the side of the road and yelled.   "Jesus, I'm sorry Snaggletooth, but you're going to have to get out and walk, you're stinking up the car. Buddy I'm not kidding, your breath smells worst than the shit-bag of a skunk. Go home my son and brush your teeth for shame's sake. And never mind chewing gum, you're only masking the problem. The Gum is not working for you Snaggletooth; it makes your breath smell like someone took a shit in a spearmint bush!"
Snots and Snaggletooth; My God when I think about it, those two guys never really had a chance.

As evening rolled into night, the chatting and laughter continued. There was nothing really organized or planned for that night because it was the first night that we had all gathered since last summer. Everyone was more or less getting a feel for each other again.

It's funny because although we all attended the same school and rode on the same bus, everyone sort of fell out of sync during the school year. Some of the older kids who would never acknowledge me in the school corridor were now tossing around a Frisbee with me and sharing a joke.

I guess when you are at school, you have a certain image to uphold as you tend to stick more with your classmates and kids your own age, but when you are just hanging out on summer vacation, there is less pressure to impress others and you can once again reconnect with those from your neighbourhood.

As the night started getting late, people began dispersing and Lenny finally announced a softball game tomorrow morning at 11:00 on Lahey's Field. Everyone was instructed to bring whatever softball bats, gloves and balls they could get their hands on.

3

Lahey's Field

I was awake bright and early the next morning, eagerly anticipating the softball game at 11:00. I dug out my old softball glove and 2 brand new softballs that I just got this past Christmas. With a black marker I wrote the name "Hickey" on each softball, just in case someone tried to claim them as their own. It was only 8:30 A.M. but Paul and I were quickly scoffing down our breakfast tea and toast in order to get our morning chores done before the big game.

"Would you like another cup of tea before you head out?" Mom asked.

"Nah thanks," I replied, "this poor ole tea bag has been passed around more times than a cheap hooker and it's been steeped out so thin that my tea tastes like hot water with milk and sugar."

Paul just Chuckled as Dad reached across the table and flicked me in the back of the head and said, "Watch your mouth, smartass".

Seriously though, why did we have to pass around a tea bag as much as we did? A box of Tea bags couldn't possibly have been that expensive; was there a global shortage on tea bags that I was unaware of? Dad would start out with a brand new tea bag and then Mom would use it, then Paul and finally me. By the time that sad, tired looking tea bag reached my cup, the poor dried out, beaten up bastard looked like it had spent the night in the Skin-Hut, getting shagged by Morris and Randy. It always pissed me off that I got stuck with the overused, weak tea bag and to this very day, I refuse to drink a cup of tea!

After we finished breakfast we ran over to the barn and started in. Paul quickly milked the cows as I gathered the eggs and let the hens outside. Not a word was spoken between us; we were machines. We both knew our routines off by heart and we were focused on the task at hand. Paul quickly shovelled the manure out of the barn, while I climbed into the pig pen to feed and water the pigs.

I cannot begin to describe how much I hated those dirty swine bastards. Twice a day for the months of June, July, August and September I would have to climb into the pen with these filthy creatures to feed them, water them and clean up behind them. All the while they would be chewing on my sneakers and getting pig shit all over me.

You have no idea how many times I laid the boots to those stupid, dirty animals. The only thing that got me through each day was the knowledge that by October, they would be nothing more than pork chops in the oven and bacon sizzling on the pan. I hated them and as payback, I would often tease the shit out of them. They loved turnip-tops and whenever Dad wasn't watching, I would entice one of the pigs to come to me with a handful of turnip-tops. Once I was confident that I had gained his trust and he was busy eating the turnip-tops, I would crack him on the snout, as hard as I could with an old picket from the fence. I got great satisfaction and fulfillment from watching those ungrateful pigs, take off running and squealing in pain. Every now and then, Dad would hear one of the pigs squeal and he would come running to the pig pen shouting, "For Christ's sake Brian, stop smacking those pigs, you're going to bruise and damage the meat."

Quite often though, Dad would turn a blind eye whenever I struck one of his pigs because he knew just how unpredictable they are to work with and how much I really hated them. Besides, he really couldn't get too upset because last summer he smacked one of the pigs so hard that he knocked the poor bastard out. I was with Dad that day, helping him make a few minor repairs to the pig pen. One of the bigger pigs kept walking over and bumping Dad, as he was trying to hammer some nails into the pen. Dad would give it a slap on the ass, make a roar at him and the pig would retreat. However, the pig finally bumped Dad while he was off balance and knocked him over into a fresh, steaming pile of pig shit. Dad jumped up all pissed off, swung his hammer at the pig and knocked him out cold.

Both of us just stood there and looked at each other, wondering if he had accidently killed it, when all of a sudden the pig popped up, spit our 2 broken teeth and took off running and screaming. I could see that Dad was relieved that there was no serious damage done to his pig as he shouted,   "Now, come near me again and I'll lose my size 10 boot up in your hole, you stupid, toothless pig bastard."

As Paul and I quickly finished our chores, we bought the milk and eggs back home to Mom, grabbed our gloves and balls and took off running for Lahey's Field.

By the time we arrived it was after 10:00 A.M. and a few people had already gathered. Rod and Greg were having a catch; Shirley and Krissy were on the swings, while Don and Gerald were digging out softball equipment. From far across the meadow, we could see Lenny, Rick, Mark, Morris and Alice all slowly making their way towards Lahey's Field.

Alice was my aunt, my Mom's baby sister even though she was only 6 years older than me. She was currently dating Mark, and although he was a bit of a womanizer, this pleased me because it kept him away from Karen, whom I adored. Finally Al, Randy and Karen showed up.   Ah Karen, even in those track pants and tee shirt, she still looked stunning with her long curly hair and her beautiful smile. Boy, what I wouldn't give to kiss those lips.

We all stood there in Lahey's Field which was located directly across from their yard. It was a small field, surrounded by trees and shrubs and there were rocks sticking out the ground that we used as bases. Home plate was actually a small hole in the ground, surrounded by rocks, which doubled as a fire-pit for those hot summer nights. This was by no means a groomed field and it wasn't uncommon to see someone topple over as they tripped over a bush or stepped into a hole. Still, it was our field, our sanctuary and it had been so for years.

Lenny and Gerald usually picked teams and because I was the youngest, I was usually the last one picked. But I didn't care, at least I was playing. I mean how often does a 12 year old get to hang out with kids 16, 17 and 18 years old?

As the game progressed it was usually accompanied by an array of insults, vulgarity and sexual innuendoes- most of which I didn't fully understand. Oh Man, but was it ever great to be a part of it. I was picking up things from these guys that you would never learn in school.

Quite often I was the pitcher for our team and Lenny had just hit a double and was standing safe on second base. Karen was next up to bat and of course, because I had a crush on her, I pitched an easy one, so that she was able to hit it. She hit a routine pop-up directly to second base, which would normally be caught. Except that when Don raised his glove to make the catch, Lenny who was still standing on second base, grabbed the legs of Don's track pants and pulled his pants and underwear down to his knees. The ball landed on the ground, Karen ran to first base and Don was left standing there with his wang hanging out.

The whole field erupted into laughter as Don struggled to pull his pants back up. Someone yelled out, "Nice catch Droopy Drawers" and the laughter erupted again.

Unfortunately for Don, his Dad just happened to look out his kitchen window at that exact moment when Don is standing in the middle of the field with his wang daggling.

Mr. Lahey came storming across the field, grabbed Don by the arm, and dragged him home screaming at him and calling him a pervert. While Don and his Dad exited the field, Lenny yelled out, "Hey Don, if you want to continue playing ball with us, you are going to have to learn to keep your pants on. I'm sorry buddy, but we can't have you pulling down your pants in the middle of the field, that just ain't right."

The hysterical laughter continued and even Don's brothers and sisters were high-fiving and enjoying the gag. As play resumed, everyone left on the field immediately tied up their pants as tight as possible out of fear of also being de-pants.

Throughout the day, we played 2 or 3 games of 7-inning softball, picking different teams after each game. We definitely weren't going to make the World Series of softball but the laughs and memories we shared were priceless. Another routine pop fly was hit to centerfield. As Snots raised his glove to make the catch, the sun got in his eyes. The ball smacked him right in face, breaking his nose and sending him running home bleeding and crying. Everyone felt bad for him until Lenny yelled, "Hey Snots, tell your Mom that I may come by tonight for a game of Birds and Muckers". The sympathy quickly vanished as everyone once again bursts into a fit of laughter.

Sadly it's always been that way for Snots; if it wasn't for bad luck he wouldn't have any luck at all. As long as I have known him, he has always been getting hurt, clumsy and very awkward. Bad luck just seemed to follow him around; here it was the first day of summer holidays and he had just broken his nose playing soft ball. Two summers ago, in a 2 week span, he got sun-stroke, almost drowned in the ocean and fell off his bike, breaking his arm. He was a nice enough type of guy, but his lack of coordination combined with his uncanny string of bad luck, often made him vulnerable to mishaps and persistent mocking.

Just this past winter, a crowd of us were sledding on the big hill on Lighthouse Road, next to Kevin Stone's Barn. Although it was a huge hill and great for sledding in the winter, Mr. Stone used this land as a pasture for his cattle and sheep in the summer time. When climbing the massive hill, it would take you a good 15 minutes to get to the top and you could reach some pretty impressive speeds while sledding down it.

A small group of us including Snots, Al, Greg, Rod, Paul and myself had all been sledding for about an hour and having one hell of a good time. We once again climbed to the top of the hill and as we all jumped on our sleds, we decided to race to the bottom. Snots and Rod were both using toboggans, Al and Greg were using those wooden sleighs with the steel runners and Paul and I each had a Crazy Carpet, which wasn't the safest form of transportation. But boy could they fly. We all agreed that on the count of 3 we would all take off and the first one down would be crowned King of the Hill, whereas the last one down would have to drag everyone's sled back up to the top of the hill.

As we took off I knew I was in good shape, I wasn't in first place but I knew several people were behind me. Then from the corner of my eye I could see Snots' toboggan veering off to the right, hitting a patch of dead grass, tipping over and Snots continuing to topple head over heels downhill. When we all got to the bottom we had realized that Greg had come in first place but Snots was still only half ways down the hill, laying in the fetal position, crying in agony.

We ran towards him and we all assumed that he could not have been too severely hurt; I mean how could anyone possibly injure themselves on soft snow?

Greg yelled at him, "Come on Snots, get up ya big sook." However, as we got closer we quickly realized that blood was gushing out of the side of his face.

Apparently when he fell off his toboggan, he landed on a frozen cow patty and nearly tore the side of his face off. If the sight wasn't so gruesome it would have been laughable. Imagine, busting your face open on a piece of frozen crap! We put fresh snow on his face to stop the bleeding and started walking him home.

We came upon a frozen river that we crossed regularly during the winter time because it provided us with a short cut home. Because the weather had been a little mild for the past week or so, we walked across the frozen river very gingerly and would you believe that out of the six of us, Snots was the only one who fell through the ice and sunk right up to his armpits in freezing water.

Absolutely incredible; can you believe this guy's luck? He screamed and bawled but we all manage to pull him out of the water and continued walking him home.

Along the way we passed Lenny who was skating and playing shinny on a frozen pond. He asked us what happened to Snots' face and we told him about how he crashed into some frozen cow shit.

Lenny just laughed and said, "Ha Snots, I always said you were full of shit, but you didn't have to go out and prove it!"

We all cried out laughing and to be honest, I think Lenny's little joke may have even made Snots smile.

By the time we got Snots home, he was well bloodied up and his soaking wet snowsuit was frozen stiff. His poor Mother came to the door screaming and was shocked to see the dreadful condition her son was in.

To make matters worse, when we finally got Snots inside his house, the heat struck him and he desperately had to use the bathroom. Unfortunately the zipper on his one-piece snowsuit was frozen solid, due to his ill-fated dip in the icy river and we couldn't get it open.

As hard as we all tried, we simply could not get his zipper to budge and Snots just danced in agony, all the while screaming frantically, "I have to pee, I have to pee"! We all continued to work in desperation until sadly, and perhaps fittingly, Snots was forced to surrender to his biological urges and reluctantly pissed himself.

When I returned home from sledding that evening, I carried in a couple of armfuls of wood for the woodstove and as I was taking off my snowsuit, I was pleased to see that my Grandfather, Pop Hickey was at our house for a visit. You know how when you're a kid and your Grandfather likes to bounce you on his knee, give you money, and spend quality time with you? Well, My Pop wasn't like that.

Pop Hickey could be described as a surly old man who didn't mince his words and had absolutely no trouble calling a spade a spade. He spoke his mind with little or no concern about offending others. He was a short, stout man with a bit of a beer belly. He wore suspenders to help keep his pants up and he always had a white cloth handkerchief in his back pocket for blowing his nose. Despite his surliness, he had a mischievous way about him and he would tell you a lie just for the joke of it. I think this was the reason why we got along so well, because of all my Grandparents, I could relate to Pop Hickey the most.

He was the janitor of my High School and he loved nothing more than to drive the school Nuns right off their heads. He complained a lot and fully believed that if it wasn't done his way, then it wasn't done right. He expected obedience and compliance from children and he also loved to see us kids doing chores and hard labour- just as much as Dad enjoyed it.

Pop Hickey was the type of guy that if you were playing road hockey or tossing a Frisbee outside his house and your ball or Frisbee accidently and innocently drifted over his fence and landed on his property; you could forget about ever getting them back. Every Summer Pop would bring us down a garbage bag full of baseballs, Frisbees, hockey pucks and soccer balls that made their way onto his property, but he refused to give back to their owner.

I remember a couple of summers of go, Dad and I were helping Pop Hickey replace the windows in his home. His old windows were still in decent shape after they were taken out of his home, so Pop decided to display the windows in his yard with a sign that read: *Used Windows 5 Dollars Each*. He figured that the windows were perfectly fine for anyone who was building an old barn, shed or garage. After about a week, there were a couple of people who showed interest in the windows but nobody wanted to pay the 5 dollars per window, even though they were well worth it.

Pop got tired of seeing the windows in his yard so he asked Dad if we would take the windows and throw them out in the local dump. Dad and I loaded the windows in the car and surprisingly, Pop insisted and coming to the dump with us. We arrived at the dump and piled the windows next to the regular garbage and all of a sudden, Pop picked up an old piece of pipe and started smashing out all the windows.

When he finished destroying every window, he looked and me and said, "If nobody wants to pay for them, then they sure as shit aren't getting them for free".

That's how Pop was; he didn't believe in free rides and he was from the old school that preached if you want something, then you are going to have to work for it. Most kids avoided him but I had always gotten along with him. I think it was due to the fact that he found me comical and mischievous and I somehow amused him.

Pop was sitting at the kitchen table with Dad, having a beer and he said hello and asked me if I had fun sledding. I couldn't wait to tell him all about Snots falling off his sled, striking his face on the shit, falling through the ice, and pissing himself.

After I finished telling Dad and Pop the whole story about Snots' misfortune, Pop just shook his head in disbelief, chugged his beer, laughed and said, "Maybe you boys should have done him a favour and let the poor bastard drown in the river!"

Our softball game had already suffered two causalities, Don and Snots. However, in the distance an even bigger distraction was about to interrupt the game. The majestic sight of a gray, grocery-delivery van pulling up the lane, passing Lahey's field captured the imaginations of everyone. All eyes were focused on the delivery van and its pending cargo of fine cuisine.

My Jesus, where was it going, the excitement and anticipation were unbearable. Was it going to Lahey's house or Kent's house or maybe Power's house? No Sir, on this Blessed day of our Lord, it was turning into George Hickey's driveway.

Without hesitation, I flung my softball glove to the ground and sprinted home like an Olympic Track-n-Fielder, pausing just long enough to mock the others by doing a little dance and yelling, "Better luck next time Suckers." I skipped and pranced all the way home singing the praises of the grocery van. I would return to the field moments later, like Royalty, just to tease everyone with a banana and an ice-cream cone, only to find that one of my jealous comrades had shown their displeasure in my absence, by taking a whiz on my softball glove.

Oh well, not to worry, the sun would soon dry the urine off my glove, besides it was a small price to pay for being King of the East End for the day!

We soon finished up with the third and final game of the day and people began to slowly disperse as they made their ways home for supper. Paul and I went home as well because it was Saturday and for us, that meant supper, shower and Church Services at 7:00 P.M.

While we were eating supper, Paul and I were racing since we both wanted to be first in the shower. I wasn't even chewing my food; I was just swallowing huge pieces of meat whole like a starving sea gull. As I gulped down the last morsel, I chugged my glass of milk, pointed and laughed at Paul, and headed straight for the shower. Before I could close the bathroom door, I heard Paul yell, "Don't use all the hot water, I need to shower after you."

He hated using anything after me and I shouted back, "Don't worry, I won't be long, I just have to scrub my arse with the soap and then you can have it".

I laughed to myself as I was showering because I knew the fact that Paul had to go after me, truly pissed him off. I stood there showering and trying to think of other ways to push his buttons. I decided that I was exceedingly dirty on this particular day and would require a longer than usual shower.   After about 15 minutes passed, Paul pounded on the bathroom door and shouted, "Will you hurry up in there! You're going to use up all the hot water".

I just laughed to myself and shouted back, "Take your time, I have to get extra clean for all the ladies in Church this evening, I'm only trying to give them what they want; a bigger piece of the Hickey Pie."   I could hear him storm away from the bathroom door, muttering to himself and again this made me giggle.

Ten minutes later he once again pounded on the door and said, "If you don't get out now, I'm going to come in there and throw you out!"

I was not worried because the bathroom door was locked and I was safe in my hot, steamy fortress of solitude.

"Give me 5 more minutes", I shouted back, "I just borrowed your toothbrush for those hard-to-reach places around my arse. Ha ha ha."

With that, I guess I had pushed him too far because with one big bang, he busted off the tiny, sliding door lock and I could see his menacing shadow just outside the shower curtain.

"Get out!" I screamed, as I assumed the fetal position in the bottom of the bathtub.

He opened the shower curtain slightly and I watched in horror as his hand entered the shower and turned off the hot water.

"Now" he said, "enjoy that cold shower for as long as you want."

The water immediately turned freezing cold and once again, I found myself screaming like a school girl. This went on for several minutes until finally he took pity on me and turned off the water. He then whipped open the shower curtain and ordered me out of the bathroom. I just thanked him and lay there in the bottom of the tub, shivering from the cold. My poor little wang had shrunken up so much that it looked like I had two belly buttons. I grabbed a towel and exited the bathroom, fully acknowledging the fact that Paul had won this round.

As our family made its way inside the Church, Paul and I veered off down stairs to the Altar Boy's room. We were greeted by Sam, Rod, Greg and several other alter boys from around the community. We all put on our red dress-like uniform which was crowned off with a white top. Leave it to the Catholic Church to dress up their Altar Boys in dress-like uniforms!

Before the service started, the Priest quickly gave each of us our duties for this evening's service and cautioned us that any horseplay or nonsense will not be tolerated on the Lord's Altar. My only duty for the service was to bring him the Eucharist so he may bless it before he distributed Holy Communion. Pretty easy job, as I had done it at least a hundred times before.

Once the Mass began, all the altar boys sat across from each other on the Altar ready to serve the Priest. From across the Altar, I could see Rod making funny faces trying to make us laugh. He was famous for this and last week he made another alter boy, Barry, laugh so hard that the priest suspended him for a full month. Last year, he made another Altar Boy, Tommy, laugh out so hard on the Altar that Tommy's Dad marched right up to him and dragged his son to the back of the Church by his ear. While the whole congregation found this amusing, poor Tommy was embarrassed to tears and never returned to the Alter again.

As Rod continued to make his faces, Greg let out a tiny snigger and that was enough for the Priest to glare in our direction with a look of disgust and anger. I knew I couldn't have any part of this, as I was already on thin ice with the Priest. He had already warned me that any more fooling around on my behalf and he would be forced to tell my father.

Dad was a member of The Knights of Columbus and took his religious practices very seriously. I didn't mind pissing off the priest because all he would do is suspend you from your Altar duties for a month or so. To piss off Dad however, was another matter altogether, especially if it had anything to do with the church. I made the mistake of crossing Dad in the past and painfully, lived to regret it.

Two summers ago I was unable to make it to church on one particular Saturday night, because I was busy helping my Grandfather weed his potato garden. No big deal really, this sort of thing happened all the time; I would simply attend the Sunday Service the next day. The next morning as I was about to leave the house and walk to church, Dad reminded me to bring home the weekly Church Bulletin.

I knew of course, what he was up to; he had already bought home a bulletin the night before, when he attended Mass. But me bringing home a bulletin was his way of making sure that I had attended the morning service. Pretty sneaky old man, but you are dealing with a professor, who has earned a PHD in slyness and skulduggery, or so I thought. If I did decide to play hooky from church, I would simply pop in after the service was over, grab myself a bulletin, bless myself with a little Holy Water-- just to get the smell of the Church on me-- and then head on home.

I had skipped Sunday church services many times in the past and always gotten away with it. It just so happened that on this particular Sunday morning, I was honestly planning on attending the service. The priest usually didn't have a lot of Altar Boys on Sundays, so I thought I might as well give him a hand. On my way to church, I passed Randy and Morris who were returning their empty beer bottles by wheel barrels to Old Man Drover's store. They each had a wheel barrel which was overflowing with bottles and apparently, this was their second trip already this morning. They told me that they figured they had at least another 5 trips each, as the Skin-Hut was loaded down with empties. As I chatted with the boys, I could see that they were hung-over and strung out and I reasoned that they were most likely returning their empties to purchase a few cold ones to relieve their throbbing heads.

The boys and I reached a deal that was beneficial to all three of us. I would help them bring back all their empties and in return they will give me two dollars; plus I get to hang out with them in the Skin-Hut for a little while. For a ten year old boy, two dollars was a nice chunk of change and the chance to experience the Skin-Hut and investigate the legendary tickle trunk was like finding the Holy Grail. I followed along with the boys with a little red wagon stacked high with empty beer bottles. It took us four trips each to finally empty the Skin-Hut of bottles. Thank God, Old Man Drover's store was only a five minute walk away.

When the boys got their money, just as I suspected, they each picked up a case of beer and pocketed the rest. True to their words, they gave me a two dollar bill and invited me back to the Skin-Hut.

When we walked inside the legendary shed, I was careful not to touch anything out of fear of getting the scent of skank on my church clothes. In a way, I felt a lot like Joseph Conrad and that I had just stepped into *The Heart of Darkness*. I did however get the opportunity to examine the boys' vast collection of skin-books-always a rare treat for a ten year old. The boys were sucking back their beers and paid little attention to me as I stumbled upon a large brown cardboard box. Taped to the box was a sheet of white paper with the words 'Tickle Trunk' written on it. I knew I had found the mysterious and elusive box of women's undergarments. There were bras and panties of all shapes and sizes and I was really enjoying my probing until I happened upon a giant pair of beige granny panties that contained shit-stains all along the arse. I cautiously stepped away from the box and made my way back to the boys.

"What time is it Randy"? Randy took a look at his watch and replied, "It's almost eleven thirty".

"Oh shit", I cried, "church is over at 11:00 and I still have to run up there to get a bulletin."

Randy and Morris just laughed because they too had played hooky from church back when they were kids.

All of a sudden, Randy said, "Hey Morris, didn't one of those girls that dropped in here last night, have a church bulletin"?

Morris thought for a moment and then responded, "I think she did buddy, check the table Hickey, I'm sure she left it on the table".

As I checked the table, it was covered with beer bottle caps, dirty ashtrays and skin-books. But in one corner, neatly folded, was this week's church bulletin.

"Take that now Hickey and go on home", Randy suggested.

"Hey Morris" he continued, "you got to love those Catholic girls; they go to church every Saturday night, trying to find Jesus and receive forgiveness, and an hour later they are right back here with us in the Skin-Hut, drinking beer, smoking cigarettes and riding the ole stiff one-eye."

I could hear the boys killing themselves laughing as I walked away from the shed and headed home. When I got home, I could see that Dad was busy cutting up wood with his chainsaw. When he saw me approaching, he turned off his chainsaw and asked, "How was church"?

I reached into my back pocket and proudly pulled out my bulletin and responded, "It was good, nothing out of the ordinary."

Dad put his chainsaw on the ground, walked towards me, ripped the bulletin out of my hand and shouted, "How would you know, you weren't anywhere near the church this morning."

My heart fell into my stomach, I couldn't form a sentence; Dad was understandably irate and I knew I was about to feel his wrath.

"I'm going to give you one chance to tell me where you were this morning", he yelled, "and if I even think that you are lying to me, I'm going to lose my boot up in your arse".

I stammered and stuttered trying to find the words. I certainly was not about to lie to him again.

I told him how I helped Morris and Randy bring back their empties and how they had paid me two dollars for helping them. I even held out the two dollar bill as a peace offering to Dad but he just slapped my hand to the side, knocking the money out of my hand and I watched my 2 dollars fall to the ground. Of course, I intentionally left out the part about how the boys invited me back to the Skin-Hut to hang out, because that would have sent Dad over the edge altogether.

Dad just glared at me and shouted, "So all of a sudden, beer bottles are more important than going to church...... and did the boys have you over to their shed?"

I wanted to lie but I was too scared and answered, "Yes, but only for a minute to give me this bulletin".

Well sir, if you ever wanted to see a man lose it, you should have been in George Hickey's yard that day.

"How many God Damned times have I warned you to stay away from that spunk-shack?" He screamed. I just stood there crying, I wanted this whole ordeal to be over, but Dad was too enraged and fuming. I knew from past experiences that once he resorted to swearing; there was no coming back. He was now in a state of irrational and irreconcilable behaviour. I couldn't remember ever being this scared as I stood there, paralyzed and in shock.

"Get in the house and change out of your church clothes", he roared, "I got a full day's work planned for you".

As I turned and walked toward the house, Dad stepped up behind me and gave me a swift kick in the arse.

"Hurry up, run, don't walk!" He shouted, as I took off running and bawling for the house, fearing for my life.   As I was in my room quickly changing my clothes, Mom came running into my room, asking what I had done this time to set Dad off.

I told her the whole story and she looked at me with pity and worry in her eyes and said, "I can't do anything for you Brian, you know how much you father hates lies and disobedience. Finish getting dressed and go outside and see what he wants you to do. And for God's sake, keep your mouth shut, do what he tells you to do and maybe you might live to see supper."

I left the house and I could still hear Dad mumbling to himself about how many times he warned me to stay away from that shed. I walked towards Dad with a bit of a limp, hoping that he would pity me and think that his kick in the arse hurt me more than it actually did.

He put his chainsaw in the shed and brought me out the little hand-held buck saw.

"Finish cutting up the rest of this wood," he demanded, "and have it all done before it gets dark tonight. Don't let any of your friends help you and after you get it sawed up, start packing it in the shed. I'm going to take a walk over to Randy and Morris's shed and have a word with the boys."

After Dad left, I started sawing the wood. There was about 2 cords left to cut, which would only take about half an hour with the chainsaw. But for a ten year old with a buck saw, it would take me the rest of the day. I went through each log as fast as I could, stopping only long enough to pack it in the shed. It took me the rest of the day to finish it but it also gave me a lot of time to think.   Dad was right in his actions, as he had been preaching since we were babies on the importance of honesty and trust. I regretted lying to him and making him angry but mostly I regretted making him feel disappointed in me. I was used to Dad getting mad and frustrated with me, but today I could see the hurt and discontent in his eyes from my deceptions and this didn't sit well with me. I didn't know if he would ever trust me again or if our relationship would forever be changed. I made a promise to myself that I would never lie to Dad again and that I would do whatever it takes to make it up to him.

It took me seven hours but I finished cutting the last log just as the sun was setting and I figured that if I was lucky, I would get the last of the wood packed in the shed before nightfall. Dad came out of the house and walked towards me.

"Oh, you've got it all packed in the shed as well," he said quite impressed, "nice job but that's enough for today, come on in the house and get some supper."

As we walked towards the house he put his arm around my shoulder and apologized for kicking me in the arse. I broke down into tears and told him I was sorry and that it will never happen again. He gave me a little squeeze, handed me my 2 dollar bill and said, "I believe you buddy, now let's just forget about the whole thing."

I could no longer look in Rod's direction on the Altar, out of fear of laughing, so I decided to focus and concentrate on the priest's Sermon. Maybe I might actually get some good out of this week's church experience.

The Priest was preaching about how God made the Heavens and the earth and how every creature on earth was sacred. This got me thinking about the roast beef that I had just had for supper before I attended church. What if God didn't intend for us to eat his creatures? What if we were all put on this earth to live in harmony with our fellow man as well as the cows, the feathered creatures, pigs and all the fish in the sea?

I then imagined God laying back on a cloud in Heaven on the 7th day, resting with a straw of hay between his teeth, exhausted after all he had created in the last 6 days, rather pleased with himself. I could envision him sending down to earth a few Angels to check on our progress and to report back to him. I wish I could have been there to see God's reaction when the Angels returned to Heaven and reported back to him in horror.

"Holy Jesus, it's crazy down there, the humans are devouring all the animals. Lord, you may have provided your human children with ample fruit, vegetables and plants, nuts and berries, but My God, they are eating everything. They feast on the cows, the chickens, goats, sheep and even the ugly pigs. It a real mess down there God, they are even using sticks and string to pluck the fish from the sea and then eat them. Lord, those gluttonous bastards, you have to see it to believe it!"

I can only imagine the look of disbelief on God's face on the realization that we were eating all his creations as he smacked his forehead with his palm and said, "Maybe I didn't really think this through!"

This daydream made me chuckle to myself and I quickly realized that I couldn't pay attention to the priest because my mind was incapable of drifting. Unfortunately, that's the way I've always coped with boring events that couldn't seem to keep my attention. My mind would drift away and I would usually imagine something that was humorous to me; it was like having my very own comedy writing team living inside my head. I could never understand why I found things funny at the most inappropriate times. Especially when it came to almost anything to do with religion; I always found humour in our Catholic teachings.

Mom and Dad were very religious, so I had to tread carefully around them when it came to religion. Even back in our own home, we had a different picture of Jesus hanging on a wall in every room. It took me the first 8 years of my life to realize that Jesus wasn't a family member. We had so many pictures of him in our home; I naturally assumed that he was one of my Uncles, living away in Ontario somewhere.

Every year right before Easter, Catholics partake in a ritual known as Lent which lasts 40 days from Ash Wednesday, right up to Psalm Sunday. Most Catholics usually give up something, or abstain for those 40 days to symbolize Moses and the Jews wandering the desert for 40 days. During this 40 day period in our home, the family got together every night and recited the Rosary; a series of 50 Hail Mary's.

We all knelt in the living room, each holding a set of Rosary beads as Dad led us into the Rosary. On more than one of these occasions, I had the sharp searing sensation of Dad's foot against my arse, as he kicked me for laughing and joking around during the Rosary. I simply couldn't help myself and, in my mind, a kick in the ass or a smack in the back of the head was well worth a good chuckle during our Prayer session. One time Al came knocking on our door, just as we were about to start the Rosary. I told him that I couldn't come outside because Georgio was getting ready to have Mass!

Once again, a smile came across my face as I sat there on the Altar listening to the Priest's sermon. I decided not to think about anything and tried instead to focus on our beautiful Catholic church. It was a gorgeous building that was built by local volunteers, including my other Grandfather, Vince Dalton, several years ago. There was a big Altar with a huge statue of Mary, Joseph and of course a giant likeness of Jesus hanging on a cross. I was quite impressed with the architecture of the building and the tremendous time and work that went into each detail.

The main aisle was in the center of the Church and on both walls walking up the aisle were seven majestic stained-glassed windows. Depicted in these 14 stained glassed windows were the 14 Stations of the Cross. Now, for any of you who are unfamiliar, the Stations of the Cross commemorate the 14 key events on the day of Christ's crucifixion. I read with great interest, each Station which was beautifully illustrated in our church windows.

1st Station: Jesus is condemned to death
2nd Station: Jesus carries his cross
3rd Station: Jesus falls the first time
4th Station: Jesus meets his mother
5th Station: Simon of Cyrene helps Jesus to carry his cross
6th Station: Veronica wipes the face of Jesus
7th Station: Jesus falls the second time
8th Station: Jesus meets the women of Jerusalem
9th Station: Jesus falls a third time
10th Station: Jesus clothes are taken away
11th Station: Jesus is nailed to the cross
12th Station: Jesus dies on the cross
13th Station: The body of Jesus is taken down from the cross
14th Station: Jesus is laid in the tomb

The object of the Stations of the Cross is to help the faithful make a spiritual pilgramage to the chief scene of Christ's sufferings and death, and has become one of the most popular of our Catholic devotions. After reading the Stations of the Cross, I suddenly realized how the depiction of Jesus, somehow resembled our buddy Randy, in fact, the resemblance was uncanny. I couldn't help but smile because every single person who lived on the East End of Bell Island has, at one time or another, bared witness to Randy staggering home completely intoxicated after having too many beers at the Skin-Hut.

I thought how Randy himself was like Jesus, but instead of carrying a cross to his place of crucifixion while being whipped and spit on; Randy was staggering down the road, carrying an open case of beer, trying desperately to make his way home. So, in my pre-adolescent, sacrilegious mind, I imagined East End's version of the 14 Stations that depicts Randy on his pilgrimage home:

1st Station: Randy gets intoxicated and is condemned to leave the Skin-Hut
2nd Station: Randy carries his remaining beers home
3rd Station: Randy falls the first time
4th Station: Randy meets his uncle
5th Station: Lenny and Mark help Randy to carry his beer
6th Station: A concerned neighbor wipes the drool off Randy
7th Station: Randy falls the second time
8th Station: Randy meets and flirts with local women leaving bingo
9th Station: Randy falls a third time
10th Station: Randy pisses himself
11th Station: Randy lays hammered on his picnic table
12th Station: Randy passes out on his picnic table
13th Station: The body of Randy is taken down from the

picnic table
14th Station: Randy is laid in his bed

This whole Stations of the Cross scenario was starting to make me laugh to myself so I decided I needed another distraction. Rather than look at our churches wonderful architecture; I endeavoured to focus my attention on strangers sitting quietly in the congregation. This hopefully should take my mind off any foolishness that was taking place inside my head. I gazed out over the huge crowd and my eyes automatically fell upon Karen, as if she had some type of magnetic hold over me. She was wearing a pretty summer dress with a white sweater on top. Her hair was beautifully tied up in a red ribbon and she looked like an angel.

She caught me looking at her and smiled at me and blew me a kiss, just to tease me. Karen had known for at least the past 5 years that I had a giant crush on her and sometimes she would tease me or get me to do stuff for her, just for her enjoyment. I didn't care because any minute I could spend in Karen's company was a minute well spent.

My mind drifted back to four years ago when I was eight and Karen was ten. All of my friends, including Karen, used to go to the Kiddie dances every Friday Night at the Wabana Boys and Girls Club for members between the ages of 5 and 13. Although I was eight, I had never been to a dance but decided that now I was ready to give it a try.

I slicked my hair back with Dad's Brylcreem, I had my shirt collar standing upright like Elvis and I totally drenched myself in my Dad's best cologne. Yes sir, I thought I was God's gift to women and the only problem I could imagine was which girl I would allow to dance with me.

Throughout that fateful night, I must have asked twenty different girls to dance with me, but not the one wanted to cut a rug with Brian Hickey. A couple of girls laughed at me, one girl called me Fonsie and another girl actually told me to "drop dead". A bit harsh, I thought, as this eight year old boy was just trying to experience his first dance.

Sadly, near the end of the night, I could be found standing in the corner swaying to the music all alone. I guess Karen had witnessed this pathetic site and found it in the goodness of her heart to ask me to dance the final song. It was a romantic song and I was nervous as hell. The lights went down low and as the music started, Karen put her arms around me and we began to slow dance. She smelled so good, I held her as tight as I could and never wanted to let her go. I wanted to kiss her so bad, but she was a good 3 inches taller than me and I didn't know how to make that happen.

Suddenly, I began to experience an all too familiar sensation within my pants. I didn't know why, but my wang decided to stand up, as I guess it just wanted to take a better look around. Even at that tender age, I was so hard that a cat wouldn't be able to stick his claws into it! I tried my best to keep it away from Karen; I figured the night was already such a disaster, no need to end it on a low note. We just continued slow dancing to The Eagle's, *Take It To The Limit*, and when the song was over, Karen thanked me for the dance, gave me a hug and walked away.

When the lights came back on, I stood there thinking that this was the best night of my life. I just had my first slow dance with the girl of my dreams, not a bad way to spend a Friday night. I wanted to jump and yell in exhilaration but in all the excitement, I guess I had forgotten about my little trouser buddy. Someone had noticed it and pointed and yelled, "Hey, Hickey's got a woody."

I wasn't really sure what this meant, all I knew was that the sundial in my pants was reading 12:00, so I quickly put on my jacket and got out of there as everyone laughed and pointed.

While I was walking home, I decided that this would be my last dance for a while. When I arrived home, I was visibly upset and Dad asked me what was wrong. I told him about dancing with Karen and how it felt good and confessed the awkward situation with my wang. I asked him why it does that, and why is it that most mornings when I wake up, I discover that my wang has been awake long before me? Dad told me that it was all part of becoming a man and not to worry about it.

He added, "If the day ever comes that it no longer stands up; then it's time to worry."

I smiled to myself at what Dad had told me four years ago but I was suddenly disturbed from my reminiscing by the priest who whispered, "Hickey, wake up and bring me the Eucharist." To my surprise, I had day-dreamed most of the service away. I brought him the Eucharist and said, "Sorry Father," and quickly sat back down.

When the mass was over the priest pulled me to the side and

said, "You should get your head out of the clouds Hickey, you might learn something".

While I was leaving the church, I noticed my Dad was outside chatting with the Principle of our school. That's odd, I thought to myself as both men were looking in my direction. When we got home that evening, Dad mentioned that the Principal had told him a story that had happened yesterday, with a young fellow named Paddy which involved disrespecting Sister Grace. I told Dad how Paddy had burst out laughing during a prayer but insisted that I had no idea what he was laughing at.

I knew Dad didn't believe me, but since I wasn't the one who had gotten into trouble, there was no need to further dwell on it.

When we arrived home, I quickly changed out of my church clothes and ran down to Lahey's field. It was almost 8:30 and it wouldn't be long before sun down. The crowd was starting to gather around and I was surprised to see Don had shown up, even after his little fiasco earlier today with his wang hanging out. We all sat around the fire pit at home-plate, which indicated that the older boys were preparing to start a little pit fire.

We younger kids were instructed to scour the field for any sticks or dead branches that would burn. I snuck off to Dad's woodshed and brought back an armful of his dry wood that was packed away for the winter. I knew Dad wouldn't mind me taking an armful, besides, Paul and I had cut up the majority of it, so I figured I was entitled to a few pieces. The boys lit a few old scraps of paper and soon we all enjoyed a nice roaring fire.

Everyone was sitting around chatting and laughing, telling jokes and sharing little stories about some of the things that happened to them this past winter and school year. Although everyone was enjoying each other's company, I couldn't help but notice that there was still a hierarchy that existed.

The older and cooler kids sat on one side of the fire and got to determine how big the fire would be and what topics were up for discussion.

The younger kids however, like Greg, Krissy, Karen and I sat on the opposite side of the fire. We were there to gather fire wood, run little errands and provide comic relief for the older kids. This however, never bothered me, for even at the age of 12, I fully understood how lucky I was to be a part of this. I was privy to information and teenage antics that otherwise never would have been afforded to me, if not for these older kids. I was hearing stories and being exposed to things to which no 12 year old should ever have access. You wouldn't dare disobey one of the older kids, out of fear of being banished from all the wonderful merriment that magically emerged on our field every single day.

For whatever reason, the topic of Christmas came up and Howie decided to tell an interesting story about this past Christmas, which involved my Dad. First of all, let me remind you that my Dad and Howie's Dad both worked for the Bell Island Hospital. Dad was a janitor and Howie's Dad, Keith worked in the kitchen. Apparently, from listening to Dad grumble for the past few years, Keith was a bit of a shit-disturber, who liked to brown-nose and tried to better position himself by stepping on his co-workers toes. From what I had heard over the supper table these past few years, Dad and Keith had butted heads quite a few times and Dad didn't trust him, nor did he like him.

Anyway, getting back to Howie's story, he looks at me and says, "Hickey, there's something wrong with your father; the man is nuts". The whole crowd was intrigued by Howie's statement and urged him to tell more.

"I'm not really sure what happened" Howie continued, "but around two days before Christmas, myself, Mom and Dad were eating breakfast at our kitchen table and the next thing we know, George Hickey whips open our door, throws a live 30 lb turkey at us and dumps a bag of vegetables on our porch floor and yells, "Here's your turkey and vegetables Keith, enjoy your Christmas Dinner you rotten windsucker!"

The whole crowd burst out laughing and looked to me to fill in the blanks. I reminded everyone how Dad raises his own turkeys and kills them every December, as well as grows his own vegetables.

"Well", I said, "This past year the hospital was having a Christmas fundraiser and selling tickets on various items."

Dad wanted to contribute and donated a complete Christmas dinner, consisting of garden-fresh potatoes, carrots, turnip and cabbage, as well as a 30 pound fresh turkey that would be delivered to the lucky winner, just before Christmas. The fundraising went very well this year and there were many tickets sold throughout the Island. When it came time to draw for all the prizes on December 20th, Dad himself actually won a bottle of whiskey. Unfortunately, when it came time to draw for the Christmas dinner prize that Dad had donated, Keith had the winning ticket. Man, was Dad ever pissed and the thought of Keith enjoying one of his delicious, fresh turkeys was too much for Dad to handle.

To make matters worse, for the next couple of days at work, Keith was really rubbing it in and teasing Dad and asking him, ""When am I getting my turkey George? The meat better be moist and tender or I'm sending it back.""

The guys that Dad worked with, got a great laugh at this because they all knew just how much Dad disliked Keith. So finally on the 23rd of December, when Dad could no longer take the joking, he decided he would make good on his promise and deliver the turkey and vegetables.

I didn't know what was going on; all I knew was that I was sitting in Dad's truck with a live 30lb turkey sitting in my lap." All of a sudden, Dad and I pulled into Howie's yard. Dad parked his truck, took the turkey from me, opened Howie's front door and pitched it towards their kitchen table. The turkey landed in the middle of their kitchen floor, spread his big wings and ran around the kitchen. Howie's Mom took off running down the hall, while Keith jumped up on the kitchen table scared to death. Then Dad dumped all the vegetables on their porch floor, and we drove away laughing."

I finished up with my story and everyone, including Howie, just sat there laughing and shaking their heads in disbelief.

"Your father really is a crazy bastard Hickey," Lenny said, as he threw a couple more sticks on the fire.

"Who's a crazy bastard?" asked a familiar voice from the dark. As they approached the fire, we could see that it was Al and Randy.

"Ahhh, Randy and Super Grover," Lenny acknowledged the boys, "What are you guys up to?"

The boys came closer to the fire and sat down; Al moved next to me, while Randy sat beside Lenny.

"Not much, just hanging out", Randy responded. "Where's Morris tonight Randy?" someone asked.

Randy started to laugh and replied, "Morris's home in bed, he had a bit of a hard night last night." We all knew by Randy's tone that something shocking or funny was about to be revealed and so we all listened intensely.

"Last night," Randy began, "Myself and Morris picked up a couple cases of beer and were sat back in the Skin-Hut listening to a few tunes and sucking back a few cold ones. We were having a good time, feeling no pain when all of a sudden we could hear a ruckus coming up the East End road. It was well after midnight and when we checked it out, it turned out to be Horny Heather Morgan staggering up the road, loaded drunk."

Now Mrs. Heather Morgan was a heavy-set woman, about 45 years old, who made her living as a cashier at the local grocery store. Her husband would go away to Ontario each summer to find work and return every fall to collect unemployment insurance for the winter. It was widely known that while Mr. Morgan was away, Mrs. Morgan would play, hence the name Horny Heather.

"Anyway," Randy continued, "Morris met her on the road and asked her back to the Skin-Hut for a cold beer. She agreed and all three of us went back, sat down and drank a couple of beers. She was very drunk and spent most of the night cursing her husband for leaving her every year and telling Morris that he was cute. Pretty soon they started sucking face, so not wanting to be a third wheel, I jumped up on the top bunk and fell asleep. I was awakened a little while later by a tremendous crash that shook the whole shed. I jumped down from the top bunk, only to find Morris lying on the floor, butt naked and knocked out cold. I turned on the lamp and could see Horny Heather; her mouth wide open, snoring away in the bottom bunk."

"She was as naked as the day she was born, with her big banana titties drooping over the side of the bed and her false teeth sitting on the table," he continued.

"She looked like someone had hit her in the face with a shovel. I went over to Morris and shook him and he eventually started to come around. I asked him what had happened and apparently he woke to go outside to take a piss, but slipped on something and banged his head off the table.   I couldn't figure out what he could have slipped on so I took the lamp and shined the light on the floor and began to look around. I came across a small streak of blood on the floor and assumed that Morris must have cut his foot open on a bottle or maybe a piece of glass. Then at the end of the blood streak, I spotted the culprit; Horny Heather's used Tampon. Apparently, her 'aunt-flo' was visiting!"

Randy began roaring laughing as he continued, "Morris stepped on her used Tampon, slid and knocked himself out, on the corner of the table".

Everybody fell into fits of laugher, but at the same time we were also a little grossed out.

"That's not all," Randy continued, "This morning Morris woke up with a wicked headache and an egg-sized lump on his head. He was hung over and hurting and got his first glance at what a toothless, 200-pound, naked Horny Heather looks like at six o'clock in the morning. He desperately wanted to go inside his house for some aspirin, but she was asleep on his arm and he couldn't get it out from under her. He didn't know whether to wake her up or gnaw his arm off! When he finally did wake her up, he went into his house and after about 20 minutes, she and I both knew that he wasn't coming back."

Randy went on with a grin, "I peeked down on her from the

top bunk and she gave me a wink and that come-hither look, as she smiled at me without any teeth. I could tell that she was hurtin' for a squirtin' so naturally, I did what any red-blooded male would do in that situation; I crawled in the bottom bunk alongside her, grabbed me a heaping handful of flabby boob and treated myself to an extra-large scoop of that Horny Heather lovin'."

As we all laughed, he continued with story. "She may not have been pretty, but it was chilly early this morning and when I cuddled next to her big, warm, hairy body, I felt like I was Han Solo in Star Wars on the frozen planet of Hoth, spooning with a Taun-Taun."

Again, everyone busted a gut laughing, even Shirley who was enjoying a can of Pepsi; suddenly spit a mouthful of her soda across the ground as she couldn't stop herself from laughing.

"Randy......", Lenny laughed, "you and Morris must have cast-iron stomachs."

Randy just laughed along with everyone, shook his head and said, "Oh well, what are ya going do, when I first got a look at her girth this morning, I thought to myself, Lord, you gave me a mountain, but what can I say, ugly women needs lovin' too."   Again, the crowd all burst out laughing at Randy's story.   "That's so gross," Shirley insisted, "I can't believe you had sex with her while she was on her period."

Randy just shrugged and said, "Ah, what's the difference, it's just like playing golf after a rainstorm. If the front greens are too chewed up and sloppy, you can always play the back nine!"

I had no idea what he was talking about, so I just laughed along with everyone else.

I couldn't help but notice how pretty Karen looked by the camp fire. Just to watch her laughing and having a good time made me feel good. I also couldn't help notice how, under different circumstances, this would be considered very romantic; sitting around a roaring fire on a beautiful summer's night. Unfortunately, Karen must have been thinking the same thing, as I watched her inching herself closer to Mark. Damned, stupid, sexy Mark, I needed to stop her in her tracks and blurted out the first thing that came to me.

"Hey, has anyone heard what's happening with The Woman in White"?

All the different conversations came to an immediate halt, as any mention of the Woman in White tended to catch people's attention.

"Yeah," Lenny said, "I heard that last night the Woman in White chased a couple of girls up the road and they ran crying and screaming into the hospital begging for help."

The Woman in White was legendary throughout Bell Island. Just about every summer, some fool would dress in a white sheet, hide in the woods and chase scared and unescorted girls up the road. Of course, as with most legends, people would embellish and exaggerate the details of a run-in with the Woman in White.

Some reports had the Woman in White being seen carrying a knife, while others said they saw her one night all covered in blood. I myself was not concerned with such foolishness. Since I was a young kid, Dad had told me that The Woman in White was only one person with a white sheet, chasing people at night.

He told me that about 10 summers ago, someone was at it again with the white sheet, chasing women.   One night one of my Dad's friend's wife was chased down the East End road and so Dad and a couple of his buddies decided to do something about it. They looked for patterns and came to the realization that the Woman in White would strike every Thursday night after bingo ended.

It made sense when you think about it; mostly women attended bingo, and many women walked home at night when bingo was over.   On this particular Thursday night, Dad and three of his friends spread themselves out throughout the woods not far from where bingo was taking place.

Sure enough, a little later that night, two girls came screaming down the road and passed right by where Dad was hiding. A few seconds later the Woman in White came running by, only to have Dad step out in front of her, cutting her off.

When the Woman in White realized that Dad wasn't afraid of her, she started backing away only to have Dad's three buddies step out on the road behind her, trapping her between the four Men.

"Now", Dad said, "let's get a look at who you are!"

The Woman in White tried to make a run for it but Dad and his friends managed to catch her, tore off the sheet.

When they discovered it was a man, they persisted in giving him a beaten.

"We laid him out on the road, all bloodied and bruised." Dad continued, "We could see that it was old Jimmy Prole from the West end of the Island. I felt a bit bad for giving him such a beaten but he had to be taught a lesson. We eventually helped him up and told him that if we ever catch him doing it again, we would put him in the hospital, permanently."

Jimmy agreed and swore he would never dress up again. I asked Dad what would make a man do something like that, what exactly is he getting out of this?

"I don't know Brian", he replied, "but you've got to understand, I've known Jimmy Prole most of my life and he has always been a bit simple minded. When we were teenagers, he dipped his cat's tail in kerosene and lit it on fire, just to see what would happen. Unfortunately, the cat ran underneath his father's barn and burned it to the ground."

He went on, "Another time, he got caught wearing an empty chip bag on his wang, trying to have sexual relations with one of his Dad's goats. He has no education, he has no social skills, he has no friends and he's never worked and although I don't like to say that the man is stupid; he is definitely not firing on all cylinders."

Jimmy actually got arrested one time for taking a dump on people's car windshields. For about an entire year, he used to sneak into people's driveways in the middle of the night and take a crap on their windshields. By the time the Police caught and arrested that crazy knobgobbler, he had shit on more than 50 cars and was known throughout Bell Island as The Shit Bandit.

Dad said, "So hopefully the little thumping we gave him that night may have been enough to scare him straight and smarten him up."

As the night stretched on, people began dispersing and heading home. Lenny extinguished the fire and shouted.

"See everyone tomorrow afternoon around 1:30; it should be a good day".

It was common knowledge that it was pointless to meet before lunch time on Sunday, because everyone would have to leave again at 12:00 in order to go home and enjoy their cooked Sunday dinner. Paul and I walked home to our house still laughing and joking about the Horny Heather story that Randy had told us.

4

The Potato Garden

The next morning, Dad had Paul and I up bright and early to get a start on our chores. His philosophy was, the earlier we get started, the earlier we finished up, leaving us plenty of time to spend with our friends. This suited us fine, we knew there was a lot to do, and the sooner we got it done, the sooner we could meet up with everyone on the field.

We raced over to the barn and did our usual morning chores of feeding and watering the animals, cleaning out the barn and collecting the eggs and milk.

What's on the go for today Georgio," I asked Dad in a playful manner. "Let's get the lead out; myself and Paul got important people waiting for us."

Paul and I laughed at my little joke. "I'm glad you're in such a good mood and full of energy", Dad responded, "because today we have to set out our potato garden and then go up to my Father's yard and set out his garden."

The smile instantly fell from my face; '*oh damn I hated setting potatoes.*' I wouldn't mind if we owned a small, sensible garden, but Dad had a piece of ploughed land which measured 150 feet by 75 feet and Pop's garden was about the same size. This was sure to take up the entire morning. Of all the chores that we did for Dad; planting, weeding and harvesting potatoes were my least favourite. I remember late last Fall, Dad decided that we were going to harvest his and Pop's potatoes all on a Saturday. It was a little chilly out that day and I desperately wanted to avoid it. So early that morning at breakfast, I faked a bad stomach, hoping Dad would take pity on me.

Unfortunately, there was no pity to be found that morning as Dad insisted, "If you have a bad stomach, then spending a few hours in the potato garden bending and stretching will be the best thing for you". Dad knew I was faking and that I just wanted to stay home all day Saturday and watch cartoons. I knew I was fighting a losing battle and I would have to take my appeal to a higher court.....MY MOM.

Mom was standing at the sink, washing dishes as I slowly walked over to her. "Mom, I don't feel so well", I said to her with the saddest, weakest voice that I could muster.

Mom just put her hand on my forehead and said, "Well Brian, you don't feel warm, hurry up and finish your breakfast, maybe the fresh air will make you feel better".

Et Tu, Brute; thanks for nothing Mudder. I could see that I was on my own for this one. From my end of the table, I could see Dad grinning at me while he was eating his toast. By God, that man knew me better than I knew myself and he couldn't help but smile at my feeble and futile attempts. However, he underestimated my resolve for I was determined to win this one not only for me, but for overworked kids all around the world. I organized my thoughts, stood up from the kitchen table and bellowed out my best argument.

"Here we are at the end of September; I go to school from Monday to Friday and I deserve to have Saturday off. Instead I have to spend half my weekend plucking potatoes from the cold ground. Why the hell can't we buy our potatoes at the grocery store like every other normal person, why does this family have to do everything the hard way? We chop our own wood, raise and kill our own farm animals, cut our own hay and grow our own vegetables. What's wrong with us; are we living in the 1980's or did we somehow get transported back to the Little House on the Prairie?"

I sat back down to the kitchen table and mumbled a few more disparaging complaints about having too many chores and I even once again criticized how weak my tea was, as USUAL. Dad just continued to eat his breakfast while grinning at me, until he calmly said, "Are you finished bitchin' now; hurry up and finish your breakfast so we can get started on the potatoes."

I wanted to tell my Dad where he could stick his potatoes, but let's face it, that was never going to happen. I mean I was upset, but I wasn't stupid. I frantically searched my brain for any plausible solution.

Dad decided to add a little more salt to my wounds as he stood up and walked away from the breakfast table, he said, "I'm only giving you 5 more minutes Brian, so hurry up, we have a full day of work ahead of us." He pulled on his boots and jacket and with a sly grin on his face, he kissed Mom on the cheek before he headed out the door.

By now I was fuming, not only had I been outwitted by the Old Man, but he was actually taunting me about it. Well, I was hoping that it wouldn't come to this but like they say, desperate times call for desperate measures. With all my focus, with all my strength, with all my will, I bared down with my stomach muscles as hard as I possibly could, just like a pregnant woman trying to deliver twins. I pushed with all of my might until finally, Eureka...... I crapped my pants.   I let out a huge cry and took off running towards the bathroom. Mom came running after me yelling, "What's wrong, are you okay?"

When she finally discovered what I had done, she quickly poured me a hot bath and informed Dad that I was too sick to help out at the potato garden.

Now, you may think that this was a bit of an overreaction on my part but in my mind, getting a full day of lazin' around on the couch watching cartoons, was well worth getting a bit a crap on me. I still recall watching Dad through the window later that morning, as he and Paul loaded the plough on the horse and cart and headed towards Pop's garden. I threw him a little wave through the window, just as a peace offering and my way of saying no hard feelings.   Although he had seen me in the window, Dad ignored my wave and rode away without even acknowledging me, which told me 3 things:

1. He knew I was faking.
2. He was extremely pissed off.
3. I would definitely pay up for this at a later date.

But for now, I was the victor and to the victor go the spoils, as I anticipated a full day of relaxing and watching cartoons, while being tended on by Mom.

We lifted about 8 buckets of seed potatoes into the trunk of Dad's car and drove over to his potato garden. The entire garden still reeked of rotten Caplin and manure from the barn. You see, a few weeks earlier Dad turned over the soil with his horse and plough and spread manure and Caplin all over the garden for fertilizer. So in reality, the process of setting out Dad's potato garden actually started a few weeks ago.

For an entire week after school, Paul and I would bring over a horse and boxcar load of manure, which had been piled up outside the barn all winter, and spread it over the garden. Naturally, once we adequately covered our garden, then we had to do Pop Hickey's garden as well.

Once both gardens were covered in manure, then we would wait for the Caplin to roll, just as they have done every June. The beach down at Number 2 Cove would come alive as millions of these tiny fish washed up on shoreline. People would be there to get their bags or buckets full of the tasty fish and take them home for a meal of freshly fried Caplin with homemade bread and butter. Many people dried and salted their Caplin so they could enjoy a meal or two over the winter months.

But not us, no Sir, when the Hickey's do something, we have to do it big! Dad would bring the horse and boxcar right down to the beach and we would load the boxcar full with Caplin. The horse would then pull the load of Caplin to the potato garden and we would spread the tiny fish over the newly turned-over ground. Once we emptied the cart, we would then rake over the Caplin with clay to keep the Sea Gulls and stray cats away from the fish. Then we would head back down to Number 2 Cove and repeat the process over and over, until both Dad and Pop Hickey were satisfied that they had enough fertilizer in their potato gardens.

"Don't forget", Dad said, "set each seed about a foot apart". As if we didn't know this; we had been planting potatoes ever since we were old enough to walk. Paul & I would race to see who could set out our row (or drill) the fastest and Dad would follow along behind us to bury them in. It wasn't hard work, but it was painstakingly slow and boring.

I would invent games while planting the seeds, so instead of planting potatoes, I was planting grenades and when we were finally finished, I was going to blow the shit out of the entire garden. Ahhhh, if only it were that easy!

There was no possible way that Dad could bury the potatoes as fast as Paul and I planted them, so by the time we finished, Dad had only buried about one third of the potatoes.

"Hurry up Skipper", I shouted out him, "If you move any slower, people are going to mistake you for a scarecrow".

Paul would be both amused and amazed at some of the things I could say to Dad and get away with it. He would never speak to Dad the way that I did, but Dad knew I was only fooling around. I think he understood and accepted that if you expected to get any mindless, physical labour out of me; you had to let me entertain myself.

"Don't worry about me, funny guy", Dad retorted, "There's two more rakes in the back of the car for you and Paul to help me bury the rest of these potatoes".

After about three hours we finally finished up with Dad's garden. We drove home to get something to drink and to pick up some more seed potatoes. As I ran inside our house for a glass of water, I could smell Mom's Sunday dinner. There was a stuffed chicken and roast of beef in the oven. The salt meat and vegetables were boiling on the stove top. For readers unfamiliar with 'salt meat,' this is the base of a meal served in many homes on Sunday in Newfoundland even today. The vegetables are boiled with a piece of beef which has been preserved in a brine solution and unnamed chemicals.

It was already 11:00 A.M. and we had at least another three hours to go to finish the work at Pop's garden. This was going to make us late for both dinner and Lahey's field. I grabbed the phone and called up Rod, Greg and Al. I never got to speak to Al however, as he was still in bed, but I spoke to Rod and Greg. I explained our situation and asked if they wouldn't mind giving us a hand. They weren't busy and said we could pick them both up along our way.

As we were getting in the car, I informed Dad that he could pick up Rod and Greg on our way to Pops because the boys were going to give us a hand. Dad just shook his head in disbelief and said, "Leave it to you Brian to con someone into doing your work".

I just grinned at him and said, "It's like I always say Old Man; never put off until tomorrow, what you can have someone else do for you today". Again, Dad just shook his head and laughed.

We picked up the boys and as we drove to my Grandfathers, the boys informed me that I would be the one working side by side with Pop. The boys all found him to be far too serious and hard to work with. I could see their point, he liked order and decorum, but I never had the same issues with him as most people did. His surly and cantankerous disposition was a source of entertainment for me, and likewise, I could always get a chuckle out of him.

As soon as he walked over from his house and met us at his potato garden he started complaining.

"I thought we were supposed to set out this garden after dinner." he stated with considerable displeasure. "The wife is home getting ready to take up dinner in about half an hour."

Dad just rolled his eyes and replied, "Me and the boys thought we'd come up and get an early start on it for you Father, you can go home and have your dinner. We can handle this."

We all knew Pop would never go home and let us do it, he had to be there to make sure every seed was equally spaced and that we weren't burying them too deep. Paul, Rod, Greg and Dad started over on the far end of the garden, while Pop and I started on the opposite end.

"Why in the blazes are they starting way over there?" Pop asked me.

I didn't have the heart to tell him that they were trying to get away from him, so I replied, "I don't know Pop, maybe they are all queers and they want some alone time." Pop just let out a big laugh as I started planting his potatoes. "Your father didn't plough these drills very straight." Pop complained, "Every one of them are veering off to the right".

I knew he would be complaining the whole time I was working with him, so I tried to speed up and put a little distance between us. He was slowly coming behind me to bury in my drill of potatoes.

"Slow down there buddy", he shouted at me. "This is not a race, besides these seeds are not equally spaced. Just look, these two are about 11 inches apart and the next one is about 14 inches apart. If you don't want to do it right buddy, then you might as well go on home".

I knew Dad would probably kill me if I went home and I also knew that Pop was going to be riding my ass for the next couple of hours.

I needed a distraction and I knew how much he loved to talk and tell stories; this at least would get him to stop complaining. "Hey Pop", I teased, "You must be really missing all the nuns, now that the school is closed for summer holidays." I knew how much he disliked working for them at the school.

"Bunch of God Damned, over educated hypocrites," Pop relied, "I tells them more lies at that school and pulls more pranks on them in the run of a day than you can shake a stick at."

It was true, just this past year in school, I watched Pop lie to Sister Grace at least a half dozen times. One time he was walking by the library he popped his head in through the door and told Sister Grace that she was wanted at the principal's office and when she left the room, Pop closed and locked the library door so that she couldn't get back in.   Then he would hide away, downstairs in the furnace room while Sister Grace spent the whole day trying to find him to get his key to the library. He told me how he always kept a bottle of Screech Rum stashed away in the furnace room at school and that two Nuns in particular were always making their way downstairs mooching free drinks off him.

"I got one of them good about ten years ago at Christmas time," Pop said, "Sister Joyce was always drinking my stash of Screech in the furnace room at school. Before we finished school for Christmas break, I invited her to drop in to our house over the Holidays for a glass of Christmas cheer."   He went on, "Sure enough on Boxing Day, I watched from my window as her little red car pulled into my driveway. She came in the house and I introduced her to the wife and the three of us enjoyed a drink. We were all having a nice chat and so I offered her another drink and then another after that."

"By the time she was ready to leave, she was half in the bag, and as soon as she left the house and got into her car, I called the police and told them that there was a small red car, driving erratically up my lane. The cops caught up with her about ten minutes later and although they let her off with a warning, the damage had already been done. The story went all around Bell Island about how Sister Joyce was pulled over for drinking and driving," Pop said.

"The best part was that she never found out that I was the one who called the police on her."

Pop and I took a little break from our work and just stood there laughing at his story. I looked across the garden and I could tell that Dad and the boys were making much better time than Pop and I. We were only on our second drill, whereas the boys already had half the garden done. I was convinced that the only reason Dad used to take me up to Pop's garden was to have me distract Pop so that the boys could finish their work in peace. So it didn't matter that Pop and I were slower than those guys, because they were just happy that I was keeping Pop busy and he wasn't standing over them complaining and stressing everyone out.

"Why are potatoes so important to you Pop?" I asked him, "and why do you grow so many, when it's only you and Nan living home?"

Pop stopped what he was doing, pulled out his handkerchief from his pocket and wiped the sweat from his forehead. He leaned forward onto his rake, took a deep breath and paused for a few moments, as if he was organizing his thoughts.

"You see Brian; potatoes have always been a big part of our lives growing up, so much so, that one of the worst things that could ever happen to you during the winter, was to run short of potatoes. I know we are planting way too many potatoes here today for just me and your Grandmother, but it's the fear of running short that keeps me growing so many every year. Besides, if we do have too many left over by the end of the winter, I will just give them to your father. I'm sure you have heard me say for the past couple of summers that this is the last year that I am growing potatoes. I say that because I'm getting older and it's getting harder on me every year. However, when the long, cold winter sets in and I can go down into my cellar any day of the week and get a meal of potatoes for supper, I forget all about the hard work that went into it. There is a certain pride in cooking something that you grew with your own two hands, but more importantly, as long as you store away a few seed potatoes for the following spring, you will never run out."

He continued, "Now, I realize that you are too young to know, but when I was your age, our potato garden was three times as big as this one. In fact, most of the land on Bell Island was set out in potatoes. Back then, potatoes were all we had; potatoes and salt fish. Salt fish was easy to come by, because so many Bell Islanders owned a small fishing boat and there was an endless supply of cod. All winter long my cellar would be filled with salt fish and potatoes. This was all people had to survive on. There were no freezers to preserve your food and even if there had been, most people wouldn't have been able to afford one."

"Before Confederation, before Newfoundland joined Canada in 1949, there were little to no Government handouts. If you didn't work hard all summer preparing for the long, cold winter, then you were on your own. Nobody wanted to run short of potatoes in the middle of February because you would still have a few cold, lean months to go before summer. Just about every year a family member, friend or neighbour would suffer an illness or death over the winter months and it wasn't uncommon for other Bell Islanders to rally behind that family; offering potatoes, salt fish, firewood and anything else they could to help that family survive," he explained.

Back in those days, during the summer months most men would put in 18-20 hour days because they had young families at home that needed to be provided for.

"I can remember my father waking up at 3:30 in the morning and walking down to the beach with his brother to take their boat out on the water," he explained.

They would return around 6:30, clean and salt-in their morning catch of cod. Then they would each have a cup of tea and a slice of bread and walk to work for a 10 hour shift underground in the Iron ore mines. After they completed their 10 hour shift they would walk back home and spend the rest of the daylight looking after their potato gardens.

Pop continued, "When the mines closed in '66, growing your own potatoes was crucial because so many people lost their jobs. All the big paying jobs were gone and it was a depressing time here on Bell Island with so many people out of work."

"Growing potatoes gave me something to do; it gave me purpose as well as it helped me feed my family during that lean and gloomy time. So you see, from the time I was a small boy, younger than you are now, it was beat into us to never run short of potatoes."

"I guess that since I have been growing potatoes for the past 50 years, it isn't an easy habit to break. Potatoes were our main staple back then; it's what kept us from starving. The great thing about potatoes is how durable they are." Pop went on with the story, while I listened closely.

"As long as you have a decent cellar or basement, potatoes can keep without spoiling all winter long. We don't have a long or ideal growing season here in Newfoundland and yet our potatoes flourish."

"I guess you can say that potatoes are a lot like Newfoundlanders; hardy, durable and sustaining. Every month of March, Dad and I would take a trip to Downtown St. John's for some supplies. We would load up our horse and catamaran with vegetables, pork, beef and salt fish and leave for Water Street, St. John's to barter and trade for flour, sugar and tea. That would take us a full day, we would leave early in the morning and travel over the ice, across the ocean, from Bell Island to Portugal Cove with the horse and catamaran and once we reached land, make the long journey downtown." Pop continued.

"When the Townies saw Dad with a fifty dollar bill they automatically knew that we were from Bell Island, because only on Bell Island could you earn that kind of cash at the iron ore mines. Dad would trade and buy so much merchandise that quite often they threw in a couple of bottles of boot legged liquor as a Thank You for Dad's business. We would then make the journey back to Bell Island across the ice, making sure to get back before the sun went down so we could see any gaps in the Bay ice," he sighed.

"If you think this job is stressful, try getting your horse and catamaran full of supplies across the frozen Bay before the sun goes down!" He laughed at the memory.

He went on soberly, "Sadly, some people weren't as fortunate as we were growing up and I've seen too many families go cold and hungry over a long hard winter. I've seen people come to Dad's house in the middle of February, begging for food, desperate and starving."

"Nothing was ever wasted or thrown out and you were thankful for everything you had. You certainly never complained because people back then knew that the difference between working hard or goofing off was the same thing as surviving the winter or starving to death," he said as he levelled a look at me.

"We didn't need a lot of luxuries or play things because as long as you had enough food and heat, you were happy. No Sir, there were no extras, but there were plenty of potatoes if you were willing to put in the work for it," he said with a shake of his head.

When Pop finished speaking, I could see that his eyes were welling up and while he continued back to work, I just stood there speechless. I had no idea that things were so different only 50 years ago. I looked over at Paul, Rod and Greg who were still on opposite sides of the garden working away and I couldn't believe the important history lesson that they had just missed out on.

"Did you know my other Grandfather Vince when you worked in the Mines?" I asked him.
Pop looked at me and smiled with a look of pride and respect on his face. "Yes Sir," he said, "I knew Vince Dalton, his brother Dick and their Father Jerry. I worked with all of them and they were excellent workers and very knowledgeable people. In fact, when I first started out as a shoveller, I chased after Vince on a daily basis. It took two shovellers to fill an ore cart. Each cart would hold 1.8 tonnes of iron ore and each pair of men would have to fill 20 ore carts in a 10 hour shift." He paused for a second.

"Just think about that for a second Brian; if two of us filled 20 carts that meant we filled 10 carts each. 10 times 1.8 is 18 tonnes of iron ore; that's what we shovelled every shift." He squinted as he did the math in his head.

"Now, the only good thing about this job was that if you and your buddy could fill 20 carts in 8 or 9 hours; you could go home early and still get paid for a 10 hour shift."

He mimed a drilling action with his hands. "Because your Grandfather Vince was such a precise driller, he could blast out a wall of iron ore and when the smoke lifted, you were left with chunks of ore no bigger than your fist. Ore that size was easy to shovel and if you had a good shovelling partner, you could easily finish in 8 or 9 hours."

"Poor old Vince never got to go home early because he had to stay the entire 10 hours, drilling and blasting. Besides, with his type of skill set, you don't get to go home early, you are far too valuable to the company. Vince didn't mind though, he loved being down in the mines and he was proud and humbled to be the guy responsible for us shovellers going home early. There is many a man still living here on Bell Island that has a lot of respect and high praise for Vince Dalton." He smiled as he continued.

"Mind you, you had some drillers who didn't have a clue what they were doing and when they blasted out a wall; you were left with junks of ore the size of a pork barrel. There isn't a shoveller alive who can shovel or even lift that, so now the shoveller has to take his sledge hammer and break apart the huge chunks of ore. This is hard work and very time consuming, which meant you could forget about finishing up early if you were unlucky enough to work with and inexperienced driller."

He nodded his head and said, "Yes sir, Vince Dalton was one of the best drillers to work in the Mines and miners always felt safe working next to him."

I had a new found respect for both my Grandfathers. It was nice coming from a family of men who were well respected and contributors to Bell Island. Both Pop Hickey and Vince Daltons had worked hard their entire lives and had successfully supported their family, their church and their community. As we finished with Pop's potato garden, he thanked us all for our help and said, "I hope to see you young fellas in about a month's time to give me a hand to weed the garden."

We all agreed that we would help out as we piled into Dad's car to head home and we dropped off Greg and Rod along the way and pulled up into our own driveway.

From outside our kitchen window I could smell the wonderful aroma of Mom's Sunday cooked dinner. I raced inside the house and was met by the overwhelming delicious and tantalising scent of dinner. We were just in time to watch Mom serve up her potatoes, carrots, turnip, cabbage, peas' pudding, stuffed chicken, roast beef and blueberry duff all smothered in her homemade gravy.

I was salivating in the porch like a starved dog as I was removing my boots. "Make sure you wash up before you eat", Mom insisted, "and leave those clay-filled boots out on the step, I just put down a new piece of cardboard on the porch floor this morning".

I laughed to myself as I exited to the step to remove my boots, and warned Paul and Dad that all dirty boots are to be taken off on the step; Mom has put down a new piece of cardboard. Dad and Paul both laughed as they both knew that this was another one of Mom's weekly rituals, changing the cardboard on the porch floor. Since our driveway wasn't paved, people were always dragging mud and dirt in on their boots; all over Mom's porch floor. So Mom would cut open cardboard boxes and spread it out on the porch floor like a mat. She would sweep and vacuum it daily, as if it were a real mat and every week when she mopped up the porch; she would discard the week-old cardboard to the wood furnace and put down a brand new piece.

You should see this woman fuss over the new cardboard on the day she first put it down. She would protect it as if it were one of her children, and God help anyone who walked in the house and sullied up her new piece of cardboard.

I ran back into the house, quickly washed my hands and sat down to the kitchen table. Mom, Jason and Jennifer had already eaten since we were about a half hour late, finishing up with Pop's garden. Mom put a plate of food in front of me that was fit for a king. She had been working on this meal since early this morning and was now tackling the mountain of dishes that accompanied Sunday dinner. She poured me a tall glass of milk and I thanked her and told her that everything looks great. I figured it was the least I could do as she had worked so hard on it.

She just smiled and said, "Thank you, there's plenty more left over if you would like a second plate".

I was soon joined by Dad and Paul and the wonderful meal

that Mom had worked on for the past three hours was devoured in about 5 minutes.

Mom just shook her head in disbelief as she washed the dishes and watched her men wolf down her dinner.

"Take your time", she would say, "No one is going to steal it from you."

When I finished what was on my plate, I went back to the stove to get myself another piece of blueberry duff, just as I had done every Sunday for as long as I could remember.

"Excellent dinner", I said to Mom as I grabbed the duff, "we may have to keep you on."

Dad finished up with his dinner and helped Mom out with the dishes as he always did. Myself and Paul finished up and took off down to Lahey's field to see if anyone else had gathered.

When we arrived on the field, we could see most of the group was there and everyone had already decided to have a game of tag in the woods. I loved playing tag because size and age had nothing to do with the outcome of the game.

Two different captains picked teams and the first team ran out into the woods, while the second team gave them all five minutes to run and hide, before trying to find them. It was more like hide-and-seek than tag, but when you spotted someone from the opposite team you had to catch and tag them. When everyone on the hiding team had been caught, then it was the other team's turn to hide.

Today, the other team got to hide first; so we gave them a five minute head start to make their way through the woods. Some teammates liked to hide together whereas other's like to hide solo. There was a big round boulder, about the size of a small car located in the middle of the woods, that we nicknamed Bedrock. The rule was that once you were caught you had to go and sit on Bedrock and wait for the rest of your team to get caught.

When the five minutes were up, we took off into the woods to find our opponents. I had only been searching a few minutes when I noticed Snots hiding up a tree.

"I see you up there Snots", I said, "are you going to come down or are you going to make me come up there after you?"

Snots started climbing higher which told me he was not prepared to give up easily. I was concerned about going up after him because just two years ago he had fallen out of a tree and broke a couple of bones.

"Why don't you come down Snots," I bargained, "If you do, I will give you a 1 minute head start to run and hide."

He continued to climb higher so I knew I would have to go up after him. I started climbing and I could hear Snots giggling as I pursued him.

"Be careful now Snots", I said, "I don't want to see you fall and hurt yourself". Snots continued to laugh and as I climbed and looked up, I could see that he was quickly running out of tree to climb. He had almost reached the top and had no place left to go.

"I'm coming for you Snots", I said confidently, "it won't be long now."

Before I knew what had happened, Snots took a swan dive out of the top of the tree and grabbed on to the next tree about ten feet away.

"Holy Spiderman", I shouted, "Snots where did you learn to do that?" Snots just continued giggling as he scurried down out of his tree like a frightened squirrel and hit the ground running. I just sat up in my tree amazed and started the long process of climbing back down.

I came to the conclusion that Snots must be half ape because he was more stable and graceful up in a tree than he was on the ground. This actually explains a lot including his lack of intelligence and antisocial behaviour; his mother must have found him in a tree as a baby, bought him home and taught him how to speak!

I took off around the corner and saw that Krissy and Rod were already sitting on Bedrock. I knew that Snots couldn't have gotten far and decided to take a look around the rock. Sure enough, on the other side of the rock, Snots was on his knees hiding.

I touched him on the arm and said, "Tag on Snots." Snots took his place on Bedrock and I continued my search for the others.

After about an hour we had rounded up all seven members of the other team and were all chatting around Bedrock. It was now our turn to hide but Snots insisted that he had to go home.

"Why do you have to go home Snots", Lenny asked, "we had to find everyone on your team and now it's your turn to find us". Snots leaned in towards Lenny and whispered that he had to go home to do his poop.

"Don't be so foolish Snots," Lenny insisted, "You don't need to go all the way home to take a dump. Go back deep in the woods where nobody hides and take a dump, we will all wait for you here."

Snots agreed and Lenny rounded up a couple of tissues from the girls and handed them to Snots.

"Now Snots", Lenny warned, "make sure you don't crap anywhere we are playing, because if I steps into your shit, I'm going to have to kick your arse. Go way back there in the woods by the marsh and crap back there". Snots left a little embarrassed and headed towards the marsh.

Once he was out of site Lenny motioned for everyone to gather in closer.

"We should sneak up on Snots while he's taking a dump", he said devilishly, "We can sneak up on him and catch him with his pants down and frighten the living daylights out of him."

The plan seemed too funny not to try so everyone got low to the ground and crawled in the direction of the marsh. After crawling through the woods for about 200 feet, we could see Snots squatting down against a tree, doing his business. Lenny motioned for everyone to stay put as he would sneak in and frighten Snots. He made his way around the back of Snots and was less than 10 feet directly behind him. The anticipation and excitement was too much to bare as we were all giggling and waiting to see what was about to unfold. Lenny crept up even closer until he was standing right behind Snots. He then let out a deafening roar and Snots popped up and spun around to face the noise, but Lenny waved his arms at him, resulting in Snots falling backwards into his own shit.

He let out a loud cry and as we all ran towards him to get a closer look, we were shocked to find Snots on the ground with his pants and underwear down around his angles, rolling around in his own shit. Of course the place went up into laughter as Snots lay there crying his head off.

He finally stood up, pulled his pants up and took off crying and yelling, "I'm telling Mom." We all continued whistling and laughing, while Lenny yelled back at him, "Go ahead, tell her. You can also tell your Mom that I will see her later tonight for a game of hide the sausage". The laugher continued as we all made our way back to Bedrock and continued our game of tag.

After several hours of playing tag, the group began to get smaller as people started going home for supper. We called the game off for the day and agreed to meet back on Lahey's field later after supper.

I ran home and met Mom and Dad in the kitchen, taking up supper. I immediately told them about Snots falling back into his own shit and as Dad burst out laughing, Mom showed her disappointment and scolded Dad and I for laughing at Snots. "You shouldn't laugh at him", Mom warned, "He may not be the brightest boy on the East End, but he has a good heart and there isn't a mean bone in his whole body." You could always leave it to Mom to find the good in people. She hated to see people making fun at the less fortunate and often warned me that my devilish and fun-making ways were going to come back to haunt me someday.

I washed up for supper knowing exactly what was going to be served. It was Sunday evening which meant Mom had made both an egg and a beet salad out of the left over potatoes from dinner. We would also have the left over roasted chicken and roast beef from dinner with a few slices of tomato. For desert, we will enjoy the usual Sunday evening Jelly and custard. I sat down to the table and discovered that I was exactly right in my prediction.

I wondered if people all over the world would eat Jelly and custard for desert every Sunday. I scoffed down my supper and enjoyed my desert before putting on my sneakers and racing off to complete my evening chores. I wanted to make sure that I could get back down to Laheys before the crowd arrived, out of fear of missing something.

I got to the field I was pleasantly surprised to find that the only two people that were there were Krissy and Karen. I snuck up behind the two girls and listened in on their conversation. They were talking about how cute Mark was and wondered how much longer he would continue dating Alice. Krissy admitted that she was developing a crush on Rod and then they both began laughing when they discussed what had happened to Snots earlier that day. "I saw his penis," Krissy admitted, "when he jumped up first when Lenny scared him." "Does he have a big one?" Karen asked and Krissy just nodded and said, "Yes, it was about the size of a wiener."

I jumped up out of the grass and shouted, "Ah ha, the girls are talking about wangs".

They both jumped up off the grass and chased me and knocked me down. We wrestled harmlessly around the grass as the girls begged me not to say anything about their conversation. I teased them and told them I was going to tell everyone, but I really wasn't going to say anything. I managed to roll the girls off me and I got on top of them.

Without even realizing it, the sundial in my pants was once again reading 12:00. I guess with all the close contact with the girls; the bumping and grinding had made me stand to attention.

Krissy noticed it first and said, "Oh my God, Brian got a woody!"

I tried to hide it but Karen noticed it as well and said, "Ha ha, Brian's a pervert!"

I was quite embarrassed until finally the girls and I came to an agreement that I wouldn't say anything about their conversation and they wouldn't say anything about my trouser-tower.

As I got off the both of them I could feel my stomach rumbling. I guess with all the cabbage and peas pudding from earlier today, my stomach was feeling bloated. I stood up in front of Krissy, who was still sitting on the grass next to Karen and blew a tremendous fart in her face.

Karen cracked up laughing while Krissy was totally disgusted, especially when the smell hit. Oh man, there is nothing that stinks more than the flatulence caused by cabbage and peas pudding. Krissy was forced to stand up and walk away from me while Karen just pinched her nose and continued laughing. After I cranked off a couple more, it was apparent that I was in for a long and stink filled night.

Pretty soon the field began filling up with people again and we decided that when the sun went down, we would have a game of spotlight in the field. After it got dark, I was nominated to go first, so I turned off the flashlight, covered my eyes and counted to one hundred. The object of the game was for people to make it back to the fire pit, without being seen with the spot light. My strategy was to keep the light turned off and sneak around in the dark field so that no one could see me coming. In a dark field, you could see a flash light a mile away, so I kept it turned off until I could hear noises.

In the distance, I could hear people whispering so I turned on the light and shouted, "Spot light on Krissy, Karen and Alice.

The three girls then had to go sit by the fire pit and wait for me to find everyone else. I quickly turned the light back off and headed towards the other end of the field. I could hear footsteps and turned on the flashlight.

"Spot light on Paul, Al, Greg and Rod," I shouted. Not bad, I had already caught seven people and no one had made it safely back to Home Base. I again turned off the flashlight and headed off in a different direction. Suddenly I could hear a couple of voices crying out, "Home Free", which meant someone had made it back safely to home base. I ran towards the fire pit and could see that Lenny, Don and Andy were safely at home.

After I took a head count, I deducted that Shirley, Sam and Howie were the only three left unaccounted for. With my flashlight turned off, I quickly took off for the far end of the field. I paused for a second and listen intensely and could hear someone running across the field. I turned back towards the fire pit and saw Sam a mere 50 feet from Home Base.

I switched on the flash light, catching Sam in its beam and shouted, "Spotlight on Sam."

Now with just two people left, I switched the flashlight back off and continued to the back of the field. I tiptoed around the field close to the tree line and for a second, I thought I could hear a low moan. Once again I paused and listened as hard as I could. There it was again, a very faint moan just off to the right of me. I tiptoed in that direction and the odd sound was getting louder and closer with every step I took. I was so close that I was almost on top of the noise that sounded like moaning and heavy breathing. I turned on the light and to my surprise Howie was lying on top of Shirley in the trees, and they were kissing.

I laughed and shouted, "Spotlight on Howie and Shirley."

I was on my way back to Home Base to tell everyone what I had just witnessed, when all of a sudden I was tackled to the ground by Shirley. As I said earlier, Shirley was very athletic and was as physical as any of the boys on the field.

She pinned me down to the ground and said, "Brian if you tell anyone about this, I swear to God I will pound the living piss out of you."

 I could feel the strength in her arms and fully realized that she could easily do it if she so desired. Trembling with fear, I insisted, "I won't say a word Shirley, I promise".

The three of us walked back to Home Base together without uttering a word. "Good job Hickey-Dickey," Lenny said, "Ok, who wants to take a turn with the flashlight?"

We played a couple more games of Spotlight until everyone got tired of it. Then we all sat around the fire pit while Lenny and Mark loaded it up with wood and got a nice roaring fire going.

Out of all the activities that we participated in, sitting around the fire and listening to stories was by far my favourite thing to do. Everyone seemed so peaceful and friendly, even when they were tormenting and insulting each other. You really felt like you were part of something special and everyone was happy and at peace with each other. Sitting around that fire gave you the same feeling you get during Christmas when everyone is just a little more forgiving, friendly and merry.   The fire reflected a warm glow on everyone's smiling face and the camaraderie was uniquely special. You could truly get lost staring into a fire and watching the flames dance over the burning embers as you experience a very hypnotic sensation, which is only enhanced by the sound of your friend's voices laughing and sharing stories.

The topic of the evening was near death experiences and as soon as this particular conversation started, Al and I automatically looked at each other. Lenny told a story about the time he almost drowned in a local swimming hole known as Green Waters.

He described how he dove underwater and got tangled up in branches and twigs. He managed to free himself but he said he still has nightmares about it. Green Waters was located way up on the other end of the Island and the Town Council was supposed to fill it in years ago because apparently the bottom of the Green Waters was cover in a thick muddy material, branches and other debris and there had already been several close calls with regards to kids drowning.   Dad had warned Paul and I several times that if he ever found out that we even went near Green Waters, that we would be grounded for life. That sold me; I wasn't going anywhere in the proximity of that swimming hole.

Don then told a story about the time he fell off his bike and skinned out the entire side of his face. Gruesome for sure, but I wouldn't necessarily consider it near death.   Tell them what happened to you last winter Hickey!" Al said to me, "When we were jumping ice pans down on the beach".   I didn't really want to talk about that and just shook my head and said, "Nah Al, that was no big deal."

"What happened Hickey?" Lenny questioned, "don't be a pussy, tell us what happened."

I thought back on the event and then I started in. "First of all, nobody can tell my Dad or Mom about this, or I will be skinned alive."

Back in March when all the arctic ice was in the Bay, Al and I decided one weekend to take a walk down to the beach to see some of the icebergs. I was amazed to see large slabs of ice sitting right at the water's edge and before I knew it, Al and I were climbing on them, jumping from one ice pan to another. Well, before long I noticed that we were a good 200 feet from shore. I couldn't believe that we had travelled that far in such a short period of time. I think what had happened was that we were so focused on making it to the next ice pan, that we weren't paying attention to how far we had travelled.

Anyway, I knew I was a pretty good swimmer but Al couldn't swim a stroke. Not that it mattered because if you happened to fall into the water, you would surely be sucked underneath one of the ice pans that were so tightly packed together. As Al and I stood on the one ice pan, I pointed out how far from shore we were and we both agreed that it was time to head back in immediately.

We started to make our way back in and we both were standing on a small ice pan about four feet wide by six feet long. This small ice pan was bobbing up and down on the ocean pretty good and I knew we couldn't stay on it for very long. About 4 or 5 feet away there was a huge, flat ice pan measuring about 12 feet by 15 feet. I said to Al that 'if we can get to that one, then we are home safe.' I jumped to it first and when I landed on it, I walked to the far end to scout out our next ice pan. When I got about 2 feet from the end of this big ice pan it started sinking into the ocean as the back of the pan came rising up out of the water. It was sinking fast and I was already about knee deep in water before I leaped to the next pan.

Just as I leaped the entire pan flipped completely over and smacked the water about a half foot behind me with a terrible crash. It came so close to rolling over on me that when it hit, I could feel the wind from it slice by my back. Just 6 or 8 inches closer and this thing would have come crashing down on top of me, squatting me like a bug.

When we finally made it back to the beach, Al was as white as a ghost. He told me that when the ice pan lifted up out of the water 12 feet and rolled over, there was a 2 or 3 second window when he could no longer see me. He thought I was dead and to be honest, there was a split second when I thought I was a goner as well. "From that moment," I told the crowd, "I swore I would never fool around with ice pans ever again." The crowd was unusually quiet.

"Jesus Hickey," Mark said, "you should have better sense than that. Don't you know how many people have been stranded or lost out on the open ice?"

After I finished telling my story, that old bloated, cramped feeling was starting to come back to my stomach. I could feel all the cabbage and turnip and peas pudding from today's dinner coagulating with the salads and custard from supper. My stomach was making some awful noises and the gas pressure was building to dangerous levels. I really needed to run home and use the bathroom but I just couldn't tear myself away from the group. Heaven forbid that I run home for ten minutes and end up missing something earth-shattering or hilarious.

Everyone continued talking as I cautiously lifted my right arse cheek and let sneak out a serious of silent farts. There was no sound that accompanied them, so I knew that with such a huge crowd present, they couldn't prove it was me. When the smell started meandering throughout the unsuspecting bodies, the effects were nothing short of animated. Some people plugged their noses while others held their breath. Some people even jumped up from around the fire and walked away to get some fresh air.

"Who shit in their pants?" Howie demanded, but no one

would admit to it. I fired off a couple more, each one more deadly than the last. The smell could only be described as a combination of rotten eggs, burnt cabbage and death.

As the second attack began taking innocent victims Lenny jumped up and said,

"Holy German Jesus somebody died, guys who's the dirty bastard?"

Everyone laughed, however no one was brave enough to come forward. Finally, Karen who had her nose tucked down into her top pointed at me and said, "It's Brian, he's the dirty pig. He was farting earlier this evening." Everyone looked at me but I was laughing too hard to deny it.

"Sorry everyone", I finally said, "Must be the Sunday dinner".

I let out another assault on my friends, which triggered a response of moans and looks of disgust. My dear aunt, poor Alice, was bent over gagging as her body urged with the dry heaves.

"Frig off now Hickey and give it up," Lenny insisted, "That smells worse than Snaggletooth's breath; somebody call a priest so we can perform an exorcism on his arsehole."

Unfortunately the laughing only seemed to make my body shake and contort even more until finally I released an ungodly malodorous cloud of toxic gas that could easily turn the strongest stomach.

"Enough of this shit!" Howie exclaimed, as he knocked me face-down on the ground and sat on my back.

"Someone grab his hands and someone grab his feet". Don grabbed my hands and Randy grabbed my feet and then Howie got off my back and pulled my pants down to my angles. I struggled as much as I could but I was laughing so much that my attempts at freedom proved futile. As the boys continued to hold me face-down on the ground, Howie found himself a nice big branch from an evergreen tree and began whipping my arse. Although it hurt considerably, I still couldn't stop farting and laughing. While Howie continued whipping me, Lenny started splashing my arse with his bottle of Pepsi in the same fashion that a priest would splash his congregation with holy water.

To add to the humour, Lenny starting chanting, "The power of Christ compels you; the power of Christ compels you. Release him Demons, get out of his body!"

As a final act of penance for my shameless and unforgiveable act, Howie ripped off my underwear and threw them in the fire as some type of offering to the flatulent Gods. When they let me go, I quickly pulled up my pants and sat up with my arse hurting, still laughing and watched my underwear burn in the fire. Although it was funny then, it definitely wasn't laughing later that night when I was home in the shower plucking evergreen needles out of my arse.

5

The End of Innocence

So that's how things went on for the next few weeks. Softball and tag during the day, followed by pit fires and fun making throughout the night. Every now and then Snots would show up, take a ball in the head and go home for a couple of more days. Dad was chewing me out on a daily basis for neglecting my chores or doing as little as possible and all the crops that we had planted, as well as our livestock were growing bigger every day.

One hot and humid day the older boys decided that it was much too hot to play sports and that a nice cool swim was in order at Green Waters. This was deemed to be a voyage for the men, with no girls allowed. I wanted to go so badly, but I knew Dad wouldn't hear tell of us going anyplace near Green Waters. Even Paul wanted to go but insisted that Dad would skin us alive.

"Come on Farmer Hickey," Lenny said to Paul, "Don't be a pussy your entire life. I'll make you a deal; we will all go to Green Waters but if anyone asks, we will say that we're going to the beach."

Paul and I agreed, knowing full well that Mom would not object to us going to the beach. I ran home, got Mom's permission and grabbed a couple of towels for myself and Paul.

"Be careful," Mom warned, "and make sure you stay with Paul at all times." I ran out of the house and met up with the rest of the group and we all headed for Green Waters.

It was a good 1-hour walk to the swimming hole and along the way Snots, who always desperately tried to fit in, decided to try his hand at telling a few jokes.

"Hey Lenny", he snickered, "what's the difference between a peeping Tom and a pickpocket?" Lenny just rolled his eyes and retorted, "shut up Snots and be thankful that we are letting you tag along."

Snots looked blatantly heartbroken that he didn't get to tell the punch line, so Rod tried to cheer him up and asked, "What is the difference between a peeping Tom and a pickpocket, Snots?"

Snots' face once again beamed with pride as he answered, "one likes to snatch watches and the other likes to watch snatches."

I personally thought it was kind of funny but for some reason Lenny didn't think so. "Hey Snots," Lenny scolded, "when we get to Green Waters, there are probably going to be a lot of people there swimming and hanging out, some of which will be pretty girls. Don't say anything to embarrass me or you will never be allowed to hang out with us ever again. That joke you just told wasn't funny, in fact, it sucked. Here's how you tell a good joke. What's the difference between a rooster and Snots' mother?" He paused before answering, "A rooster says cock-a-doodle-doo, and Snots' mother says any-cockle-doo."

Everyone was bursting out laughing, except of course for Snots. He turned as red as a beet and probably would have started crying, if not for the fact that Lenny would have made him go home, had he done so.

"Don't feel bad", Lenny joked, "I'm only kidding about your Mom. Besides, who cares if she blows harder than a hurricane? I mean does it really matter that she likes to give free blow jobs just to get a hot meal into her stomach?" The harder people laughed, the more Snots looked like he wanted to cry.

Lenny really loved making sex jokes about Snots' mother and to give him credit, he was quite good at it. What always amazed and astonished me was the fact that the worse the boys treated Snots, the harder he tried to win their approval and acceptance.

I guess it was partially due to the fact that Snots never had a Dad; perhaps this was the reason that he kept seeking the approval and friendship of guys that constantly treated him like crap. To be honest, I always felt sorry for Snots and sometimes felt frustrated with him for putting up with the boy's bullshit. If it had been me, I would have told the boys to go to hell years ago. I probably would have gotten my ass kicked for it, but at least I wouldn't be their doormat and would have maintained some level of self respect and dignity. I constantly lectured Snots on the importance of standing up for himself and how it was better to die on your feet than to live on your knees. Unfortunately, with Snots it always fell on deaf ears and he was satisfied to be everyone's flunky.

When we finally reached Green Waters, it was like a whole new world. It was my first time ever being there and it somehow beckoned me with the promise of forbidden pleasures. This must have been how Charlie felt when he first entered Willy Wonka's Chocolate factory. There were at least a hundred people hanging out, most of whom were 18 years and older. A few people were smoking, drinking beer and even passing around marijuana cigarettes, but for the most part it was just innocent kids enjoying a hot afternoon.

I recognised a lot of the kids from my School, but there were also a good number of kids there from the Protestant High School. I didn't know a lot of kids from the Protestant School, but there was one guy, Barry Lawrence, that threw me a wave from the lake where he was swimming. I had met Barry last year at the Boys and Girls Club. He introduced himself to me because apparently his younger sister thought I was cute and wanted to meet me. I didn't know much about the guy except for the fact that we were the same age and seemed fairly friendly.

Someone had brought along their ghetto blaster and the tunes were ringing out across the lake. There were girls in short shorts and halter tops and even a few in bathing suits. Some girls were swimming in their tee shirts and when they came out of the water, you could almost see their *ta-tas*, as their nipples stared out at you like tiny hidden treasures. If this place was as wrong as Dad said, then I didn't want to be right.

Our group slowly dispersed into different directions, so I sat down at the lake's edge with Al, as we both tried to take in all the majestic wonder.

"Look at the set of jugs on the missus in the white shorts!" Al commented, "They're bigger than my head."

I nodded in approval and retorted, "Her nipples are big enough to hang your towel on." Of course, I wasn't exactly sure what I was talking about, but I did know that I liked what I was seeing. "We should come here every day", I commented, "This place is awesome".

Through all of the excitement of watching the beautiful, scantily dressed women, Al and I didn't even bother to get into the water. Instead we simply sat back and enjoyed the sights and sounds that Green Waters had to offer. Besides, it was bad enough that I was up hanging around the forbidden lake, if I dared venture into the water and Dad was to find out about it, not even the sanctity of my Happy Place would save me. There was so much going on, you needed your head on a swivel. I felt like a kid in a candy store and for a brief moment, I had forgotten all about the chores that awaited me at home.

Green Waters on this particular day was like my new Happy Place, only better. This place was real and tangible; you could reach out and touch it, hear it and smell it. Perhaps this was the reason so many kids hung out here, maybe it meant more to them than just a swimming lake, and maybe it was their escape from reality: their Happy Place.

When it came time to leave, I realized that we had been there for over three hours and it struck me as funny how relative time can be. Three hours of planting potatoes can seem like a life time, yet three hours of watching beautiful women in wet bathing suits, skips by like the blink on an eye. On our walk back to the East End, everyone had a different story to share about the perfect set of breasts or the wicked arse that they had just experienced.

"Did you guys catch the muck on the missus in the skin-tight orange shorts?" Lenny joked, "No problem to spot the camel-toe on her. You'd have to tie a piece of board across your arse to keep you falling into that big muck."

Everyone laughed, except for me and the reasons for my serious disposition was twofold. First of all, I hadn't the slightest clue what a camel-toe was and secondly, I was still blown away over what I had just witnessed. For me, it was more of a sexual awakening rather than just some random, meaningless event. I knew I had always been interested in, and attracted to girls. I spent more than my fair share of time daydreaming about Karen, who has always made me feel warm and fuzzy all over.

I remember when I was five, Dad caught me underneath his bed giggling and acting very suspiciously. He pulled me out from under his bed by my ankles only to discover that I had my pants and underwear pulled down to my knees and was sporting a raging woody while skimming through the bra and panties section of the Sears catalogue.

"What the hell are you doing? He shouted, "put your pants back on and give me your mother's catalogue".

The strange thing about that whole ordeal was that I couldn't give him an answer. I didn't know why I was doing that; I was only 5 years old at the time and all I knew was that it felt good. I'd noticed this past year in my grade seven class that some of the female classmates were starting to develop and that was invoking certain thoughts, but nothing like what I just saw at Green Waters. These were women; tanned, firm and built to last. I knew I had just experienced some wonderful epiphany and that I was on the cusp of entering in to my teens and all the crazy unknowns that accompanied it.

I was happy when we finally made it back to the familiarity of our East End road, close to home. Although Bell Island is a small community, I always felt most comfortable close to our own neighborhood. Everyone on the East End waved hello to us and called us by name. I knew everyone in our neighborhood and there was something very safe and reassuring about that. Mr. Whalen was mowing his lawn and Mrs. Smith had a full line of bed sheets drying on the clothesline that was snapping dry in the warm summer breeze.

Along our way, we were all surprised to find two teenage boys from St. Boniface, carrying large white buckets and going from door to door selling fresh fish fillets. How dare these dirty Protestants come into our neighbourhood, peddling their wares to us wholesome, God-fearing Catholics? You must keep in mind that the East End of Bell Island was predominantly Catholic. There were a few Protestant families in our neighbourhood, but for the most part they had married their way in, so there was really nothing you could do other than accept them. However, this was something entirely different; these were outside Protestants trespassing on our turf.

As I've already mentioned, there were two High schools on Bell Island; my Catholic school St. Michael's and the Protestant school St. Boniface. Twice a year we went to war with St. Boniface; in the Fall they kicked our arse in soccer and in the Winter, we slaughtered them in hockey. The whole community would come together, especially to watch the hockey and it could get pretty serious; even the Nuns would show up at the rink to cheer on their beloved Catholics. There has always been segregation with the Protestants and the Catholics, to the point that Dad used to tell me that he had Catholic friends whose family disowned them because they fell in love with, and married a Protestant. It was common knowledge that Protestants didn't take their religion as serious as us Catholics; we said far more prayers than Protestants and we were much more hard core in our beliefs. For example, Catholics believe, without question, that Jesus walked on water. Protestants acknowledge this as well, but they skeptically think that it may have been during the winter, when the water was frozen! Now, here we were face to face with these Protestant heathens trying to make a buck off us hard working Catholics.

"How are you boys doing today?" Lenny asked with a big smile.

"Not too bad," one of the boys answered, "just selling a bit of fresh fillet."

Lenny looked into one of the buckets and said, "nice looking fish you got there boys, are you selling much?"

"Selling a fair amount", one of the guys responded, "thought we would try our luck on the East End."

As we walked away from the two guys, Lenny said, "best of luck to you boys." and we continued on our way.

That was unusually kind and civil of Lenny, I thought to myself as we walked away. When the two protestant boys were out of site, Lenny and Howie ducked into the bushes and when the two guys left their buckets of fish on the side of the road to knock on someone's door, Lenny and Howie snuck up on the beautiful cod fillets and pissed in the bucket.

The rest of us nearly died laughing as Howie and Lenny ran back to us, just in time to see the two Protestant boys walk back to their bucket of fish and continue carrying it down the road. When we got home for supper later that evening, I told Mom that if anyone happens to come to our house selling fish, don't buy it. I told her all about the boys pissing in the bucket of fish and mom just shook her head in disgust and disbelief. She immediately ran to the phone to call her Mom and her sister and next door neighbors, to warn them about purchasing any fish

The next morning I went to the breakfast table as usual but when I met Mom and Dad I knew immediately something was wrong.

"What's going on?" I asked with my heart up in my throat, "Has something happened to Nan or Pop?"

Dad just shook his head and said, "No, Nan and Pop are fine but Jake Lawrence's young fellow drowned in Green Waters last night."

I slowly sat down and couldn't believe what I was hearing. It took me some time but I finally found the words and muttered,

"Not Barry Lawrence was it?" Mom and Dad looked at me in total surprise.

"Yes, the boy's name was Barry Lawrence," Mom responded. "I didn't realize you knew him," she said.

"Yeah, I met him at the Boys and Girls Club," I responded.

I couldn't let either of them know that I had just seen him yesterday at the lake.

"How old was he Brian"? Mom asked. "He is my age, 12". I said in disbelief.

"Oh my, that poor little Angel." Mom continued, "Apparently he didn't come home last night and when his parents called his friends looking for him, they told them that he had been swimming at Green Waters all day yesterday. The parents called the police and they found the boy's body late last night, tangled up in the weeds at the bottom of the lake. I can only imagine what his mother and father are going through. May God have Mercy on his poor, little soul."

While we sat there eating breakfast, hardly a word was spoken. I just couldn't wrap my mind around the fact that I had seen Barry yesterday, laughing and having fun and now he was dead. It just didn't seem fair that God would take someone like Barry, while there were so many bad people out there. The silence was broken by Dad slamming his fist on the kitchen table.

"God Damned Green Waters", he said, "the Council should have filled in that deathtrap years ago, but like everything else, they have to wait until some poor bastard dies before they do anything about it. Well Sir, I'm getting a petition started to get that God forsaken lake filled in once and for all."

Dad spent the next while on the phone, trying to get some action on having the popular swimming hole filled in, while I sat their quietly thinking about Barry. How could a kid my age no longer exist? Where is he now, in heaven or eternal sleep? If only I could have yesterday back, to perhaps talk with him up at the lake and warn him that he had only hours left on this earth. It was all so confusing to me, I had faithfully attended church every week for the past twelve years and I still had no concept of death. I had attended a few funerals as an Altar boy, but never for a family member or a friend. Up until now, they were just strangers in a coffin and I never really gave death too much thought.

I thought to myself; how does a family cope with the loss of a 12 year old son and brother? Are we better off staying in our homes where we are safely out of reach from any accidents and death's cold hand? In my short life, I had already climbed cliffs, jumped ice pans and entered the old abandoned mines shaft, any one of which could have easily ended in tragedy. How do God pick and choose who's number is up and who lives to tempt fate another day?

My lamenting was interrupted by my Mom's soft voice who said, "finish your breakfast now sweetie and head out for your morning chores, keeping busy will help take your mind off things; it's not good to think about death too much."

I headed out to do my chores with nothing on my mind only the thought of Barry Lawrence. While I was milking one of the cows, I could hear Dad walking towards the barn, still cursing Green Waters. He walked into the barn, picked up a shovel and starting shovelling the cows manure out of the barn. "When we are finished here," he demanded, "we are taking a walk through the East End and getting some signatures for a petition to have Green Waters filled in. If that deathtrap had been filled in years ago like people wanted, that young Lawrence boy would still be around today."

I continued milking the cow in silence but the more Dad ranted on about Green Waters, the more the urge filled me until I could no longer contain myself.

"I was at the lake yesterday too," I blurted out. I stood up from the cow and laid my pale of milk to the side because I had no idea what Dad's reaction was going to be. He turned at looked at me and I could see rage in his eyes.

"A bunch of us walked up there yesterday, but I swear I did not go into the water. I just sat around the lake with Al and we hung out listening to music and watching the crowd swimming."

Dad threw down his shovel and grabbed me by the arm.

"How many times have I told you not to go near that place" he screamed at me. I fought back the tears and yelled back at him,

"I'm sorry, I didn't go in the water but I saw Barry there. He was in the water and waved at me, but I wouldn't go in."

Dad immediately let go of my arm and the look on his face quickly changed from anger to sorrow. He got down on his knee so that we were face to face and calmly said,

"Now you see why I don't want you hanging out at places like that. I'm not trying to ruin your fun; I just want to make sure that you come home every night in one piece. You think nothing bad can happen to you, but I'm telling you right now my son, in my opinion our small island is every bit as dangerous as a big city, perhaps even more treacherous. We have open mines, unsafe swimming holes, high cliffs and lots of other temptations for a fool-hearted, bored and curious kid to press his luck. Only problem is that sometimes your luck runs out and you have to pay the ultimate price. How do you think your Mother would react if she was faced with the knowledge that your body was found, drowned in a lake; it would tear her apart and she would never be the same woman again. You seem to forget that I grew up on Bell Island and I know all too well about some of the trouble an innocent, unsupervised kid can get himself into. This is why I assign you and Paul so many chores; to keep you busy and to give you something to do. Every day while I'm at work, I take comfort knowing that my kids are home at the vegetable garden, or sawing up a bit of wood, instead of out doing God knows what. When you are around the house, I know you are safe."

Everything Dad was saying was making sense. I guess I never considered his and Mom's role in trying to protect us and keep us safe. I honestly thought that he was just being a grumpy old bastard who hated seeing us having fun, when all along he was doing everything in his power to protect us. Just the two of us spent the whole afternoon together, walking the East end and we collected over 300 signatures for our petition. Other petitions around the island were also collected and it was decided unanimously that Green Waters would be filled in as soon as possible. Dad never even grounded me for going to Green Waters, as I guess he figured that with Barry's death, my lesson had been learned.

Later that evening the gang had gathered at Lahey's field and all the conversation naturally surrounded Barry Lawrence's drowning. Not surprising, everyone had a different story about what they had heard; how he got tangled up underwater, how he looked when his body was recovered, and the reaction of his family.

Of course, everything that was being said was pure speculation and hearsay, but for some reason when speaking of someone's passing we all need to feel part of the drama. We all like to think that we knew that person better than we really did and that their death has affected each of us on some profound and personal level. I listened to everyone's anecdotes and recollections of their experiences with Barry and when it was all said and done, I came to the conclusion that for the most part, they were all full of shit. They hardly knew Barry, just as I hardly knew him. When we went to Green Waters yesterday, not one person from our group talked to Barry, or even acknowledged him for that matter. He was simply a kid from Bell Island who went to a different school than us and lived on a different part of the Island from us and yet his passing had touched all of us. Had he been alive and walked on Lahey's field today, we most likely would have shunned him back to his own neighbourhood. It's strange how we speak so highly of someone after they are gone, when we really couldn't be bothered to give them the time of day while they are here amongst us.

Later that night as we lit the pit fire, there was a solemn quietness that surrounded our group. There was no one cracking jokes or insulting someone's mother and even Lenny was a lot more subdued. We talked about what would become of Green Waters and discussed the fact that Barry would be getting buried in a couple of days. I was kind of hoping that the whole conversation would take a more religious and spiritual turn so that I could find out who amongst our group believed in heaven and the great hereafter.

Finally, Don made the comment, "Oh well, the poor fellow is in a better place now."

I listened with great intensity as everyone debated the notion of God and Heaven.

"I can't see how that young fellow is in a better place," Howie retorted, "He's dead and in a couple of days he is going to be six feet under the ground where he will eventually become worm food."

"That's only his body," Shirley remarked, "His spirit and his soul have already gone to heaven."

"How do you know that?" Howie questioned, "I say that when you're dead-you're dead and heaven is just a made up fairy-tale to keep people on the straight and narrow with the promise of being rewarded with everlasting life. I say there is no heaven and no hell; you are simply born, you live and then you die, end of story."

I couldn't believe it; I've never heard anyone actually say that they didn't believe in God before. I was never a big fan of Howie but at least now I respected him for putting it out there what he believed, fully aware that his beliefs were in a very small minority with us Catholic crowd. But what if Howie was right? What if there was no God and what if Heaven was just a made up Happy Place that people conjured up to take the sting out of losing loved ones? There is definitely a lot of comfort in the belief that we will all meet again one day in heaven. But what if this was all a fairy-tale and there was nothing after death? The thought of this just made me shudder and I refused to believe that there wasn't a higher power out there somewhere.

"Well I think God exists," Karen responded, "Because it says so in the bible. Besides, why would there be so many churches built all around the world if there was no such thing as God?"

"Well I believe in God too," Krissy said, "but not the devil. I think the devil is just something made up to scare you into being good."

I sat there with great interest listening to everyone's point of view. There were many different takes on God and heaven, all of which I found fascinating. "Well, I think Jesus must have been a homosexual," Lenny said with a smile on his face.

Everyone booed and hissed at Lenny for his sacrilegious remark. "No seriously," Lenny continued, "there are a couple of times in the bible when Jesus says, *Get thee behind me Satan!*" Sacrilegious or not, everyone cracked up laughing at Lenny's joke.

"Come on people," Lenny continued, "I know a young fellow drowned yesterday but we are not doing him any good by sitting here all sad on this beautiful night, debating the existence of God. Hey Hickey, tell us a funny story to lighten the mood."

I thought hard for a minute and then remembered a story I had developed around my birthday, back in November.

"Ok." I started, "last November I turned 12 years old and when I got home from school that day, my Dad called me aside and told me that now that I was 12, we needed to have a little talk about sex. I placed my hands over my ears and began screaming, NO Dad NO, Please NO, I don't want to talk about sex. When my Dad asked me what was the matter I responded; when I turned 9, you wanted to talk to me about the tooth-fairy and you told me that the tooth-fairy didn't really exist. When I turned 10 you wanted to talk to me about the Easter Bunny and you told me that the Easter Bunny didn't really exist.

Last year when I turned 11 you wanted to talk to me about Christmas and you told me that Santa Claus didn't really exist. Now that I'm 12, you want to talk to me about sex and if you're about to tell me that people don't really FUCK.........................then I have nothing left to live for!"

Surprisingly, I received a lot of laughs for my little anecdote, which always scored points with the older kids. I always had a knack for telling stories or jokes and making people laugh. I learned very early, that when telling a story, it's always best to do so in the first Person, as it makes it more personable. I enjoyed being the center of attention and loved the fact that I could hold everyone's ear. I felt like I was Lord of the Flies and as long as I held the conch, I could easily keep people entertained with my comical stories.

"Ha ha, that was a good one Hickey," Lenny remarked, "Do you know anymore?"

I thought about it for a minute and said, "Alright, now this tale took place during the summer when I was 5 years old and my Grandfather used to take me down fishing off the wharf every Sunday morning. Nan used to pack us each a little lunch; cookies and milk for me and a couple of beers and cigarettes for Pop. While we were fishing, Pop pulled out one of his cigarettes, lit it and began smoking it. I looked at him and asked, may I have one of your cigarettes Poppy?"

"Pop just looked at me and smiled and said, 'I don't know Brian; can you touch your dicky bird off your bum?'

I thought about it for a minute and finally said no. 'Well then,' Poppy said, 'I guess you are not old enough to smoke cigarettes.' As a little more time passed, Pop reached into his lunch box and pulled out a bottle of beer. 'May I have one of your beers Poppy?' I asked. 'Well,' said Pop, 'with a little smile, I don't know, can you touch your dicky bird off your bum?' Once again I replied No and Pop said, 'then I guess you are not old enough to drink beer.' A little later I was feeling hungry, so I pulled a chocolate chip cookie out of my lunch box and started eating it. Pop saw this and asked me if he could have one of my cookies. I looked at him with a big smile on my face and said, 'I don't know Poppy, can you touch your dicky bird off your bum?' He grinned at me with a smug look on his face and said, 'yes my little buddy, I can.' 'Well, then' I said, 'GO FUCK YOURSELF Poppy, these are my cookies!'

Again the whole crowd erupted into laughter. Although I sat there quite pleased with myself, I couldn't help but think what Dad would do to me if he ever heard me telling these types of jokes and using such bad language. Others took turns telling a few jokes, lightening the mood and cheering each other up.

All of a sudden Al, who was sitting next to me, elbowed me in the arm and motioned for me to look over to the right. As I glanced over, my heart sank as I watched Rod and Karen sitting together next to the fire holding hands. I guess a tragedy such as death has a way of bringing people closer together. Krissy noticed this too and made it known to everyone by shouting, "Oh my God, Rod and Karen are holding hands"! Everyone stopped talking and looked at Karen and Rod. Rod turned blood red and tried to pull away his hand, but Karen sat there as pleased as punch and squeezed his hand all the tighter.

"Yes, it's true," Karen admitted proudly, "Rod and I have been chatting on the phone these past few nights and have decided to start dating."

I just sat there with the wind knocked out of me. For some reason I felt betrayed by the both of them. I mean, this was my girl and here she is announcing to the world that she is dating my cousin. This must have been how King Arthur felt when he discovered Guinevere was having an affair with Lancelot.

As everyone headed home that night, they were all feeling a little better than when they first arrived here earlier this evening; everyone of course, except for me. In my Happy Place, Karen was always right there by my side, I never pictured myself with anyone else. Now the love of my life has a new boyfriend and I would have to learn to live with it. I cried a little that night when I went to bed, for two reasons. First of all, for losing Karen before I even got the chance to kiss her. And secondly, I couldn't help but feel so selfish for letting something as small as this upset me, when not too far away, there is a family mourning in turmoil over the loss of their son. I decided right then and there that I would be strong while dealing with my own minor loss, out of respect and honour for the memory of Barry.

A couple of days later, Dad and I were driving home from the lumber yard when in the distance we could see the big black hearse slowing coming towards us with a long procession of mourners following. Dad pulled off to the side of the road and took off his ball hat as a sign of respect as the funeral drove passed us. I tried my best not to stare, but I could see Barry's younger sister in one of the cars, crying her heart out as they drove by. This was the same girl that Barry once tried to set me up with, just last year. I respectively declined her invitation to dance that night at the Boys and Girl Club and that is something I will forever regret. If I could only go back to last year at the Boys and Girls Club, I would gladly talk to and dance with Barry's younger sister, make friends with her and try to bring a little laugher to her life.

I asked Dad why the hearse and funeral were driving up on this end of the Island if the cemetery was in the opposite direction. As we drove off, Dad put his hat back on head and said, "They are taking the young fellow on his final run around the Island before they bring him to his resting place."

I was surprised to see a tear running down Dad's cheek as he tousled my hair and we headed home. For the remainder of our drive home, I drifted off to my Happy Place where there were no accidents, death or sorrow. Kids played carefree and happiness enveloped everyone. The one thing that could always be counted on in my Happy Place was good friends and good times that lasted forever. You kept your innocence and the notion of pain and suffering never existed. It was a utopia filled with never ending pleasures and bliss.

Still, not even my Happy Place could banish my questions surrounding death, God or heaven and no matter how much I tried to ignore them, they would task me for the rest of my life.

6

A New Love Interest

A few more weeks passed and I had come to grips with Rod's and Karen's relationship and I was accepting it as best I could. I felt a little jealous whenever I saw them both together, but at least no one else knew how I was feeling. This morning I had all my chores done early and I decided to go for a nice long bike ride by myself to try and clear my head. I planned to ride up through the old wooden path known as Long Harry which takes you from Lighthouse Road to the Beach Hill. Not too many people used this road and I really wanted to be alone.

I was flying through Long Harry, immensely enjoying the warm summer breeze, the sound of birds chirping and the sweet smell of evergreen trees, wildflowers and fresh berries. That's when it happened; I spotted perhaps the prettiest girl I had ever seen in all my 12 years. She looked to be about my age, dark complexion, beautiful brown hair, dark eyes and a gorgeous white smile. She was so breathtakingly stunning, that I couldn't bring myself to make eye contact with her. In short, she was perfect, a perfect, gorgeous, amazing angel who just happened to be right here on Long Harry Road. She was walking her bike and I sensed that something was wrong. I pulled up beside her and I could see that she was walking a very old bike, the type that had front and back fenders. I managed to muster up the nerve and asked her if she needed help, and with the prettiest voice I'd ever heard, she told me that her front fender had come loose and was rubbing off her front tire, making her bike impossible to ride. I got off my bike and slowly walked over towards her. "Nice Bike", she said with a smile, and my heart instantly melted. I checked her front fender and sure enough, it was loose, but I couldn't tighten it without a wrench. After about 30 seconds of fiddling with it, I pulled the red lace out of one of my sneakers and used it to tie up her loose fender to her handlebars, preventing it from rubbing off the tire. "There you go", I said, "That should hold until you get home". She smiled and thanked me and then sat on her bike and began to peddle away. For the next couple of seconds, I just stood there on Long Harry Road, with the sun on my shoulders and I watched this elegant, beautiful young girl, ride off into the distance, taking with her a piece of my heart. She paused just long enough to look back, smile and wave her hand goodbye and then she was gone. I knew right then and there, at that exact moment, that life would never get any more perfect than that.

As I was riding home, I was pretty upset with myself for letting such an opportunity slip by. I was just in the presence of one of God's most beautiful creations and I didn't even ask her name...... IDIOT!!! The farther I rode away, the more I panicked over the fact that I knew absolutely nothing about her and I might never, ever see her again. When I got home I was so upset with myself that I threw my bike on the ground in frustration at my pathetic lack of courage.

I ran into the house and questioned my Mom on who that girl could possibly be, riding through Long Harry on a bike all by herself. Mom asked me how old she was and who she looked like. I had no idea, I figured she was around my age and she looked like a precious gift from God.

"I'm sorry honey", Mom said, "I haven't got a clue who she could possibly be. Why don't you ride back through Long Harry and see if she is still there?"

Mudder, you magnificent creature, I thought to myself. Of course, the solution was simple; I would ride back up there, casually bump into her and strike up a conversation. I ran into the bathroom and brushed my teeth, fixed my hair, splashed on some of Dad's cologne and ran back outside to get my bike.

On my way out the door, I bumped into Dad, who roared,

"Slow down my Son, where's the fire? Where are you running off to in such a hurry? I can use your help with a couple of chores."

I jumped on my bike and shouted to him, "I have to do something for Mom, I'll be back shortly," and I took off as fast as I could.

Nice try Old Man, I thought to myself as I rode off, but not even Dad was going to stand in my way. In all my years of bike riding, I didn't think it possible to make a bike go as fast as I did that day. I was picking up so much speed; I actually thought I was going to take flight. I made it back up to Long Harry in record time to the exact spot where I had encountered her earlier this morning. She was no longer there, so I quickly rode up the path a little further, hoping to catch up with her. Damn, she was nowhere to be found.

All of a sudden, I became the Great White Tracker, looking for any indication as to where she might be. After about an hour of searching, I finally gave up and reluctantly returned home. Dad was there waiting for me with two shovels to help him spread a load of topsoil over our lawn. He was yammering on about the different flowers and shrubs that he was going to plant in the yard for Mom, but all I could think about was that incredible, beautiful, mysterious girl and how I let her slip right through my fingers.

As usual, summer was flying by and we were already getting into August. This always made me feel sad for a couple of reasons. First of all; it signified that summer holidays were half over and that in four short weeks we would be making our way back to school. Secondly, it was the beginning of the hay cutting season and trust me folks, there is nothing in this whole wide world that Brian Hickey hates more than cultivating hay.

We started, as we always did with cutting the hay off my Grandfather's yard on Lighthouse Road. This was my Mom's father, Vince Dalton, known around the Island as being very knowledgeable and a bit of a Jack of all trades. Vince was a lofty, slender man over 6 feet tall, in fact, one of the tallest people

I knew. I remember in grade 3 telling my teacher Miss Power that my Grandfather Vince was a giant. She laughed and said, "I know your Grandfather Mr. Dalton Brian, and while he is very tall, he is not a giant. However, he is a giant amongst men!" At that age, I never really understood what Miss Power meant by that. Vince always drove the most up to date vehicle and wore the most stylish leather jackets. He was a proud man and he had worked so hard his entire life, that he was finally able to enjoy the fruits of his labours. He always had his hair slicked back and wore a huge smile on his wrinkled, weathered face.

Vince was also known for making some of the finest, most potent, homemade booze known to man. He moved to Bell Island with his family when he was a young boy from Harbour Main as his Dad took a job in the Bell Island Mines. Like his Dad, Vince also worked in the Mines until it closed in 1966.

I've known my Grandfather Vince since I was born. He lives a short ten minute walk from my house and I can't remember a single day when he hasn't driven down to our house for a visit. Since I've known him, I've always called him Vince and that's not out of disrespect or anything; it's just that I grew up calling him Vince and everyone accepted that.

In the mines, Vince was a Blaster, in fact, he was so highly skilled that when he worked in the mines he got the reputation of being a precision blaster, a bit of a maverick. After the mines closed he just did local contract jobs around the Island, but he was also hired by blasting companies all across the Province to do a precision blast. When everyone else said it couldn't be blasted; Vince Dalton would blast it!

We pulled into Vince's Yard with the horse and hay mower and I noticed that Vince was busy making repairs to his fence. When he spotted us, he stopped what he was doing and walked towards us. I looked across his huge yard at the prime grass that was waist high. The warm summer breeze danced over the long grass and as it blew, it resembled waves on the ocean. There was a lot of work ahead of us but as much as I hated cutting hay; I didn't mind cutting their hay because Vince would always help

Dad out, while Nan would feed me ice-cream and soda.

This day was particularly hot and when we finally had the hay cut, Vince went into the house and bought out two bottles of homemade beer for him and Dad. This beer was as clear as water but it was said that it would hit you like a tonne of bricks. I never tasted it, but I knew it must be potent, because last year after we cut the hay, Dad drank two bottles of Vince's beer and got so intoxicated that he ordered me and Paul to take the horse home while he laid back in the hay and fell asleep for a couple of hours.

Now when it came to drinking beer, Dad was no light weight, so for only two of Vince's homemade beers to put Dad on his arse, I knew that it must have had a high alcohol content.

Dad and Vince drank a beer and when Vince offered him another one, Dad just laughed and said, "No Thanks Skipper, after what happened last year, one homemade beer is my limit. We will be back first thing tomorrow morning to turn the hay over."

I knew we would be leaving soon to go to another meadow and start cutting more hay. I was desperate to get out of the hay racket for the day and boldly blurted out, "Do you need a hand fixing your fence Vince?"

Dad just looked at me and I think he knew how much I hated the hay because he replied, "Yes you stay up here and help Vince with his fence and me and Paul will go on to the next hay garden."

Poor ole Vince looked at me with a little disappointment in his eyes. Even I knew that he would much rather have Paul stay behind to help him; after all, I'll most likely just get in his way. Ah well Skipper, you're stuck with me because I had the foresight to grasp an opportunity to get away from the hay and I took it.

We watched Paul and Dad walk the horse down the road and as soon as they were out of sight I said, "I'd better get another glass of Pepsi off Nan before we start Vince, no sense in risking dehydration."

Vince just rolled his eyes and headed back towards his broken fence while I went inside to have a nice sit down visit with Nan. Before I go any farther, let me tell you a little bit about my Nan Dalton. This was probably the sweetest, kindest woman I have ever met in my life. She loved to spoil you and would give you anything you requested.

When I was five, Paul and I had to live with Nan and Vince for an entire summer because my younger brother Jason got sick and Mom and Dad had to take him to a children's hospital in Ontario. I think that it was during that particular summer that my relationship with Nan first blossomed. She had several grandkids by now, but I felt a real connection with her while I lived with her. She would take me berry picking and for long walks up through Long Harry. She told me about some of the men she dated before Vince and shared secrets with me that are only shared between Grandmothers and Grandsons. At bedtime she would always sneak me extra ice-cream and treats.

"What are you still doing here sweetheart," she asked all excitedly, "I thought I saw your father and Paul leave already with the horse?"

"Yep, I stayed behind to help Vince with his fence," I said with huge smile. It always made her laugh when I called my Grandfather Vince.

"Well then," she said, "Let me get you a glass of Pepsi and a couple of cookies."

"That would probably be for the best Nan," I responded and she just looked at me at laughed.

"Let Vince fix the fence now Brian," she continued, "you stay in the house with me and keep me company; there's no need for you to be out there helping him."

I took a mouthful of drink and responded, "That was the plan all along Nan, besides, who am I to argue with you?"

Ahhhh, Nan Dalton understood me. She realized that I wasn't built for manual labour. She understood how to enjoy the simple pleasures that life had to offer. It truly is a special relationship between a boy and his Grandmother.

I've always maintained that I would never allow any adults

into my Happy Place, but Nan Dalton may very well earn herself a free lifetime membership there. We sat there in her kitchen chatting and laughing for the next hour as she periodically looked out the window to check on Vince's progress.

While we were chatting, my Great Grand Father, Jerry Dalton walked in from the living room. Jerry was Vince's Father and he was well into his 80's. He was losing some of his faculties, so he was now living with Nan and Vince. He would mostly just wander around the house in his pyjamas and eat cheesies.

"How are you doing today Jerry?" I roared at him as he was hard of hearing. He just smiled and waved at me and asked Nan for a bowl of cheesies. Nan gave him his snack and he slowly returned to the living room.

"How's Jerry doing Nan", I asked her after he left the kitchen?

"Don't be talking", Nan said as she laughed to herself. "He's not any trouble, except for the fact that I have to wash out my curtains at least once a day. He goes around the house all day eating cheesies and wiping his hands in the curtains. Every time I look, my lovely curtains are full of cheesie stains." She chuckled, "Last week he mixed up his Denture cleaner with the Dish Detergent. He washed the dishes in Polident and soaked his teeth with Palmolive!"

Nan and I just laughed and continued chatting about some of things that were going on in my life. I can't even calculate the countless hours I have spent with Nan Dalton as she told me about the 'Good Old Days'. We would sit on her front porch on those warm summer nights and we would watch the light from the Lighthouse encircle our little Island and then make its way back over the black, silent ocean. She would tell me what things were like when she was a little girl growing up on Bell Island. She would also talk about how she and Vince first got married and moved into a house together.

She told me how they had no electricity and how every morning when Vince left to walk to his job in the Mines, she would hand him his lunch, kiss him goodbye and tell him to make sure he comes home later tonight safe and sound. She said as soon as the sun began to set, she would light a candle in the window to ensure that Vince could easily find his way home from work each night. Believe me when I say that the irony of the fact that my Nan Dalton lived on Lighthouse Road was not lost on me. She herself was like a lighthouse, a beacon guiding and welcoming her family safely back home.

When she finished telling her stories, she asked me what I have been doing all summer. I eagerly told her about the beautiful girl I had met at Long Harry a little while ago and since Lighthouse Road leads into Long Harry; I asked her if she knew who this girl could be.

Nan had no idea and suggested that I keep going back there every once and awhile and maybe I will bump into her again.

"Don't give up on her Brian, if you like her that much, go back to that spot every day until you find her again. Who knows, maybe she goes back there from time to time looking for you. People give up too easy today; don't be afraid to tell her what's in your heart."

Nan turned her attention back to the kitchen window and when she noticed that Vince was putting up the final rail on the fence, she directed me to go outside and help him finish up. She gave me a pocket full of candy and kissed me on the cheek as I left her house.

I walked over to where Vince was working just as he was hammering the final nail in the fence. "All finished up," I commented.

"Yes," he remarked, "No thanks to you, where did you disappear to?"

"I was inside helping Nan," I responded, "Do you want me to get you a beer?"

Vince just nodded and I ran to the house and got him one of his homemade beers. We both walked to his shed to put away his hammer and nails and we sat down while he drank his beer. Two hours and eight beers later, Vince was feeling no pain and I was just glad to be away from the hay. It didn't take long before Vince started talking about working in the Bell Island Iron Ore Mines.

He loved working in the mines and he loved talking about the mines.

Now when Vince Dalton tells you a story about the mines, he doesn't just remember the story; he acts it out and relives it to the point where you feel like you are actually there to experience it.

He would take a deep breath, make a big sigh and then he would start his nostalgic tale. "The last mine closed in 1966 and that was the saddest day in the history of Bell Island. There was a lot of depression on the Island after '66, we didn't just lose our jobs; many of us lost our way and lost hope. The Government was trying to relocate us and everyone was pissed off especially when you consider how much iron ore still exists down in those mines. In the early years, we used to work 10 hour shifts, six days a week, all year long. It was simple, if you didn't go to work, you didn't get paid. There were no sick days or vacation days, so if you wanted to earn a pay cheque; you worked." I settled in for the long tale.

"There were big Clydesdale horses that worked in the mines and the men would never have been able to do what we did without those horses. There were rats down there as big as small dogs; so big that we were forced to hang our lunchboxes from the ceiling with a piece of rope, just to stop the furry bastards from stealing them." I know now this is true from similar stories I have heard.

He continued, "In fact, the rats were so big and plentiful that whenever a new, young guy started working underground for the first time, the older guys would make wagers and take bets on how long the new guys would be able to last amongst the rats. More often than not, these new guys would come underground and experience the pitch black and the hundreds of rats, and when they finished their shift after the first day, they would never return."

"I've even seen guys come down for their first shift, work a few hours, get freaked out by the rats, leave and never come back. Personally, I was glad to see the rats; in fact the rats actually saved my life one time."

"I was busy drilling into the iron ore face, preparing it to be blasted, when my partner suddenly tugged on my jacket to get my attention. As I turned off my drill, he pointed out this huge group of rats that were all running away from us. He was totally amazed at this, since he had never seen it before," he said with a gleam in his eye.

"Of course I had seen it before and without hesitation, I dropped my drill, grabbed my buddy by his arm and took off running after the rats. Just as we got about 100 feet from the very spot where I was drilling, the entire area caved in. So you see, the rats were a good thing because they would always warn you of any pending danger. To this very day, I am always suspicious of a place that has no rats. There were 106 men who were killed in the mines and countless numbers of injuries," he said as he shook his head.

"Many of the men would say that any day that you made it out of the mines in one piece, was a good day. Every now and then, someone would sneak a bottle of rum into work and you would run into them later that day, hiding out behind a pillar, passed out, loaded drunk," he said this with a smile.

"Everyone who worked underground had a rag hanging out of their arse pocket. You see everything underground, such as the wheels and axels on all the ore carts, as well as the drills and the drill bits, were all made of steel and everything steel constantly had to be greased. Everything underground is wet and if you don't keep your steel equipment greased, then it will rust and seize up and it won't work. So after you greased your equipment, you pulled the rag out of your arse pocket and wiped the grease off your hands and got back to work. Now this meant that everyone in the mines had a greasy rag hanging out of their arse pocket." He glanced at me again as he paused, as if deciding whether he should go on.

He was grinning widely now as he said, "It didn't take long for some of the veteran miners to devise a little prank to initiate any new guys that started working in the mines. The older guys would wait to get one of these new guys underground, sneak up behind him in the dark and light his greasy rag on fire. The new guy wouldn't know anything until all of a sudden, his arse was burning and he would let out a loud scream and throw his fiery rag on the ground. Then all the other men would let out a big laugh and yell, welcome to Bell Island mines."

He looked sidelong at me, continuing, "Now this practice of lighting the new guy's rags on fire went on for years. One time this new guy from St. John's started working in our mines. He was a big, strong young fellow, about 21 years old and a real hotshot. He bragged about how he worked in mines all across Canada, but he never worked on Bell Island before. Just for the fact that this guy never shut up bragging and he was a townie from St. John's, meant that the local boys didn't really like him very much."

Taking a casual sip of the beer, he went on, "So we decided to get him with the fiery rag. As he walked by us one afternoon, we lit his rag on fire and as soon as he felt his arse burning, instead of throwing the fiery rag on the ground, this poor guy took off running and screaming through the mine with his arse on fire." He barked a laugh at this.

"We had never seen this reaction before, so we all ran after him and when we finally caught up with him, he had found a pool of water and jumped into it!" He was laughing and talking at once.

"So now this poor guy was neck deep in water. I felt bad for him, so I helped him out of the water and when he got out, he was soaking wet, froze to death and pretty well pissed off. He pulled the wet rag from his back pocket and threw it to the ground and then reached back into that same pocket and slowly pulled out 5 dynamite blasting caps!"

"These dynamite caps had been in the same back pocket that was just on fire!" He shook his head at this.

"This is why he took off running and screaming, the poor guy just panicked. Now, this story naturally travelled quickly throughout the mine and it didn't take long for the bosses to hear about it. The Bosses knew that we had been lighting each other's rags on fire for years, but nobody cared because no one ever got hurt. However, after this incident with this particular guy and his dynamite caps, the Bosses put out a new rule that stated; any man who gets caught lighting another man's rag on fire, will be FIRED!"

"Needless to say, that was the last time anyone ever lit another man's rag on fire. We had a lot of good times in the mines; it was dark, wet and cold but I loved it and I would go back to work there tomorrow if it reopened." Vince stopped talking, continued to laugh to himself and took a huge mouthful of beer.

I could see in his eyes that he was gone back to the mines. "So, 106 men died in the mines?" I said, "Did you ever see anyone die?"

Vince took another mouthful of beer, let out another sigh and started in again.

"I personally never saw anyone die, although I helped carry a few bodies out from the mines. Your Great Grand Father Jerry, he had a man die in his arms one time in the mines. He's told me about it several times and although it happened a lifetime ago; I don't think he ever got over it."

I was very intrigue and asked, "What Happened?"

"Well," Vince continued, "It was in Number 2 Mine, around 1913, Dad was 15 or 16 years old. The mine went underground on a 10 degree slope and there were 2 sets of railway tracks on the main slope. One track carried full ore carts from underground, all the way to the pier to load the ore ships and the other track brought back the empty ore carts to the miners underground. All of these carts were being pulled by a one inch steel cable." He was animated as he estimated the size of the cable.

"On this particular day, one of the two-tonne ore carts was loaded with ore and while being pulled up the slope to the surface; the cable snapped. There was no braking system and you can imagine how much speed a two tonne ore cart could pick up on a 10 degree slope. Dad just happened to be walking out to the main slope for a cigarette break when he saw this runaway cart go whizzing by him. Dad took-off chasing after it, yelling at anyone on the main slope to look out." The tempo of his speech increased as the story became more intense.

"Of course no one could hear him because of all the drilling and blasting going on. At the bottom of the main slope there was a Driller who had his back turned to the tracks, drilling the wall, preparing it to be blasted to make the tunnel deeper. Dad continued to chase the cart, screaming at the Driller to look out, but he couldn't hear him. Unfortunately, the cart had picked up so much speed that it was pulling away from Dad, who couldn't catch up to it on the wet, slippery slope."

"By the time Dad reached the end of the tunnel, the cart had smashed into the Driller and crushed his body. He breathed his last breath while being comforted in Dad's arms before his body finally succumb to his injuries," he finished sadly.

Vince and I just sat there quietly as he finished off his beer, trying to hide the fact that his eyes were welling-up with tears. It was hard for me to believe that the old man eating cheesies in Nan's house had been through something so terrible. In an attempt to comfort Vince, I patted him on the shoulder as he stood up and motioned for us to leave his shed.

I deduced that by now, Dad and Paul must be finished cutting the hay and it's probably safe to return home. Later tonight a few of us were going to be sleeping out in a tent and I was really looking forward to that.

I helped Vince lock up his shed for the evening and told him I would see him again tomorrow. Pop nodded and handed me a five dollar bill for helping, although I really think he was paying me for my company; my time and attention and the chance for him to tell old stories about the Bell Island mines.

It always struck me as odd as to why Vince spoke so highly about the mines. I mean he spoke of it like it was the Shangri-La. Somehow the Bell Island Iron Ore Mines had become Vince's

Happy Place. Other people would describe the mine's deplorable cold, wet, rat invested conditions, whereas Pop Dalton talked about it as if it was Disney Land. Was it possible that since he had spent over 20 years of his life working underground, forging relationships with his coworkers, providing him with a means to support his family that it somehow grew on him?

Perhaps when you work in a place long enough, it becomes a part of you, it's all you know and recognize and maybe eventually you depend on it to sustain your way of life. When it is taken away from you, it becomes nothing more than a fond memory and as you get older, you begin to miss and crave that familiarity.

All the stories that my Grandfather's Vince Dalton and George Hickey Sr. had told me over the years, inspired me to write a poem for a Grade 12 poetry competition, and I'm proud to say, I won first place. I would like to share that poem with you as a tribute to my Grandfathers and every other man who worked in the Bell Island Iron Ore Mines:

A Gentle Man

The whistle blew at 2 a.m., men scurried from the mine.
An explosion down in Number 2, was the word from down the line.
I watched my Nan light her lamp and rush right out the door.
To number 2, to check on Pop, like many times before.
So I knelt, beside my bed and prayed with all my might.
Please God, keep Poppy safe and bring him home tonight.
Just then, the door blew open and I watched my Pop walk in.
His clothes, all torn and dirty, iron-ore colored skin.
He sat in his favorite chair, beside the fireplace.
I asked him what had happened, a blank look came on his face.
He described the large explosion, in the backslopes, level 10.
And how he lost his buddies, hard-working, family men.
As a tear ran down his cheek, he whispered, "Where's your Nan"?
I told him, "Once the whistle blew, out the door she ran".
Pop stood up and wiped his tears, so I hugged that gentle man.
"Now go to bed", he whispered, "I'm off to fetch your Nan".
But just as Pop walked out the door, I could hear my Nanny cry.
Weeping uncontrollably, "Why Jesus, WHY"?
I ran out to the porch and asked her what was wrong.

She could barely say the words, "Your poor Poppy is gone"!
"NO", I cried, "this can't be true, I was just with Pop".
Nanny knelt and hugged me, just as the whistle stopped.
Three days passed, we buried Pop and he took his place in line.
Amongst a list of brave, loved men who never left the mine.
So years flew by, the mines closed down, now I look after Nan.
She often talks about my Pop, her one and only man.
But every time that whistle blows, tears still fill my eyes.
And I think about that gentle man when he said his last goodbyes.

I approached the boys and I could see that Paul was still pissed off because I had managed to squirm my way out of cutting hay. I handed him the five dollars that Vince had given me and told him that he can buy us whatever snacks he wanted for camping out. This seemed to rectify the situation and as the boys continued setting up the tent, I collected a pile of firewood. While gathering the firewood, Greg secretly called me over to the tent and pulled a couple of skin books out of his sleeping bag. Rod pulled a flask of Rum out of his sleeping bag and I could tell immediately that tonight had the potential to be a good time.

This would be an excellent night for sleeping out since all the older kids were going to a teen dance tonight, there most likely wouldn't be anyone to hang out with on Lahey's field. With the tent set up and the firewood collected, Rod and Greg headed home for supper and we all agreed that we would meet back at the tent in about an hour.

After we finished supper, Mom and Dad decided to go for an evening drive and they asked me to keep a watch over Jason and Jennifer until they got back home. Paul went outside to meet the boys and walk to the store to buy some snacks for tonight. After Mom and Dad left the house I began to feel guilty for not having anything to contribute to our campout. I then remembered that every January Dad bottles off a couple of cases of homemade wine and stores it in the attic for the following Christmas. I made sure Jason and Jennifer were busy watching television before I climbed up into the attic to investigate.

The attic was traditionally off limits and the only times I was ever permitted up there was to retrieve Christmas decorations and of course to help store Dad's wine. There were two boxes which contained seventeen 26 oz bottles of wine in total. I knew Dad wouldn't miss one bottle so I grabbed one, climbed down out of the attic and stashed it in my rolled up sleeping bag. Now I just waited for Mom and Dad to get home so I could join the boys out into the tent.

After they arrived home, Mom and Dad got settled in for the evening, so I grabbed my sleeping bag and flash light and ran outside. As I was going through the door Dad made a yell at me and told me that he would have us all up bright and early tomorrow morning to help him turn over the hay.

"No problem Georgio," I yelled back, "see you tomorrow!"

I jogged over to where we had our tent pitched, which was about a 200 yards away from the house, in the woods just down past our barn. As I neared the tent, I could hear the boys already giggling, so I snuck up on the tent and in my best George Hickey voice I roared, "Get out of that tent you bunch of nob-gobbling windsuckers".

The tent went deathly quiet until I let out a loud laugh and I could hear the boys retort, "Arsehole." I unzipped the tent and entered what could only be described as the playboy mansion. There were two flashlights hung in opposite corners of the tent; one emitting a red light and the other emitting a blue.

There were at least three skin books being passed around and in the center of the tent there was a mound of candy, bars, suckers and assorted junk food that would make Willie Wonka envious. The boys passed around a flask of rum and we all took turns taking sips. Rod had bought along his Ghetto Blaster and we rocked out to some Bob Seger. It may have only been a cheap nylon tent but to us on that particular night, it was better than the Taj Mahal.

We were like kings; we wanted for nothing and tonight we would rule the world. We each polished off a can of Vienna Sausages and as we were finishing up the tasty treats I asked the boys to give me their empty sausage cans. They did so a little curiously until I pulled out the bottle of homemade wine from my sleeping bag and filled up everyone's empty Vienna sausage can with the beverage. I handed everyone their cup and raised my can.

"Gentlemen", I started, "tonight I would like to propose a toast to friendship. I know I piss you guys off a lot, but tonight we are all of one accord. Thank you for letting me camp out with you guys tonight, thanks for helping me and Paul with the hay tomorrow and let us now offer Thanks to God for this wonderful bounty of food, wine and skin books. Let me finish by saying please raise your glasses and here's hoping that the best of our past is equalled to the worst of our future........ Cheers."

The boys all said "Cheers", as we touched our Vienna sausage cans together and downed the homemade wine.

We laughed and told jokes throughout the night. By midnight, we were all sitting outside, around a small fire, drunk as skunks, trying to keep warm. Since Rod was the only one of us with any experience with the ladies, we asked him about a girl he was dating this past winter. Her name was Mary Carter and she went to our school. She was 2 years older than Rod, very pretty and she would often sing at our church services. She wasn't allowed to go to any parties or dances, as her Dad was very strict and overprotective. Apparently, no guy had ever gotten past first-base with her and as a result, everyone called her Virgin Mary. It was said that you needed a note from God to get into her pants. Rod had been dating her for about five months, but he said that the constant badgering and accusations from her dad was too much for him to handle.

"How far did you get with her Rod?" Greg asked with a dirty grin, "Did you let the Virgin Mary take a ride on the ole baloney-pony?"

We all laughed as we waited for a response from Rod, but he was a real gentleman; quiet and respectable he would never say anything to criticize or disparage anyone. "Don't worry about it Rod," I interrupted, "You got a really nice girl now in Karen."

"Yeah," Greg added, "You're better off Rod, not even Moses

could part Mary's legs! Besides, I heard that she's hurtin' in the titty-department as well. A guy in grade 12 said that he dated Mary for about a year, and the one time he convinced her to take off her bra; she looked like a 10 year old boy! So, I guess it's true what the bible says: It is easier for a camel to pass through the eye of a needle, than it is to get inside Mary Carter's pants!"

We all laughed and chugged another can of wine. I asked Rod how things were going with Karen and he said things were fine. I could tell he liked her a lot and I was actually feeling happy for them. Maybe it was the alcohol talking but I told him that they make a nice couple and I was happy for them.

Of course I was bursting to tell the boys about my encounter with the beautiful young girl at Long Harry a few days ago. I described her to them as best I could, but not one of them had any idea who I was talking about.

"She might be just here on Bell Island visiting Brian," Rod said, "You may never see her again."

What a horrible thing that would be, I thought to myself. I could still picture her there standing next to her bike, looking beautiful. No, I decided, she lives here somewhere on Bell Island and I will just have to find her.

A couple of different times during the night, I couldn't help notice Greg rubbing his left arm. Finally I saw him once again rub his bicep and I asked, "What's wrong with your arm Greg, did you hurt it?"

Greg just shrugged it off, stood up, walked away and responded, "Nah, it's nothing, I'm going to take a piss."

While Greg was gone, Rod began telling Paul and I that while we were gone today cutting hay, Howie gave Greg a bit of a beating. This really pissed me off, I had my share of run-ins with Howie and he was nothing more than a big bullying arsehole.

"Someone needs to teach that guy a lesson," I protested, "he is almost five years older than me and he tosses me around like a rag doll. Only for Dad, that idiot would have put me in the hospital long ago."

Both Paul and Rod nodded in agreement and I guess Greg

must have overheard what I said because as he walked back to the fire, he sat down and asked, "Who's an idiot, who are you talking about?"

I threw another couple of sticks on the fire and said, "Howie is a friggin' idiot. Rod just told us how he beat you up today, what happened anyway"? Greg poured himself another sausage can full of wine and started in.

"Today while you and Paul were gone cutting hay, I rode over to Lahey's field on my bike. Howie was there having a cigarette and putting on a show for the rest of the boys. As I rode up closer to them, Howie grabbed the handlebars on my bike and tipped me over. Then he took my bike from me and said, 'Thanks for the bike needle-dick'."

"Everyone was laughing so I said, 'Yeah Howie, well my dick was big enough to fill your mother's mouth last night!' Everyone laughed even harder at that and I could see that Howie didn't like it."

'Run along now needle-dick,' he said, 'before you gets hurt'. I couldn't leave without my bike so I told him to give it back. 'Ah, needle-dick wants his bike back,' he said, 'Is needle-dick going to cry?'

Greg continued, "He gave me back my bike with everyone laughing but before I left I said, '*Thanks for the bike ass-wipe, and tell your Mom that me and the boys will pop over later tonight for another round of head!*'

"With that, his friends laughed even harder and he got mad and knocked me down, sat on top of me and punched me in the arm over and over until I said I was sorry. I held off for as long as I could but after about 50 punches in the arm, I finally apologized, but only because it felt like he was going to break my arm. Then he told me that the next time he sees me with my bike, he's taking it home with him and selling it."

This was classic Howie; he didn't have the guts to pick on anyone his own size, so he targeted us.

"We should all get together and beat the shit out of him," I said, "or better yet, make Dad think that Howie did something to him and let Dad pound the shit out of him."

We all relished the idea of uniting forces to kick his ass but we also realized that if we gang up on him, he will get us all back individually.

"If we get him, we've got to get him good," I demanded, "I'd like to push the arsehole off a cliff, but he's not worth going to jail for. Wait a second, I got it !!! I know what we can do; who would like to see our ole buddy Howie guzzle down a mouthful of piss?"

I could see that I had everyone's full attention as I picked up our empty rum flask that was lying next to the fire.

"Let's all take a piss in this rum bottle and get Howie to drink it."

Everyone laughed and agreed to the idea, so we left a small amount of rum sitting in the bottom of the flask and then we all took turns filling it with urine. The remaining rum left in the bottle was enough to give the flask a nice rum-smell and the color of our urine matched the rum-color perfectly. We devised a plan that involved skin books, cigarettes and a flask full of piss and agreed that tomorrow night on Lahey's field; Howie would finally receive his much deserved comeuppance which would hopefully atone for years of bullying and beatings that he had administered to each of us.

The next morning, as good as his word, Dad showed up bright and early at the tent for us to help him turn over the hay. Dad made a yell at us to get up while he made his way to the barn to milk the cows. We had only slept for about 3 hours and I was still feeling the effects of the homemade wine.

Everyone was sat up in the tent feeling groggy and hung-over and it was only when I pulled the flask of piss out from under my sleeping bag, did the atmosphere change. Everyone began giggling and very excited as we left the tent and I carefully stashed the flask, empty wine bottle and the skin books in the woods.

We walked to the barn and each grabbed a hay prong and

walked up towards my Grandfathers to turn over the hay. Along the walk, we fine-tuned some of the details of our plan, which we code-named; "Operation COCK-tail" and we were all in agreement that if we pulled this off, Howie would be the laughing stock of the East End.

We arrived at my Grandparents yard and turned over the hay in record time. Then we left there and walked down to the second meadow of hay and turned that over just as quickly. With the warm sunshine and light breeze, the hay would most likely be dry enough to put in the barn by tomorrow morning. We finished up and were relieved to find that we had everything done by lunch time. Everyone was tired and agreed that we will all go home and have some lunch and meet up again by the tent later that afternoon.

We all met up at the tent and everyone was filled with exhilaration and nervous energy over what would hopefully take place tonight.

"Remember everyone," Greg interjected, "Howie is going to be totally pissed off and humiliated and will more than likely be looking to get back at one of us. It will probably be me since I am the smallest. I don't think he will go after Brian, because he knows Georgio will find him and kill him; and I can't see him trying to take on Paul or Rod because either one of the boys would probably give him a run for his money. No, it will definitely be me that he goes for first, so I am going to need you guys to be there with me and help fight him off. We all have to stand strong, if one of us runs; the whole plan will go to shit and I will be the one who gets the worst of it. The moment he makes a grab for one of us, everyone attack."

We all agreed and I added, "Don't worry buddy, if Howie makes a move towards you, we will be all standing at the ready."

We walked into Dad's barn and Greg pulled out 3 cigarettes that he had taken from his father and planned to give to Howe, along with the flask. He walked towards one of Dad's cows, lifted the cow's tail and gently started rubbing the butt of each cigarette against the cow's shitty arsehole. Everyone watched in disgust and I commented, "Well, they may not be as refined as liquor tipped cigars, but I think bovine-ass tipped cigarettes will do just fine for Howie!"

We all burst out laughing and after we rehearsed our plan several more times, we wished Greg good luck and waved goodbye to him as he rode away on his bike.

Rod, Paul and I walked towards Lahey's field excited and nervous all at the same time and as we approached we could see that Howie was already there, bragging about something to Mark and Lenny.

As we approached the group, Howie commented, "look at the three fairies' coming, did you queers have fun sleeping out in your little tent last night, did you curl each other's hair and do each other's nails?"

Oh man, I thought to myself, I can't wait to see this arsehole go down, what an idiot! It was so ironic because after hearing Howie's comment, Mark replied, "Ease up on the boys Howie, or one of these days they are all going to get together and pay you back...........Big-Time."

You got that right Mark, I thought to myself, in fact, hopefully tonight's the night! Howie just sniggered and said, "I would like to see these little Queers try".

The usual crowd had gathered around the field that night but I noticed that Al was nowhere to be found. Too bad, I was dying to fill him in on what we had planned for Howie. I looked across the field and I could see that Greg was standing on the side of Lahey's house waving at me, which meant it was time to put our plan into motion. I walked up to Howie and discreetly asked him if I could talk to him for a minute. I got Howie alone and he looked at me and said, "What do you want Queer?"

I told Howie that Greg was over by Lahey's house and he had a couple of cigarettes, skin books and some booze he wanted to give him, as a way of making amends for what he had said about Howie's mother yesterday. I also told Howie that Greg wanted to give it all to him, but he was too afraid to bring it over because he thought that Howie was still mad at him.

Howie's eyes widened with anticipation at the thought of free booze and cigarettes and he responded, "No problem Hickey buddy, tell Greg to come on over and I won't bother him anymore." Howie walked away and immediately went over to Lenny, Mark, Don and Gerald and started bragging about how Greg was about to bring him some goodies out of fear and respect. I waved Greg over to the field and he quickly jogged over and handed Howie a brown paper bag and muttered, "I'm sorry about yesterday."

Howie took the bag and said, "No problem ass-wipe, but next time watch your mouth or I'll kick your arse again."

Howie opened the bag and pulled out the three cigarettes all neatly wrapped in tin foil. He lit one of the cigarettes and Paul, Rod, Greg and I all looked at each other, desperately trying to prevent ourselves from laughing. While enjoying his smoke, Howie pulled out a couple of skin books and said, "Well, well, well, what do we have here, looks like a bit of reading material for later tonight."

Finally he pulled the flask of rum out of the bag and his eyes lit up like a Christmas tree.

"Yes by," he said, "looks like I'm in for a free drunk tonight boys."

We watched with great anticipation as he twisted the top off his flask. He took another puff from his cow-arse-cigarette and raised his flask in a toasting motion and said, "Here's to being the East End Bad Boy."

He put the flask of urine to his lips and gulped down a huge mouthful. I could no longer contain myself as I burst out laughing in disgust. The look on Howie's face was priceless, the flask looked and smelled like booze but he wasn't quite sure what this stuff was. The strong smell of rum was still in the bottle so he must have figured that it had gone weak.

"Holy shit," he said, "how old is this rum Greg? It tastes like it's been watered down?"

Before Greg could even answer, Howie took another huge mouthful and as he swallowed it, alarms must have gone off inside his tiny brain.

"This ain't booze!" He shouted, "What the hell is this shit?"

"Not shit," Greg replied, "PISS, you are drinking a bottle of piss, you big, dumb bastard"!

Everyone just looked at each other in shock as the four of us busted a gut laughing.

"What the hell is going on?" Lenny asked, as he took the flask out of Howie's hand and sniffed its contents.

"Me and the boys pissed in the flask," Greg said between laughs, "and Howie drank it. Not only that, the cigarettes that he is smoking were up a cows ass."

Everyone laughed except for Howie who turned as red as a beet. You could see the hatred and humiliation building in his eyes as he lunged at Greg knocking him down on the ground. I was paralyzed with fear and before I could even react, Rod and Paul threw themselves on top of Howie and pulled him off Greg. Nervous and scared, I also dove in on the mound of bodies and grabbed both of Howie's legs and held on for dare life. Rod and Paul each grabbed an arm and Greg administered a choke hold. Howie was bigger than us, but there was no way in the world that he could take on the four of us.

Everyone just stood around and watched as Greg slowly chocked Howie into submission. No one tried to interfere mainly because everyone, especially the older kids, knew that Howie had this coming.

"Now ASS-WIPE," Greg shouted, "if you ever mess with one of us again, we will all get together and beat the living shit out of you." Howie was gasping for air and nodded in agreement. When we all let him go, he coughed and tried to catch his breath.

Everyone that was on Lahey's field that evening remained deafly quiet, and as I was picking myself up, I felt a sharp, swift pain in my back, that sent me tumbling to the ground and I realized that Howie had kicked me from his seated position.

"You are all going to die," he shouted, as he got to his knees and was reaching out to grab a hold of me. I let out a scream and in a split second, before he had his hands around my throat; Paul leaped in and kneed him in the face. Howie fell back to the ground, spitting out blood and then Rod stepped in and, as hard as he could, he landed a solid kick to Howie's ribs. You could hear the loud THUD of the kick echo as the force of it knocked the wind out of Howie. He rolled around the ground in pain, trying desperately to catch his breath and as he and I looked directly at each other, I could see that his eyes were still filled with rage and revenge.

I didn't want him to be filled with rage and revenge, I wanted him to be filled with fear; the same fear that he had made me live with for so long. Years of being bullied by him had finally spilled over and now I wanted him to know what real pain and fear were all about. An overpowering, uncontrollable surge came over me and I felt like I was Captain Ahab and Howie was my Moby Dick; I would not rest until I had him. He lay on his back clutching his ribs in pain and I jumped on top of him and started raining down punches and elbows to his face. I'm ashamed to say it, but a small part of me wanted him dead that evening; for all the pain and humiliation I had suffered at his hands. I could see that he was bleeding and I liked it; in fact, I wanted more. I continued wailing down on him until finally Lenny and Andy each grabbed my arms and pulled me off him.

"That's enough Brian," Andy whispered, "The guy has had enough."

When I finally calmed down, the boys let me go and I looked over at Howie lying on the ground bleeding and crying in agony. I walked over towards him, lifted my foot and stomped down on his nuts as hard as I could. Then I spit on him and walked away as he screamed out in pain. *To this very day, I often wonder how far my rage would have taken me if Lenny and Andy had not pulled me off him. I have never since felt that kind of rage or uncontrolled desire to hurt someone; and I hope I never experience it again.*

Greg walked over to him and slapped Howie in the face a

couple of times. "Did you hear what I said Arsehole, if you mess with one of us, you mess with all of us. Now, go home and don't come back here anymore."

Howie was still sobbing and limping from the kick in the nuts and he muttered,

"This ain't your field, you can't make me go home." With that, Rod leaned in with another kick to his stomach and as Howie dropped back down to one knee, Paul landed another punch to his face, bringing about a small trickle of blood from his nose. Again Howie rolled around the ground, crying in pain.

"Ok, ok", he shouted, "I'm going home; just give me a second to catch my breath." We all looked at each other relieved.

"Before you go", Greg said, "I have something for you." He pulled down his pants and sat of Howie's face until Howie's nose went half ways up Greg's arse. "Kiss my arse you friggin loser," Greg said to him and Howie was too weak and defeated to do anything about it. Everyone killed themselves laughing again and finally Howie picked himself up and limped off Lahey's field in disgrace.

"Hey Howie," Greg shouted, "Tell your Mom that I will drop by later tonight to play Sesame Street."

Howie suddenly paused for a second and turned back to the crowd and gave Greg a puzzled look.

"What the hell are you talking about.........Sesame Street?"

"You know," Greg replied, "Sesame Street; I'll be Big Bird and your Mom can be Mr. Stuff-it-up-her-muss!"

Everyone laughed at Howie, who continued to slowly limp away in pain. Lenny and the older boys walked over towards us and gave us all high fives and said, "Well done boys, Howie had that coming".

Howie never came around much after that fateful evening. Stories spread through Bell Island like wildfire about how Howie drank a flask of piss, smoked shit-tipped cigarettes and had his arse kicked by a couple of 12 and 14 year olds. His shame followed him around and thankfully, none of us ever had any further dealings with him.

Later that night, the four of us went back to our tent filled with excitement as we celebrated our victory over Howie. I joked and said, "I never figured Howie for a brown-noser, but after Greg sat on his face, we may just have to start calling him that."

Everyone laughed and Greg added, "Yeah, I think his nose finally dislodged a peanut that's been stuck in my arse for the past six months."

The laugher continued, but we were all starting to feel a little hungry after tonight's events.

"Anyone up for a free feed of fish and chips?" Greg asked.

We all knew exactly what he meant. You see, about a 20 minute walk up the road there stands Dwyer's Snack-bar; well known throughout Bell Island for their fine fish and chips. The Take-Out restaurant is owned and operated by Mr. and Mrs. Dwyer, perhaps one of the kindest, sweetest old couples you could ever meet. My Mom actually worked at the snack-bar every Friday and Saturday night, when it is the busiest. From Sunday night through Thursday night however, only the elderly couple work at the snack-bar and it is during this period that the boys and I have helped ourselves to an occasional free meal.

During the summer months the kitchen in the snack-bar gets too hot with all the stoves on high and the deep frying that goes on. So, they usually keep the outside door to the kitchen open, to let in some cool air. This kitchen door is located on the back of the restaurant and is off limits to the general public. We all knew that when someone phoned in a take-out order, the Dwyer's cooked the order, packaged it brown paper bags and placed in on a table next to the kitchen door until the customer arrives to pick up their order. With this door remaining open on warm summer nights, it was pretty easy to reach in around the open door, grab a hot order and take off without being seen.

"Ok," I said, "If we are going to do this, we better get a move on, it's getting late and the snack-bar closes in about 2 hours."

We all ran down to Rod's house and snuck into his basement

to use the phone. I dialled the number to the snack-bar and Mrs. Dwyer soon answered. I lowered my voice and tried my best to sound like an older gentleman.

"Yes hello," I said, "I would like to place an order for some food. I would like 3 large fish and chips, 1 large chicken and chips, 4 cheeseburgers and 4 cans of coke please."

Mrs. Dwyer asked for my name, to which I replied, "John Butler." "Yes Mr. Butler," she said, "your total comes to $43.55 and your order will be ready for pickup in about 25 minutes."

"Very good," I replied, "I will come pick up the food in half an hour, see you then."

I hung up the phone and the boys and I started laughing. "Shhhhh," Rod said, "you're going to wake up Mom upstairs; let's all go back to the tent."

We left Rod's house and ran back to the tent to work out the rest of the details to our Snack-bar plan. It was decided that I would walk into the store and distract the store owners by ordering a can of drink and a chocolate bar from off the top shelf, while the boys would grab the food in the kitchen. With our plan all worked out, we headed towards the snack-bar. We ducked in the trees, just behind the snack-bar and we stayed outside until we made sure there weren't any more customers inside. The boys all gave me their money and I walked into the restaurant.

"Hello Brian," Mrs. Dwyer said as she greeted me with a big smile, "how are you doing tonight?"

"I'm good Mrs. Dwyer," I replied, "a couple of my friends and I are sleeping out in a tent and I thought I would come in for a can of drink and a bar."

I could see Mr. Dwyer out in the kitchen bagging up some food.

"What type of drink would you like sweetie?" Mrs. Dwyer asked me.

"I will have a can of root beer please," I replied. Mrs. Dwyer was quite a short woman and I scanned the bars on the shelf behind her to find one that was out of her reach.

"May I also have a Mars Bar, please?" I asked as I pointed to the top shelf. She turned around and looked up at the bar which was well out of her reach.

"Jim," she yelled to her husband, "can you please come here and reach a chocolate bar for me?"

Mr. Dwyer came out to the front of the store and when he saw me he said, "Hello there young Hickey, what kind of bar can I get you?"

Again I pointed up to the Mars bars on the top shelf. I chatted with the couple for a few minutes and while I had them both distracted and out of the kitchen, I assumed that the boys should already be grabbing the food.

"That will be 95 cents Brian, please," Mrs. Dwyer said. I counted out the money and handed it to her.

"Here's a bag of chips to go along for your little camping trip," she said, "no charge for the chips."

What a kind old lady I thought. I thanked her and walked towards the door. "Say hello to your Mom for me," she shouted as I was leaving.

We all raced back to the tent, the boys were each carrying a brown paper bag while I carried my can of pop, bar and free bag of chips. I couldn't help but feel guilty about what we had just done. We just cheated these nice people out of food and to make matters worse, they rewarded me with a free bag of chips. Oh well, I thought as we neared the tent, the Lord helps those who help themselves. We sat in the tent and the smell of all the wonderful hot food was intoxicating.

"Let's see what we have", Greg said as he began tearing open his bag. Much to our delight, Greg's bag contained the 3 plates of fish of chips and 1 plate of chicken and chips. Paul ripped open his bag and it contained the 4 cheeseburgers and 4 cans of pop. Rod ripped open his bag and his jaw nearly dropped when he discovered that it contained a box of drinking straws and a pack of paper napkins. Everyone busted out laughing at the sight of Rod's wares.

"Nice score there Rod," Greg teased as we shared out the food. "I'll trade you a plate of my fish and chips for a couple of your napkins and straws."

We sat there like kings eating our wonderful feast and reliving what had happened to Howie. We laughed and carried on as if everything was perfect. The only thing that would make the night better was if it wasn't so bloody cold. We were into August and the summers nights were cooling down, almost too cool for sleeping in a tent.

"You guys should build a shed," I said to them. "Build a nice warm shed like Morris and Randy's and that way we won't have to sleep on the cold ground."

I could see that my idea was being well received and we spent the rest of the night planning out how our new shed will look.

The next morning we woke up in the tent bright and early when we heard Dad in the barn, hooking up the horse and hay cart. We quickly made sure that we had burned all the evidence from last night that could in any way tie us to the acquired food. Satisfied that we had covered all our tracks the four of us climbed outside our tent and was faced with yet another warm and sunny morning.

To everyone's surprise, Al was walking towards our tent and as Rod looked at his watch he said, "What are you doing up so early Al, it's not even seven o'clock in the morning?"

Al came closer to us with a strange look on his face and I knew that there was something wrong.

"Hey boys," Al said, "what day is it today?"

We all looked at each other a little dumbfounded until finally Rod answered in his best British accent, "Why it's Christmas day Mr. Scrooge!" We all laughed at Rod's Joke but I could see that Al did not find it one bit funny.

"It's Friday morning Al," I said, "Is there anything wrong"?

Al just sat there scratching his head until he finally mumbled, "Wow, Friday morning, I have been asleep since Wednesday night!"

We couldn't believe it; Al went to bed 11:30 Wednesday night and didn't wake up until 6:30 Friday Morning. That's a total of

31 consecutive hours of sleeping, how was this even possible?

"I don't know what happened," Al said. "All I know is that I woke up this morning and had to take a 2 minute piss. When I finished in the bathroom, I ate two bowls of cereal and 4 slices of toast for breakfast".

When dad emerged from the barn, we quickly told him about Al's marathon sleep-fest.

"Al my Son," Dad stated, "you couldn't have been asleep for that long, you must have been in a coma." Everyone laughed as Dad continued, "Anyway, since you're awake and you've had your beauty rest, you can help me and boys with the hay today."

We all followed behind Dad on the horse and cart as we walked towards my Grandparents yard to collect the hay. Along the way, we told Al all about last night's adventure of finally getting back at Howie and yet another successful heist at Dwyer's Fish and Chips.

7

The Miners cave

Later that afternoon, we finished putting the hay in the barn, so we all decided to go down to Freshwater for a nice refreshing swim. Freshwater was a swimming area on the ocean that was located on the East End of Bell Island, not far from where we lived. It was a little tricky getting down over the cliff, but it had a magnificent beach for swimming, as well as a picturesque waterfall that cascaded off the cliff and onto the beach rocks.

Once we arrived at the ocean, I kicked off my sneakers, pulled off my tee shirt and ran out into the cool ocean. I was still sweaty and sticky from being at the hay all morning and the cold ocean water was wonderfully refreshing. Pretty soon the boys were all in the water, as we swam around laughing and joking. We soon climbed out of the cold water and sought out the warmth of the hot sun and dry beach rocks. We lay back on hot rocks and soaked up the hot rays as we watched the local girls frolic in the water.

There wasn't as many good looking ladies at the ocean as there had been at Green Waters, but there was still enough to catch your eye. Once the cold ocean water made contact with the girl's sun-baked skin; we were in nipple heaven. We spent many a hot afternoon down at Freshwater, cooling off in ocean.

Two years ago, it was late into the summer before all of the Northern ice left Conception Bay. I can remember actually swimming out to the ice pans, climbing up on top of them and then diving back into ocean. The water was particularly cold that summer, but it didn't stop us from swimming in it.

What always made me laugh was how Mom insisted that you weren't allowed to go swimming in the ocean until July 21st. That, apparently was the official day that the chill magically left the water. We weren't allowed in the water on July 20th but on July 21st the chill was gone and the water was fine.

After a few hours of swimming, we would climb back over the cliffs of Fresh Water and start our journey back home. With our jean shorts soaking wet and the hot sun on our backs, we would stop throughout Fresh Water path and pick and eat a few blue berries and raspberries, just to get the taste of salt water out of our mouths.

Along the way, we could hear that unmistakable 4 o'clock Town whistle that sounded across the Island. For many of us, that town whistle meant that we had about half an hour to get home before supper. We hurried up the path to get home, each of us excited about the thought of building our own shed. Paul and I said goodbye to the boys as we headed home for supper.

While we were at the supper table, I ran the idea by Dad about us building a small shed, much like the one Morris and Randy had.

Dad's first reaction was to naturally yell and rant, "If you boys were to build a shed, there wouldn't be any booze or whores in it like Morris and Randy has in their shed, I can promise you that. Now, where do you plan on building the shed and where would you get the lumber?"

I told Dad that Rod, Greg and Al all have access to some lumber at home and between the five of us, we should have enough.

"Well then," Dad added, "I have some extra felt left over from when I re-felted the barn last year; I guess you can have that to put on your roof. There are plenty of nails and tools out in the tool shed, so I guess you can borrow those. Where are you planning on building this shed? It has to be somewhere on my property."

Paul cleared his throat and answered, "We were planning on

building it next to your wood shed, that way we can run an extension cord to it at night for a lamp and a radio."

Dad thought it over for a minute and said, "Sounds good, as long as it don't interfere with your chores; crack onto it."

After supper, I called all the boys and told them that we had the okay from the old man. That evening Dad drove Paul and I to the boy's houses to load up whatever old lumber each person had. Between the five of us, we had several trunk loads of old plank and boards. Before nightfall, we actually had the shed framed out with a floor built. We used some of Dad's spruce firewood that hadn't been cut up yet for the wall and ceiling joists.

When we were finishing up that night, Dad came out to inspect our work and he placed his hands on one wall of the frame to see how sturdy it was. I could see that he was surprised and impressed to find that he couldn't shake it.

"You won't be able to shake our shed Georgio," I said to him with a smile, "The boys and I are master carpenters."

Dad just laughed and said, "Nice job on the frame boys, I can see that she's good and sturdy. I noticed that you're using my firewood to frame it up."

None of the boys knew what to say, so I stepped in and said, "Yes Sir, and as soon as we finish the shed, me and the boys are going to cut up all your wood and pack it away in the shed for you."

Dad just smiled and walked away and said, "Good, and make sure all my tools go back in the tool shed as well."

The next morning, Dad had nothing on the agenda for us to do. It was Saturday, which meant Dad was off work today and Mom would be working later tonight at Dwyer's Snack Bar. All the boys came around bright and early the next morning to get started on the shed. Even Al showed up before 9 A.M. which surprised the shit out of everyone. Dad got in on the act and helped us board up the walls. I'm telling you; we all worked together with great precision and cooperation. The only one who was really slowing us down was Dad who had to make sure everything was perfectly square and level. Finally, I couldn't take it anymore and I shouted, "Hurry up Georgio, we are trying to build a simple shed, not raise an Amish barn!"

By lunchtime we had all four walls sheeted up and Paul, Rod and Greg were on top of the shed, building the roof, while Dad was framing out a storm door. Vince drove into our driveway for a visit and offered a few suggestions on how to make the shed stronger.

"Why is it that you and Al aren't up on the roof with the boys?" Vince asked me, "As usual, the boys are doing all the work and every time I see you; I can' help but notice that you are always standing around with your hands in your pockets."

Everyone just laughed, but I wasn't about to be humiliated by my Grandfather, so I just looked at him and said, "I'm the foreman on this Project Vince, and Al is the lead-hand. The two of us drew up the blueprints for this shed and hired the boys to build it for us. Now, for safety reasons Vince, I'm going to have to ask you to move along, because this is a construction site, not an old age home."

Both Dad and Vince just laughed at my response and I decided to use this opportunity to secure a 5 dollar donation from Vince to go towards the purchasing of a few snacks for myself and my hard working colleagues. Vince gladly handed over the 5 dollars and Al and I headed in to Old Man Drover's store to buy some refreshments. That's one thing I have to say about Vince; he was not cheap with his money.

A few years ago he asked me to pick him a cup of blueberries so that he could make a nice blueberry duff to go along with his Sunday Dinner. It must have taken me all of 5 minutes to pick a cup of blueberries and when I gave them to him, he gave me a ten dollar bill. I snatched the money from his hand and took off running like a bat out of hell. I thought he must surely be going senile in his old age and I got out of there as fast as I could before he realized his mistake. I didn't stop running until I hit the grocery store and I went inside and purchased a frozen pizza, a 2 liter bottle of Pepsi, a family sized Jelly-Roll and a container of Ice Cream. I then ran home with my purchase and proudly put the groceries on the kitchen table in front of Mom and Dad and said, "Here you are guys, supper is on me today."

Later that evening we enjoyed a slice of pizza and a glass of Pepsi for supper and believe me, food like that was a rarity in my house. We grew up on fresh meat and potatoes and fresh milk and the only time we had soda to drink was around Christmas time. The Hickey's ate well that night though, as we even had Jelly-Roll and Ice Cream for dessert. It was an unexpected treat and I tell you, I felt as though I was ten feet tall for being able to provide my family with that meal as well as a nice little change of pace.

While we were passing Al's house on our way to the store, Al's Grandfather called us over and asked where we were going. Al explained to him that we were building a shed at my house and that we were on our way to the store to buy some snacks.

"If you're going into the store," Al's grandfather said, "Drop off these bag of books to Johnny for me."

He handed us a huge, heavy brown paper bag and said, "Give this bag to Johnny and he should have a similar bag to give you to bring back to me. Bring the bag right back here and don't look inside it." Al took the bag from his grandfather and as soon as we were out of sight from his house, we looked inside it. Holy German Jesus, the bag was filled with skin books! He had everything; Penthouse, Hustler and Playbook, it was like Al and I had won the lottery. Here we were on a hot and sunny summer's day with a 5 dollar bill in our pocket and a full bag of skin books. I hadn't been this excited since Lionel Richie was *"Dancing on the Ceiling."*

We continued walking towards the store and as we passed a wooded area, Al grabbed a handful of the skin books and stashed them in the woods. When we reached the store, Mr. Drover was there and Al handed him the bag of books.

"Here's a bag of books that Pop asked me to give you Mr.

Drover," Al shouted, since Mr. Drover was old and losing his hearing. Mr. Drover thanked Al and handed him a different bag.

"Here you go, give this bag to your grandfather."

We purchased 5 dollar's worth of soda and potato chips, licorice, bars and candy and headed on back down the road. As soon as we left the store, we peeped inside the bag and sure enough, it too was filled with skin books. Apparently Al's grandfather and old Old Man Drover were involved in a Bell Island sex trade; Skin Books that is!

Once we passed the wooded area, Al grabbed another handful of skin books and stashed them in the woods along with the others. We then walked back to his house, gave his grandfather the bag of books and then ran over to my house with the snacks.

We reached my house and I was pleased to see that the boys already had the roof sheeted up and was busy nailing on the felt. Dad and Paul were laying the felt, while Rod and Greg were coming along behind them, tarring over the nail heads.

When the boys noticed us returning, Dad shouted, "What took you so long my Son, I thought you had gone to a store in St. John's."

Al climbed up the ladder and handed over the bag of snacks. The boys each grabbed a can of soda and a bag of chips and Dad instructed me to run into the house and bring him back a cold beer. I did so and on my return I grabbed myself a can of soda and some licorice.

We were all done by late that afternoon as Dad nailed on the last strip of felt and Rod followed behind him with the tar. When we were finished we all stood there on the roof and admired our fine work. We all took turns climbing down the ladder and as I was the last one off, I passed down the tools and bucket of tar to everyone before I climbed down the ladder. We all walked around the shed and commented on the craftsmanship and then we all walked inside the shed. It was pitch black in there and it appeared very spacious and empty, since there was no furniture. We agreed that we would build a couple of sets of bunk-beds in it tomorrow and Rod said that he had an old couch and coffee table that we could have.

It wasn't the greatest shed ever constructed but it was warm, waterproof and most importantly; it was ours. Dad exited the shed and said, "Good job boys, I'm going inside to help your Mother with supper, don't forget we have Mass tonight."

We all agreed that we would meet back to the shed after mass with our sleeping bags. The boys left to go home and Paul and I went into the house for supper and to get cleaned up for mass services.

We all met up again in church later that evening as we were all Alter Boys; everyone of course except for Al. Al didn't attend a whole lot of mass services. He would go to church at Christmas and Easter or to a family funeral, but other than that he didn't frequent the church very often.

Al had a unique way of looking at spirituality. One time in grade 4, we were getting ready to have our lunch and our School's Principal, Sister Carol suggested that we have a little prayer and give thanks to God for the wonderful lunch that we were all about to receive.

Without thinking, Al blurted out, "But Sister, God didn't provide me with my lunch."

The class looked at Al in astonishment as Sister Carol walked right up to where he was seated and demanded, "If God didn't provide you with your food, then where on earth did it come from?"

Al just smiled at her and said, "I got my lunch at Old Man Drover's store!"

The whole class room erupted into laugher as Sister Carol dragged Al, kicking and screaming down to her office.

Rod, Paul, Greg and I met up in the downstairs of the church and put on our Altar Boy uniforms. While we were waiting for mass to begin, we were discussing sleeping out in the new shed later tonight.

"If only we had a few alcoholic beverages for later," Rod suggested, "to christen our new shed."

"Hey Brian," Greg suggested, "Can you nab another bottle of homemade wine from Georgio?"

I thought about it for a minute and responded, "I better not boys, we took a bottle from him earlier this week, I'm afraid he will notice it gone."

We all sat there trying to figure out a plan to get some booze, when suddenly Greg said, "Don't worry about it boys, I got it covered."

The priest suddenly called for us and mass services began before Greg could reveal his idea.

When church ended for the evening, we drove away and dropped Mom off to work at Dwyer's Snack-bar before the rest of us drove home. I quickly changed out of my church clothes and ran out to the shed with my sleeping bag.

Pretty soon all the boys showed up and we decided to take a walk down to Rod's house to get his couch and coffee table. Paul, Rod and Greg carried the big couch, while Al and I carried the coffee table. When we returned to the shed, Paul ran and extension cord from the tool shed to our shed and plugged in Dad's trouble light and hung it from the corner of our shed. That provided the shed with plenty of light and now all we needed was entertainment.

I ran back in the house and grabbed Paul's radio-cassette player that he had gotten for Christmas this past year. I remembered that Dad had two old wooden chairs in his tool shed, so I grabbed them and set them up in our shed. We stood around admiring this ugly, green couch that, despite its appearance, was in pretty good shape.

We closed the shed door and hooked it in for the night. Paul, Rod and Greg took the couch, while Al and I each got a wooden chair. In the middle of the shed sat the oval coffee table. There were still plenty of snacks left over from earlier today, so I grabbed the bag of goodies and dumped them all on the table. Al went over to his sleeping bag and pulled out eight skin books,

"Here you go boys," he said, "My contribution to the new shed."

Everyone was amazed at the wonderful condition the dirty magazines were in, as Al told everyone how he and I acquired them earlier today. We began riffling through the skin books and showing each other the big guns on this lady and the tremendous arse on that girl. I couldn't help but notice that of all the magazines we had, Al grabbed one that I was not familiar with. The name of it was *'Plumpers'* and when I looked over his shoulder to see what he was so interested in, I was mortified at the realization that these were extremely large women.

"Ha-ha boys," I shouted, "Al is sizing up fat women in his Plumpers magazine."

Everyone quickly put down their magazine and ran over to Al to see what he was looking at. Everyone, including Al burst out laughing.

"Yes boys, it's true", Al confessed, "I do enjoy the site of a naked big-boned lady."

Everyone continued to laugh as we all got back to our seats. We were all close friends that shared a table full of junk food and a king's ransom in skin-books, while we rocked out to a bit of CCR; life doesn't get any better than that.

"It's too bad we didn't have a couple of beers," Rod said, "Hey Greg, I thought you said you have us covered for tonight?"

Without saying a word, Greg reached into his sleeping bag and pulled out a large bottle of wine. Immediately, all the Altar Boys in the shed recognised it as being the wine that our priest uses for the Eucharist.

"Holy Shit, Greg!" Rod exclaimed, "That's church wine!"

We all looked at each other bewildered as Greg said, "Yeah, the priest never pays us for our services, so I figured one bottle of wine is not going to kill him."

We all started laughing again and Al spoke up, "Right on Greg, I haven't been to mass since Easter, so hand over the bottle, that I may taste ever-lasting life and fill me boots with the blood of Christ."

We all knew that this was sacrilegious and that we were probably all going to hell, but we couldn't help but laugh as Al gulped downed the first mouthful. We began passing around the bottle but we were abruptly interrupted by a knock on the door. We quickly scrambled to hide the wine and skin books and when Paul finally unlocked the door; in walked Snots.

"What are you doing here this late at night Snots?" I asked, "It's 9:30 in the night, you should be home."

"I heard you guys built a shed," Snots said, "and I just wanted to see it before I go home."

Snots had a quick look around, took a couple of candy off the table and headed on back out the door.

"See you tomorrow guys," he said as he walked away.

"Hey, maybe one night me and snaggletooth could sleep out in the shed with you guys?"

We all just looked at each other before Paul finally answered, "We'll let you know Snots, maybe you can sleep out one night but not snaggletooth; he'd only stink up the entire shed."

We all laughed as Paul locked the door when Snots left. "We need to build a trap door in the floor or wall tomorrow boys," Rod said, "To hide away our skin-books and booze."

Once the coast was clear, the boys pulled out the skin books and once again started passing around the bottle of wine.

Over the next hour or so, we were all having a good time drinking the wine and telling jokes until suddenly there was another knock at the door. I could tell by the loudness of the knock that he had to be Dad. Rod quickly grabbed the remaining half bottle of wine and stashed it behind the couch. I opened the door and Dad walked in holding a six-pack of beer.

"There's nothing on that T.V. tonight," he complained. "Jason and Jennifer are gone to bed for the night, so I decided to pop out and see if you boys wanted to join me in a beer?"

The boys and I just looked at each other dumbfounded as Dad opened his six-pack and handed each of us a beer. He sat in my chair so I just took a seat on the floor. Everyone opened their beer proudly and Dad raised his bottle and said, "You all did good work today boys, cheers to you and this nice shed that you've built and for Christ's sake, don't say anything to your parents about me giving you all a bottle of beer."

Everyone laughed as we took a mouthful of beer. I couldn't believe it; we were actually sharing a beer with the Old Man!

"So, what are you fellows up to tonight?" Dad asked.

"We are not at much," Al said, "just listening to a few tunes and having a chat."

Dad reached for a liquorice on the coffee table and immediately spotted one of the skin books sitting on the table. He picked it up and asked, "What's this?"

My heart went up into my throat and I thought we were all going to be killed, but Dad just skimmed through the pages and put it back on the table and said, "Better not let your Mother see that, keep it out of sight."

We all looked at each other, totally amazed that he didn't get upset.

"So Al," Dad joked, "how are you doing with girls in real life, or is that the only kind you can get...........in a magazine?"

We all laughed and finally Al answered, "To be honest, I'm not doing too well on the girl front there Georgio; I haven't had a date in a year."

Dad just shook his head and retorted, "Wow, that's rough buddy, I know of some Catholic Priests who can't go that long without a bit of tail!"

Once again, everyone in the shed burst out into a fit of laugher. "I can bring you out one of Jennifer's stuffed animals, Al," Dad continued, "If that will help you make it through the night." The laugher continued as Al sat there embarrassed.

"Now, what's this I'm hearing about you guys pounding the shit out of Howie the other evening?" Dad asked.

Again, we all looked at each other and nobody knew what to say. "From what I hear," Dad continued, "You all pissed in an empty flask and got Howie to drink it."

With that, Dad let out a loud laugh and guzzled down a mouthful of beer.

"Then you guys all jumped him and beat the crap out of him; serves him right I suppose, he's an idiot just like his father."

Dad's tone was getting a little more serious.

"You know," he said, "I've never advocated for violence, but there comes a point when you can't be pushed any further. I watch what goes on down there in Lahey's field and for the most part, they are all a decent group. Everyone except for Howie; he is the one rotten apple in the bunch. You boys did the right thing by ganging up on him, but make sure you keep an eye out for each other. He's going to be looking to get you alone and get you all back one at a time.

It took teamwork for you to get him and it's going to take teamwork for you to protect each other. Just like today when you built this shed; everyone had a job, everyone knew their part and all hands got along and look at the result… A dandy little shed built in less than 24 hours. As you get older, you will learn that the five of you can accomplish a lot if you look after each other and stick together. Now, I'm not saying that you shouldn't have any more friends but believe me when I tell you that work-friends and different colleagues that you will meet throughout your lifetime will never be as solid as you boys are today. The way that you guys came together today to build this shed, and got together the other evening and kicked Howie's arse, is a testament to your friendship. So you boys can take comfort in the fact that you can look at anyone of your four Buddies and know that you can trust them and depend on them with your life. I've always said that I would much rather have four quarters, than one hundred pennies."

Dad finished off his beer, stood up and walked towards the shed door.

"I must head back into the house and have a nap," he said. "I have to pick your mother up at the snack bar at 3 A.M. Brian, I will have to come get you around 3 o'clock to come into the house, just in case Jason or Jennifer wakes up while I'm gone to pick up your mother."

"No problem," I said as I watched Dad walk out the shed door.

"Hey Georgio," Al shouted jokingly, "Next time you visit our shed, bring a dozen beer and don't cheap out with a six-Pack."

Dad just laughed as he walked away and shouted back, "Go to sleep Al, and try not to get all the pages stuck together in those skin books!" We all laughed and finished off our bottle of beer.

I locked the door behind Dad and sat back on the chair where he was sitting. The boys turned the radio back up and went back to their skin books and laughing but I was really taken back by what Dad had just said. Although I was the youngest in the shed, I think I understood the most about the point he was making. I looked around at my four buddies or "four quarters" and I decided to join in on the fun and felt grateful for the bond that existed between us.

I stood up, took a huge mouthful of beer and shouted at the shed, "I christen thee the *'Miners Cave'* as a tribute to all of our Grandfathers who worked in the Bell Island Mines." The boys all yelled and cheered as we officially adopted the new name Miners Cave for our beloved shed.

We continued to tell stories and laugh throughout the night but as it got later and the wine kicked in, everyone began drifting off to sleep. I was the last man standing and I lay there in my sleeping bag, browsing through one of the magazines. I looked at my watch and it was 2:15 A.M. It was no sense going to sleep because Dad would be here shortly to get me to come into the house while he goes to pick up Mom. Plus I was feeling really hungry and the junk food left on the table wasn't going to cut it. I needed something with real sustenance. I decided to sneak into the house and order me a free feed from Dwyer's.

Now, it's one thing to call an old lady and disguise your voice, but it is something entirely different when you do it to your Mom. I hated calling the snack-bar and ordering food on the weekends, because Mom would always answer the phone and I thought for sure that she would recognise my voice on the other line.

You see, I got this idea last year when Mom came home from work one night with a big bag of food. She said that someone phoned in an order about 2:30 in the morning. Mom and Mrs. Dwyer prepared the huge meal but by the time 3:00 rolled around, nobody came by the Snack-bar to claim the food. The restaurant was getting ready to close for the night and since they already had the food bagged for pick up; Mrs. Dwyer suggested that Mom go ahead and take the food home for her and Dad. So, every once and awhile, I call the Snack-bar on nights when Mom is working, about 30 minutes before it closes for the night. That way, they can't simply leave the food for another customer at a later time when no one comes to claim the food that I ordered. When I call the restaurant late enough, and nobody picks up the order; Mrs. Dwyer tells Mom to take it home with her, free of charge.

The only problem with this little plan is that if Mom or Dad ever found out about it; Dad would definitely kick my arse for stealing, and rightfully so. I picked up the receiver of the telephone and held a dish towel over the mouth piece, trying my best to disguise my voice. There was also the stress of listening to Dad, snoring in the very next room. We only had one corded telephone in the house and it was in the living room, adjacent to Mom and Dad's bedroom, where Dad was presently sleeping. I had to talk low enough so that Dad wouldn't wake up, and with a bit of an accent so that Mom couldn't tell that it was me.

I dialled the number and like clockwork, I could hear my Mom's voice, "Hello, Dwyer's Snack-bar, how may I help you?"

I cleared my throat and with my best impression of a drunken old man, I placed an order for a three-piece fish and chips, onion rings and a Pepsi. Mom took my order and instructed me that it will be ready in 20 minutes and the total cost was $14.39. I thanked her and assured her that I would be there to pick it up in exactly 20 minutes.

The timing of my call couldn't have been better because the moment I hung up the phone, I could hear dad fumbling around in his bedroom. I quietly turned on the T.V. and wrapped a blanket around me on the couch. When Dad appeared from his bedroom, I could see that he was surprised to see me and asked, "What are you doing in the house, I thought you were sleeping out in the shed with the boys?" I told him how I was getting cold and I didn't want to sleep on the floor and decided to come into the house.

"You might as well stay in now anyway", he said, "I have to leave in a few minutes and go pick your mother up for the night".

We sat there for the next few minutes watching T.V. until he finally got up and left the house and went outside in his car. I waited with patience, eagerly anticipating Mom's arrival with her bounty of hot, greasy goodness. When Mom and Dad arrived home, I peeked out through the hallway and I could see that Dad was holding a large brown bag, which could only mean one thing; Tonight I would once again feast like a King. Mom walked into the living and was surprised to see me.

"What are you still doing up," she asked, "It's 3 o'clock in the morning?" I told her how I was spending the night in the shed, but I got cold and a headache and came back into the house.

"You poor baby," she said, "Here, you and your father can share this fish and chips and onion rings that someone ordered and didn't pick up."

She laid the feast on the coffee table and got us a couple of napkins before she headed into her bedroom to get into her pyjamas. Dad and I tore into the food; it was piping hot and delicious. I sat there stuffing my face and eyeballing Dad. If I had known the old man was getting in on this, I would have ordered a couple of cheeseburgers to go with it. By the time Mom returned to the living room in her pyjamas, Dad and I were finishing of the last of the onion rings.

"You boys don't have that gone already," she asked in amazement, "My sweet virgin Mary, I'm living with a bunch of vultures."

Mom sat down next to Dad and the three of us shared a quick laugh.

"Well," I said as I stood up from the couch, "Now that the food is all gone, I shall retire to the bedroom. Goodnight to you all and hold all my calls." I walked to my bedroom as I could hear my Mom giggling in the back ground.

The next day was Sunday and as I woke up, I was surprised to see that the skies were so cloudy and heavy. It hadn't really rained in weeks but you could see that sometime today, we are really in for a downpour. I got dressed, brushed my teeth and ran out to the Miner`s Cave. I skipped breakfast, as I was still full from last night's feast. I woke up the boys and convinced them to give us a hand with our morning chores.

Once we left the shed, Paul noticed the gray sky and commented, "Looks like rain later today boys, this might be a good day to get Dad's wood sawed up and packed away."

With that I could see Al's facial expression change. There was no way you were getting Al to give up his day sawing and packing up wood.

"I have to go home boys for breakfast", he said, "I'll be back in about an hour to help you with the wood." We all chuckled as Al jogged away; we knew that we wouldn't see him anymore today.

We finished our chores in the barn pretty quickly and returned to Dad's enormous wood pile. My God there was a full winter's burning right here just waiting to be cut up and packed away. "Well," Paul sighed, "Might as well get going, the quicker we start, the quicker we'll finish."

`That's a stupid attitude to have 9 o'clock on a Sunday morning,` I thought to myself as Paul handed everyone a pair of white cotton gloves.

We all knew our jobs, because we performed this ritual every year. Rod loaded the big, heavy sticks of wood onto the wood-horse and continued to feed it ahead, as Paul sawed off 1 foot long, junks with the chainsaw. Greg and I would take turns grabbing the junks of wood and packing them into the woodshed. Any junks that measured bigger than 8 inches diameter were tossed aside and would later have to be split in two. Thank God the boys were there to give us a hand because when it's only Paul and I, it's twice as hard and takes twice as long.

As we spent the next while toiling away with this mindless

task, I couldn't help but daydream about the little beauty that I had encountered at Long Harry. I simply could not get her out of my head. I could still picture he long curly hair and piercing brown eyes. She was a beautiful vision who was destined to take up permanent occupancy in my Happy Place. Does she live on Bell Island? Will I ever see her again? All I had were questions without any answers.

My daydreaming was interrupted by the sound of the chainsaw coming to an abrupt stop. We were about an hour into it and the Chainsaw needed to be refuelled. Greg and I had kept pace with the boys, as every single junk of wood was packed neatly into the shed. About 10 feet away, there stood about 20 large junks that would have to be split with an axe. All in all, we were making good progress and I certainly appreciated the boy's help.

While Paul was refilling the chainsaw with oil and gas, Dad took that opportunity to come out to us and check on our progress.

"You're getting 'er done boys," he commented, "Good job, another couple of hours and you'll have it all conquered."

We all stood there proudly. We liked to please the old man, and believe me, he wasn't the easiest to please.

"Hey King George," I commented, "How about coming out of Windsor Castle long enough to give us a hand. Those bigger junks are starting to pile up and they're not going to split themselves!"

The boys started to laugh at my joke. I knew of course that Dad was inside helping Mom prepare Sunday dinner, but still, if there was any way of shaming him into giving us a hand; that would mean less work that Paul and I would have to do later.

Dad walked into the woodshed and retrieved his axe. He kept it as sharp as a razor and it weighed a tonne. As Paul started the chainsaw, I watched Dad off to the side, splitting the pile of big junks. I could watch Dad split wood all day. What aim, what precision, what concentration and determination, but most of all, what pure brute strength. With one mighty blow he would split those huge junks right down the middle.

As he swung that heavy axe over his head you could see his giant bulging arms, massive shoulders and rippling back force that axe deep inside the wood. Dad may not have had a bodybuilder's physique, but let me tell you, in his hayday; George Hickey was no one to mess with. Years of hard labour had made him exceptionally strong and I watched in amazement as he split those huge junks as easy as a hot knife slicing through butter. He finished the huge pile, wiped the sweat from his brow and handed me his axe.

"Now my Son, are you satisfied? Put my axe back in the shed for me," he said, "I'll come back out after dinner to split the next pile."

As Dad walked back to the house, the boys just stood there in awe at what they had just witnessed.

After another 2 hours of steady sawing and packing, Paul finally shut off the chainsaw to give his arms a rest. He had been sawing wood continuously for more than 3 hours, only stopping long enough to refuel. Not too many 14 year olds around that could keep up Paul when it came to work; then again, there weren't too many 20 year olds around that could work like him.

We were now about three quarters of the way done and as we all stood around admiring our progress, Mom yelled to us that dinner was ready and asked if Rod and Greg would like to stay for Sunday dinner. The boys quickly accepted Mom's invitation and we all walked into the house and washed up.

Jason and Jennifer were already at the table eating and the smell of oven-roasted chicken and beef and fresh vegetables filled the air. We were all starving since we had worked so hard all morning without breakfast. I asked Mom if we could each take up a plate and go back outside on the picnic table. Mom agreed and before long the four of us were sitting at the picnic table with a huge plate of hot dinner all smothered in homemade gravy. All I could think about was poor ole Al; his certainly missed out on this. Mom walked out to the picnic table with 2 large glasses of fresh milk and quickly returned to the house to retrieve 2 more. The moans of delight came from everyone as we filled our bellies with Mom's Sunday dinner.

"You know Brian", Greg said, "Sometimes I don't think you or Paul realizes how good you guys got it. Just look at these four tall glasses of milk. This is about a full carton of milk that your Mom just gave away. I bet you don't even know how expensive milk is, or the last time you guys had to buy milk. The same goes for pork and beef and chicken and eggs. This is all very expensive and yet you guys have your deep-freezer stuffed full with different fresh meats."

He was shaking his head in amazement as he said, "Man, I hope you guys appreciate what you have, because I can promise you, not all the families on Bell Island are sitting down to a meal like this every day. If I had gone home to dinner today, do you know what I would be having? Fries in the oven or maybe a peanut butter sandwich. I'm not trying to rag on you guys or nothing, but all I am saying is that you guys are very lucky."

Greg went back to eating his meal and I really thought hard about what he was saying. He was absolutely right, and to be honest, I did think that all families ate like we did. We didn't have a lot of money, but there always more than enough food to go around and I couldn't ever recall in my lifetime being hungry. I guess that since I've never experienced feeling cold or hungry, I wasn't sure how those less fortunate may live. As long as I can remember, we always had an abundance of food and heat.

I remember last Christmas, visiting some of my friend's homes and it felt pretty chilly inside their houses. I mean, it wasn't freezing; but you certainly needed a sweater on to feel comfortable. I was beginning to realize that these homes were heated by electric heaters and in the dead of winter when it's minus 20 outside, electric heaters are simply not going to cut it. You could come to our house on any bitter cold night in February and Dad and Paul and I were usually going around the house with no shirt on. The heat from our wood stove kept our small house warm and cozy even on the coldest nights.

I remember one night, someone left the butter out on the

kitchen table and it actually melted because of the heat from the wood stove. Many a winter's night, I can recall sleeping on top of the blankets because it was too warm to get underneath them. One cold night Vince was visiting and he joked that it was so warm in our house that a snowman was outside banging on our kitchen window, shaking his fist, shouting "Turn down the heat ya bastards!"

On a cold winter's day, heat was everything; when you could come in out of the cold and stand next to the blazing wood stove, it didn't take long to get the chill out of your bones. We would take the lining and vamps out from our winter boots and our gloves and hats and lay them next to the wood stove and they would be toasty warm for the next time when we wanted to go outside.

I began to better understand why Dad had created all these chores for us. I always figured that he liked to punish us, but maybe he wanted us to experience the fruits of our labours. I already knew the satisfaction of eating vegetables that we had grown with you own hands, as well as heating our home with wood that we cut last winter. Now I was seeing that even the pigs and cows that we helped look after, would bring that same level of self satisfaction, once we butchered them later this Fall.

From now on, instead of complaining about, and trying to avoid my chores, I will think about those out there who sometimes go hungry and don't have enough money to heat their homes. I'm not sure if he realized it, but Greg really opened my eyes; and for that, I will always be grateful and more appreciative of everything we had.

We all finished out meal and I encouraged the guys to follow me back inside and once again fill their plates. They all did so and we sat back down at the picnic table with our second offering.

We finished our meals and we were all stuffed to the gills. Nobody wanted to go back to sawing wood, what we really needed now was a nap, but Paul insisted that we get it finished.

He started the chainsaw and just like that, we were right back at it. After about another hour, I was very pleased to discover that we were nearing the end and there was only one log left on the ground. I knew that Rod must have left this log until last because it was the biggest of the lot and he would undoubtedly require help lifting it onto the wood horse.

When Paul saw how big the log was he turned off the chainsaw and set it down on the ground and grabbed the big end of the log. Rod grabbed the other end and although both guys struggled, they managed to lift it off the ground and walked it towards the wood horse. I guess, that with the anticipation of almost being finished, I got a little over excited because while Paul and Rod were carrying the large log, I snuck up behind Rod and dropped his track-pants and underwear down around his ankles. Greg immediately let out a loud roar of laughter and once Paul realized what I had done, he was forced to drop his end of the log laughing. Rod quickly dropped his end of the log as well, as he scrambled to pull his pants back up.

"Hey Rod," I shouted, "You didn't do a very good job of wiping your arse; you got a couple of dingle-berries dangling from your arsehole!"

Again the scene erupted into laugher but it was drowned out by the sound of Dad yelling from the front porch step as he shook his head with disapproval. By the time Dad reached us, the boys had the log picked back up onto the wood-horse and Paul began sawing the huge log. Dad got his axe and began splitting the big junks and Greg and I continued packing the wood in the shed.

Before we knew it, Paul had all the wood sawed up and Dad was splitting his last junk. After he finished, Dad handed me his axe, thanked the boys for all their help and made his way back to the house, laughing to himself and uttering the word "dingle-berries."

What an example of perfect timing; just as we finished up with the rain started. I was so happy to have our new shed as a place to hang out, especially on rainy days when it felt like prison to be barred in the house. Take today for example, it's Sunday which means Dad has gone inside to pull off one of his famous Sunday afternoon naps on the couch. Now usually Mom would make all the kids go outside and play while Dad sleeps, but because it's raining, Mom is left with the daunting task of trying to keep Jason and Jennifer quiet while Dad naps.

As everyone in our house had learned, one of the worst things you could possibly do is to wake up the old man during one of his Sunday afternoon power naps. If you were to wake him, he would be cranky as hell and inevitably find you a chore to do to keep you busy for the rest of the afternoon. How many Sunday afternoons did we spend in the house, tip toeing around the sleeping bear, trying not to disturb him.

On Sunday afternoons, Mom also liked to catch up on the laundry and in the winter or rainy Sundays; she could not hang the clothes out on the line because it was too cold or wet. Since we didn't own a dryer, Mom made a makeshift clothesline in the living room from one corner to the other. So on a Sunday night, if the weather was still bad and you were forced inside, you spent the night watching *The Beach Combers*, followed by *The Littlest Hobo*. We only had two television channels available to us; C.B.C. and N.T.V., so this provided us with a very limited program selection. I can't even count how many rainy and winter Sunday nights I had to sit at home and watch *The Beach Combers* with a wet pair of Dad's bucket underwear hanging over my head. So as you can see, normally, poor weather on a Sunday was like a prison sentence, but now all that would change because we had our shed where we could all hang out and stay warm and dry.

We all headed over to the Miner's Cave to escape the rain and for a much deserved sit-down break. As we sat down to relax, we began thumbing through some of the skin-books.

"Well," Rod said, "At least that's all the wood taken care of for this year."

Paul just looked at me and laughed. "It might be all the wood for you and Greg," I said, "But Paul and I will have to cut down twice as much as this for next year."

I could tell that Greg was sceptical of what I had said and he asked, "Why would you need to cut twice as much?" I explained to him that for every load of wood that we cut and brought home; we cut an identical load for our Pop Hickey.

Neither Rod nor Greg's families burned firewood, so although they helped us cut up the wood once we had it home, they never participated in, or fully understood the process of going and cutting down trees for firewood.

"It's true," Paul added, "Believe it or not, what we did here today is the easy part; the real work is going up into the woods and getting it."

The boys just sat there looking puzzled. "Yes," I reiterated, "let me tell you guys what real work is all about."

I tossed my skin-book back down on the coffee table, got comfortable in my chair, and started my story.

"First of all, we only cut down trees in the winter time because you have to go so far back into the woods that the paths are knee-deep in bog and water. So we wait until the winter when all the bog and water is frozen solid enough so that a horse and cart can walk on top of it. The winter is also preferable because the weather is not too hot and there are no mosquitoes in the woods during the winter. Of course during the winter, Paul and I are in school, so Dad waits for Saturday and Sunday for us to go into the woods." I had their full attention.

"Let me make one thing perfectly clear; I hate going into the woods and cutting down trees. Most kids, like yourselves, look forward to the weekend so that you can sleep in and relax a bit, after a long week of school. Not us, no Sir, Dad has us up bright and early Saturday mornings to start our day. He wakes us around 5 A.M. and instructs us to get breakfast, while he heads off to the barn to fetch the horse and cart. We quickly eat breakfast, get dressed and head outside," I said shaking my head.

"Buddy, there is nothing in this world that can prepare you

for the sharpness of the North-East wind at 5:30 A.M. on a frosty February morning. It cuts right through you, and if you weren't fully awake by now; you can be damned sure that you were awake once that wind hits your body. We run over to the shed and retrieve the chainsaw and axes as Dad comes back to the house with the horse and cart. You have to understand, it's not even daylight yet and I am already half-froze to death." The boys look at one another, not sure whether to believe it.

I continued, "We load the gear onto the cart and climb on ourselves. Dad keeps a brim-bag of hay packed for the horse to munch on, after we reach our destination. There are also a couple of woolly sheep-hides for us to sit on to keep our arses warm for the long trip. The only place that you are allowed to cut wood on Bell Island is way up in Lance Cove, on the other side of the Island. As we head off, we have to stop for Pop Hickey along the way, who is usually waiting for us with his axe in one hand and a thermos of hot tea in the other." I look at each of them to make sure they are listening.

"After we pick up Pop on Murphy's Lane, we cut through the Sports field and take the dirt road up behind the arena, straight through to the Trade School. Every now and then, I jump off the cart and run a long side it, just to keep warm. Once we pass the Trade School, we face the long and windy Wack Road. By now, it is getting daylight and the wind can literally take your breath away. Along the Wack Road we pass Franko's bar and shortly thereafter we reach our destination."

I continued, assured of their full attention, "The only good thing about actually reaching the wooded area was the fact that it was a heck of a lot warmer, with all the big trees protecting you from the wind." I continued to describe the scene.

Once we reached the wooded path, we began seeing some familiar faces of other folks from around the Island who braved the elements every Saturday to get their share of the free firewood. We knew all the players, as over the years we had built a friendship with our fellow lumber jacks. There was Uncle Stan

Hickey; Pop's brother with his two grandsons. Next, came Mr. Jim McCarthy and his two sons, followed by Mr. Bill Hibbs and his family. There was the entire Jackman family and finally Mr. Ed Thompson, with a couple of his sons.

Everyone stops by to say hello and talks about how cold it was before finally dispersing off into their secret spots in the woods. Dad brought us to a nice run of black spruce and quickly untackled the horse from the cart and tied him to a tree, a safe distance from where there would be falling trees. He gave the horse his bag of hay, started up his chain saw and began cutting down trees. Every time he cuts down a tree; Pop, Paul and I would chop the limbs of it with our axes and load it onto the cart.

Dad would cut the trees down so fast that we would all each have our own tree to limb and carry. After a couple of hours, we all stopped for a drink of water and a quick sandwich. It always amazed me how whenever one group would stop, almost everyone else would stop and come and check on your progress.

After a short break, everyone would get right back at it. What I always liked the most about being in the woods in the middle of the winter; was how fresh, crisp and clean the cold air was. There's not a breeze in the woods but the air is so pure that you can smell someone smoking a cigarette from a half mile away, or when someone lights a small fire, to boil their kettle for a mug up.

"With the four of us hard at work, it doesn't take long before we have the cart loaded down with one damned fine load of wood. But we are only half finished, because now we have to cut another load of wood for Pop," I pause for emphasis so the boys could take in the huge scope of the task.

I tell them that it would have been too late to get the load home today, so we just cut it, limbed it out and piled it up against a huge stump. We would come back tomorrow morning to get Pop's load. When Pop was satisfied that there was a good load of wood on the ground for him, we would put all the gear up on the cart of wood, hook the horse to the cart and start our long journey home.

"If you thought coming up was long, going home is even longer because now the cart is loaded down with wood and the horse has to take his time and walk home with the heavy load," I said.

On the way home, I would usually use the time to tell Pop a couple of jokes such as: 'what do farmers and homosexuals have in common? They both get shit on their rubbers!'

"Pretty soon we reach Pop's house and let him off the cart and then we ride home to our own house," I continued.

Once we arrived, Paul and I would unload the cart of wood and pile it up against the woodshed, while Dad unhooked the horse and walked him over to the barn. The next morning Dad would wake us up around 8A.M. There was no need to get such an early start on Sunday as we would on Saturday, because Pop's wood is already cut and ready to come home. All we need to do is ride up and load it on the cart. We don't pick Pop up along the way on Sunday, because it only takes about 20 minutes to load the wood onto the cart and there is no need to disturb Pop for that. I said, "By the time we returned to Pop's house with his wood, he would usually come outside to meet us and helps us unload it. He would thank Paul and I for helping him out and sometimes he would give us both a dollar each for all the work."

As I finished my story I could see that both Rod and Greg were both quite impressed with the amount of work that goes into cutting your own firewood.

"Why is it," Greg questioned, "That nobody steals your grandfather's load of wood that is left on the ground over night?"

I myself wasn't sure of that answer, but Paul spoke up and said, "Because every man is on the honour system and can be trusted. Every person up there knows how hard each man works and would never dare steal wood from each other. Don't get me wrong, there are a few arseholes around the Island who would love to get their hands on a free load of wood, but they are smart enough to know that if they were ever to get caught at it, by the likes of a George Hickey, Bill Hibbs or Ed Thompson; then they would most likely get pounded into the ground."

You could hear it in Paul's voice, how proudly he spoke about the men that sawed their own wood. Even as I was telling the story, I couldn't help but notice that Paul was sitting there, listening intensely with a little smile on his face. Make no mistake about it; Paul loved in the woods just as much as Dad.

As for me, I didn't care if I ever saw another stick of wood again and would rather spend my Saturdays and Sundays sleeping in and watching cartoons.

8

St. John's Adventure

During the next couple of weeks, we spent the days doing chores, playing ball and swimming at Freshwater, while we spent the nights on Lahey's field and sleeping out in the Miners Cave. The summer quickly rolled by and before we knew it, we were nearing the end of August. In only one week, school was scheduled to reopen.

Today was one of my favourite days of the year; the day the whole family goes to St. John's to buy our new school clothes for this upcoming school year. We only got to go to St. John's about twice a year; once for school supplies and again for Christmas shopping. So on this day, the entire family all piled into the Dodge Dart and drove down to the Ferry. After Dad parked the car on the Ferry, *The Katherine,* we all went upstairs and waited for the Ferry to leave for its 20 minute run.

I grabbed a window seat and looked out over the crowd of people standing on the dock, enjoying the beautiful sunny day. I imagined that we had just boarded some foreign luxury cruise ship and we were getting ready to set sail for someplace exotic.

Holy Crap, wait a second, from the corner of my eye I thought I spotted a familiar face on the dock! I jumped out of my seat and moved down to the back of the Ferry for a better view. Jesus, Mary and sweet Saint Joseph, it was the pretty girl that I had met in Long Harry. She was standing on the dock with a gray-haired gentleman. I tried waving to get her attention but it was of no use, she couldn't see me. I decided to run down to her and at least find out her name. As I started down the stairs, the ships horn sounded and I could see that the Ferry was already pulling up its ramp. I was too late, so I ran back upstairs to catch another glimpse of her. Ah, yes, it was definitely her and she was simply beautiful.

As the Ferry pulled away from the dock, I kept walking towards the back of the Ferry so that I could keep her in my view as long as possible. Suddenly it hit me; the way to her was to find out who that grey-haired gentleman was! I raced back to my seat and tried to point him out to Mom and Dad, but we were moving so fast that now they were lost in the crowd. DAMN, DAMN, DAMN, once again I missed out on my opportunity to find out who this girl was. To say that I was pissed off was an understatement, but at least I knew that she was still on the Island.

When the Ferry pulled into the dock at Portugal Cove, our family piled back into the car. Jennifer was sitting on Mom's laps in the front, Dad was driving and the three boys were in the back. I was still pissed at myself for not pointing out the girl and her companion on the dock to Mom and Dad sooner. While we drove in the Cove Road on our way to St. John's, Jason was launching a farting assault on the rest of us from the back seat that was so bad, that we had every window in the car open. Normally, I would have found this hilarious, but now I was just too upset to even laugh. I vowed that starting tomorrow; I will comb the streets of Bell Island until I find out who this mystery girl is.

I then made the grownup decision that I couldn't let this unfortunate event spoil my trip and realized that I should consider myself lucky for having the opportunity to see her again. The thought of her once again ended my sulky mood and bought a smile to my face. "Who's shitting in their clothes back there?" Dad shouted, as Jason unleashed a second wave. "Give it up or you can get out of the car and walk to St. John's!" This made me laugh and pretty soon we were all laughing, joking and having a great time.

Driving through St. John's was like a whole new world to

me. Bell Island was so small and we didn't have any of the amenities like McDonald's, Dairy Queen or Burger King. St. John's had sidewalks and traffic lights and movie theatres. They had museums, malls, and car dealerships. Everything was paved and men dressed in suits and ties, carrying briefcases, driving expensive cars as they rushed around with important things to do.

You never realized how much you were sheltered from the real world by living on Bell Island until you took a visit to St. John's. Last summer on a visit, I saw a black kid for my very first time. Can you imagine, being 11 years old before you see your first black person? I loved the city and as soon as I graduate from high school, I planned on leaving Bell Island and heading for St. John's.

We reached the K-mart on Torbay road and our family exited the car and entered the building. This was a far cry from the small clothing stores on Bell Island. I quickly started rummaging through the merchandise, looking for new clothes. I knew from past experiences that Georgio had little to no patience when it came to shopping and it would only be a matter of time before he blew a fuse. Mom was helping Jason and Jennifer try on different outfits, while Paul and I fitted ourselves with new jeans, tops and footwear.

After about an hour or so, we were all satisfied with our new finds so we all headed up the checkout counter to purchase our merchandise. What a relief it was for me to be getting new clothes. Most of my clothes were hand-me-downs from either my brother Paul, or my cousin Rod. While I didn't mind wearing their shirts or pants, I refused to wear their underwear. I don't care how little you may have in life; a guy should never be forced to wear another man's drawers; especially ones with old crap stains embedded into them.

The lady rang in all our clothes and as she tallied up the prices, she smiled and announced that our total was $489.63.

"Ah for Christ's sake," Dad shouted as he reached for his

wallet, "that's more than what my car is worth."

Dad reluctantly handed over the cash and as the cashier girl handed us our bags of merchandise she smiled and politely said, "Thank you and have a nice day." Dad put his change in his wallet and walked away mumbling, "How can I have a nice day when I feel like I just got mugged?"

We all put our merchandise in the trunk of the car and headed off to Mom's favourite store, Pipers. Now that we have our school clothes purchased, we have to get our school supplies; exercise books, pens, pencils, erasers and even some crayons and coloring books for Jennifer. Mom loved going to Pipers and always advocated that someone should open a Pipers store on Bell Island.

"After Pipers can we go to the Mall," I asked "and have a look around?"

Dad just glared at me through the rare view mirror, before shouting, "No Moneybags, we can't go to the Mall. After we finish up at pipers, I have to pick up something at Canadian Tire and then we are going to McDonald's for something to eat, before we head back to Bell Island."

Dad liked to spend the least amount of time in St. John's as possible. As we drove through the city, the three of us in the back were joking and tormenting each other and this was only periodically interrupted from time to time when Dad would roar, "Shut up and keep it down back there, I'm trying to drive."

Every now and then, when we got too loud, he would suddenly slam on the brakes and as we lunged forwards, he would reach back with his hand and take a smack at all 3 of us together. The whole while Mom was just sitting there in the front seat smiling, with Jennifer perched in her lap, but with every passing minute that we spent in St. John's, you could see Dad's blood pressure rise a little more.

After we finished at Pipers, I actually looked forward to going to Canadian Tire. This was one of the few stores that Dad liked to go. He could wander through the aisles for hours at Canadian

Tire, in awe of all the new, shiny tools. Yes Sir, for my Dad; Canadian Tire was his Happy Place as he slowly strolled through each tool aisle, fondly stroking and holding different tools and carefully putting them back on their shelf. I always wished that I had enough money to stock Dad's tool shed with whatever tool he wanted.

Dad never asked for much but a new tool for Christmas or Father's Day would always bring a smile to his face. Most of Dad's tools were old and used but he still took great care of them. We went inside the store but Mom decided to stay out in the car with Jennifer and enjoy the sunny day, rather than go prancing around in a tool store. Paul and Jason headed over to fishing rod section to check out the new poles, but I followed Dad to the bathroom section. He wanted to secretly purchase Mom a new vanity and mirror for the bathroom. We looked around until he found the one he liked. I was surprised to see the high price tag and I pointed out to Dad that this particular vanity and mirror was over $200.00.

"That's okay," Dad said, "Your Mother never asks for anything, but she mentioned she would like to have a new vanity for the bathroom; so I'm getting her a good one. Happy wife, happy life, you might want to remember that Brian."

Dad was a pretty impatient man with a short fuse, but he always had patience for Mom. This little trip to Canadian Tire actually calmed him down considerably and now it was time to head off to McDonald's.

When we walked into the doors of McDonald's, you could feel the excitement in the air. Dad got us all situated at a table and asked what everyone wanted. We told him our order and Paul accompanied him to the service counter to help him place the order and carry it back to the table. A few minutes later, Paul and Dad returned to the table, each carrying a huge tray of food. They sat it down on the table, and we dove into it like vultures. I grabbed my Big Mac, fries, coke and sundae before Jason had a chance to eyeball it. At one point, I dropped fry but before it even hit the floor, Jason snatched it up with lightening speed, like a Grizzly bear grabbing a salmon that's jumping upstream.

What a real treat it was to have McDonalds for lunch. I looked around the restaurant as I was eating my food. I wanted to soak in all the ambiance and I decided that this must be how the other half lives. I couldn't even fathom having so much money that you could eat lunch at McDonald's everyday and dine out for supper every night. Yes Sir, St. John's, in all its marvel and mystic was surely the place where I would hang my hat in the future.

We left McDonald's and started our drive back to the Ferry for Bell Island. Along the way, the mood was sombre. For us kids, we knew that we wouldn't be coming back to St. John's for at least another four months to do our Christmas Shopping. Dad was in the driver's seat, mentally calculating just how much money he had blown today and Jennifer was fast asleep in Mom's lap.

I listened in on the conversation that Dad and Mom were having about money. "I wish I could win enough money so that I could quit my job at the hospital and concentrate on farming and livestock," Dad said.

"Don't get me wrong; I'm thankful enough for having a Government job but being cooped-up in that hospital for 8 eight hours a day makes me feel like a trapped rat. I miss being outdoors, working with my hands, doing my own thing without the hassle and bullshit of co-workers, bosses and Unions."

It was true, Dad loved being left alone. As long as I had known him he was a hard working, solitude man who enjoyed being left alone. He would often say that he chooses to live on Bell Island for the seclusion and privacy. "Bell Island is an Island within the Island of Newfoundland," he would comment. "That's how much I love being alone; I live on a secluded Island, within a bigger secluded Island".

I knew that Dad would never last in a city like St. John's. Houses built on top of each other, no land to call your own; Dad would crack up within two months. Still I felt bad for him, because I knew how much he wanted to work outside in the fresh air, so I tried to lighten his mood.

"Go on Dad", I said, "If you won the lottery tonight; you would still show up for work, first thing the very next morning. Besides you just can't quit, you have to put in your two week's notice!"

Dad just laughed as he looked at me through the rear view mirror. "Yes", he said sarcastically, "that's all I would be worried about after winning the lottery, is putting in a two week's notice at work. If I won the lottery tonight, I would call work tomorrow and tell them that in about TWO WEEKS, they are going to begin to NOTICE that I haven't been coming to work! That's the only notice they're getting from me."

We all laughed at Dad's sarcastic reply and before we knew it, we were boarding the Ferry and on our way back to Bell Island.

When we arrived home, Paul and I helped Dad unload the trunk of the car and bring all the bags into the house. Mom went inside the house with Jennifer and Jason and started packing everything away. We saved the vanity set for last because up until now, Mom still hadn't seen it, or knew anything about it. Dad and Paul both carefully lifted the vanity out of the trunk and carried it into the house. I couldn't wait to see Mom's reaction to her new gift.

Dad and Paul placed the vanity gently on the kitchen table and Dad said, "Here you go Mary, a little gift from me and the kids."

Mom's eyes welled up with tears. Other than Christmas, Mother's Day and her birthday; she wasn't used to receiving many gifts.

"Oh George, it's beautiful," she said, "I can't even imagine a prettier vanity." Dad unpacked the vanity from its cardboard and bubble wrap container and he immediately ordered Paul to run out into the tool shed to fetch his tools so he could install the new vanity. Dad carried the vanity into the bathroom and I picked up the huge, empty cardboard box and handed to Mom and said, "Here you go Mom, it even comes complete with a brand new door mat for your porch floor." I could hear Dad laughing from the bathroom as he overheard my joke.

After about two hours, Dad and Paul had finished installing the vanity and he yelled out for everyone to come and see it. He had it wired to the bathroom light so now when you turned on the bathroom light; it also turned on the 3 new lights on the vanity. It had two full sliding mirrors and behind the mirrors were storage spaces for make-up, hair brushes and other toiletries. The new mirrors and lights really brightened up the bathroom and it was not hard to see that Mom was very pleased with Dad's work.

"It's absolutely beautiful George", Mom said, "I can't wait for Mom and Dad to come down to see it." Mom slid open and closed the mirrors as she marvelled at all the storage space. After everyone took turns getting a closer look at the new vanity, we all exited the bathroom and sat down for supper at the kitchen table.

While we were eating supper, Mom was going on and on about her new vanity. "I'll have to get you to paint the bathroom walls and ceiling now George before Christmas," she said, "To make our new vanity really stand out."

As Mom continued obsessing about her vanity the thought of Christmas filled my mind at the supper table. I always loved Christmas, as it is the wonderful time of the year when everyone seems happy and at peace with one another. As Dad always said, "Christmas is that one magical time of the year when you welcome people into your home, that you normally wouldn't allow in your yard!" I loved everything about Christmas; the gifts, the food, the visitors, the break from school but most of all, that warm, loving feeling.

A couple of days before Christmas; Dad, Paul and I would cut down a couple of Christmas trees and bring them back to the yard and stand them up in front of the living room window so that Mom could pick out which one she liked the best. Then we would bring it in the house, stand it up in a small bucket of water and tie it to the corner of the living room. The only part of decorating the tree that Dad was responsible for was putting on the lights. My God, how I dreaded helping Dad untangle the huge ball of lights and putting them on the tree. What always amazed me was that every year the same problem seemed to occur.

We would finally get one set of lights untangled and then plug them in to make sure that were working. Once we were satisfied that they were all working, we would painstakingly place the lights on the tree and once we plugged them in while they were on the tree; they would never work. Then we would have to take them back off the tree and try every single light, one at a time, until we found the one broken light that was preventing the entire string of lights from working. We would replace that light, put all the lights back on the tree, plug it in and again it wouldn't light up! Oh the language as Dad cursed the tree and on more than one occasion, I witnessed Dad throwing the entire tree across the living room in frustration, because he couldn't get the lights to work! Although you had to walk on eggshells around the old man for the rest of the evening, it was still pretty funny to watch. We had a Christmas saying at the Hickey household; Every time a Christmas Tree gets thrown across the room, another Angel gets his wings!

Once we finally had all the lights placed on tree in working order, Mom would usually decorate the tree. We never had a Christmas tree skirt, so Mom would place used Christmas wrapping paper underneath the tree to make it look pretty. After the tree was all decorated, Dad would lift Jennifer on his shoulders and let her place the Angel on top of the tree.

When Christmas Eve came, we would all get dressed up for Christmas Mass. The whole house had that unmistakable Christmas smell of the evergreen tree in the living room, and homemade raison bread baking in the oven. I loved Christmas Mass Service and the church would be filled to rafters with standing room only. During the service the congregation would sing hymns such as Silent Night and Oh Come All Ye Faithful.

When Mass ended, we would take turns shaking everyone's hands and wishing each other a Merry Christmas. As everyone returned to their vehicles the sound of the church bells ringing filled the air. It was a magical time indeed.

When we arrived home, we quickly got Jason and Jennifer settled away in their beds with the promise of Santa Claus's arrival. Dad would pop his fresh, 20 pound turkey into the oven on a low heat and let it slowly roast throughout the night. Nothing says Christmas Eve like the smell of a turkey in the oven and a ham boiling on the stove.

Early the next morning around 4 A.M., Jason and Jennifer would wake up Paul and I so that we could see what Santa had left us under the tree. The first thing Paul would do is throw a couple of logs into the woodstove to get the heat around. Pretty soon everyone was busy unwrapping gifts and Dad and Mom would usually appear and join in on all the Christmas wonder.

My God, it seemed like there was a king's ransom in toys with everything from a new game of checkers, to new hockey sticks and a couple of dolls for Jennifer. The first thing I always went for was my stocking because I knew it was filled with candy and grapes and fruit and shelled nuts. The only time of the year that we could ever afford grapes was around Christmas time and I looked forward to those juicy treats every year. After all the gifts were open and everyone was satisfied with what they had gotten, Dad would make everyone go back to bed for a couple of hours.

When we awoke again around 9 A.M., we would all go right back to our Christmas toys. I can't remember ever eating breakfast on Christmas morning. We were all too excited and besides we were having a giant turkey and ham with cooked dinner around 12:00, and nobody wanted to spoil that meal with breakfast. At dinner time, we all sat around the table, in front of perhaps the best turkey dinner known to man. We bowed our heads and said Grace and then we all raised our wine-glass, with just a taste of Dad's homemade wine, and said Cheers and Merry

Christmas.

Christmas turkey dinner at my house always resulted in two things; one was a fight between me and Dad for the turkey neck, and two was a fight between Jason and Jennifer over the wishbone. After dinner, Mom and Dad cleared away the dishes as the kids went back to our toys.

Later in the afternoon, the whole family would meet up to our Nan Dalton's house. The house was filled with Aunts and Uncles and cousins and with enough gifts to choke a horse. I passed old Jerry in the Hall in his pajamas and I shouted, "Merry Christmas Jerry". He just walked away and said, "Yeah", as he retreated to his bedroom with his bowl of cheesies.

All the men would sit in the kitchen and drink beer and liquor as all the women sat in the living room, eating chocolates and chatting. Nan was in the living room with the other ladies, showing them the $600 watch that Vince got her for Christmas. Now here was a woman who never left the house, so why he got her such an extravagant gift was beyond me.

"Nice watch Nan." I said to her.

"Thanks Love," she replied, "although I don't know where I will ever wear it. I guess I can wear it this summer when I'm out in the yard feeding the Blue Jays," she laughed. "Or perhaps I'll model it the next time I'm having high-tea with the Mucky-Mucks!"

Vince was in the kitchen having a drink with his brother, Uncle Dick. When two of these guys got together for a drink, you could be assured that stories from the Bell Island Mines were the main topic. In fact, the more they drank; the further back in the mines they went. You never knew what would come next; a funny anecdote about "Johnny Smith" who snuck three bottles of homemade blueberry wine into the mines and went missing for two days, or a tragic tale of one of the many mining accidents that resulted in some unlucky family losing a loved one. Whatever the story was, it was a safe bet that I was right there listening attentively, soaking it all in.

"Have a Drink," Vince would say to me as he poured himself

another.

"No thanks," I replied, "I'm only 11!" After a full afternoon of drinking, Vince would usually retire to his bedroom for a nap while everyone slowly begin to make their way home for supper.

As we returned to our own home for supper, I knew exactly what we would be having before Mom even served it up. Potato salad, turkey, ham and sliced tomato and that was alright with me. For the rest of the evening, it was pretty quiet. Not a lot of visitors on Christmas Day, as it was sort of an unwritten rule that Christmas Day and Christmas Night were for families.

However, we all knew that starting tomorrow; Boxing Day, the house would be a flood of visitors of family and friends and even the occasional harmless drunk, just looking for a drink as he was staggering his way home. I never one time witnessed my Dad turn anyone away for a Christmas drink. I've seen people come into the house, get drunk and loud and Dad have to put them out on their arse, but he would welcome them back again next year.

It occurs to me that during the Christmas Season, everyone seems to find their Happy Place. People are merry and any old scores are soon forgiven and forgotten. Even people's houses look brighter with their Christmas trees and lights in the windows and outdoor Christmas lights. Every house, including our own is lit up like Las Vegas. Usually Dad is screaming at us about his high electric bill and complains if one of us forgets to turn off the bathroom light. However, during Christmas, Dad doesn't even care that the old wheel on the outside electric meter box is spinning so fast that you can sharpen a pair of skates on it. It is truly a warm and magical time of the year. As we were getting settled in for the night, I was looking forward to the next couple of nights when Dad's friends would visit, because this would indeed be fun times.

The next day, Boxing Day, we would usually pay a visit to our Nan and Pop Hickey's. Nan Hickey's house was a lot different than Nan Dalton's house. At Nan Dalton's you could run and play whereas Nan Hickey's house came with a very specific set of rules. First and foremost, "Don't Touch Anything."

Nan and Pop Hickey loved to play cards too; it wasn't uncommon for us to all sit around the table and play a hand of cards. Pop would tell the same joke every Christmas.

"When I was your age, we didn't get gifts for Christmas. In fact, when you woke up Christmas morning, the only way you would have something to play with, was if you were lucky enough to wake up with an erection!"

God Love 'em, Nan and Pop Hickey could sit at the kitchen table, drink tea and play cards all day long. They constantly had one of those old flat-bottom kettles on the wood stove. They called their kettle "the old Slut." I can still hear Pop say to Nan, "Put the old slut on Doll, I get's a cup of tea." Poor old Nan burned the arse out of more kettles than I can even remember.

After a couple of hands of cards and several glasses of whiskey, Pop began reminiscing about the mines and he asked Dad if he could remember a Mr. Hubert Jesso, who lived just off Main Street.

Dad thought about it for a minute and replied, "No, I can't recall that name, I think he moved on before I was born."

"Anyway", Pop continued, "Mr. Jesso came from the West Coast of the Province and he found work in the mines as a maintenance man. He was very good with his hands; he could weld, and he was an excellent carpenter and a very hard worker. He was a big man, around 6 feet 2, 260 pounds. Because of his big stature, he liked intimidating some of the smaller men and it didn't take long before he set his sites on me. He had a wife, who also came from the West Coast. She had jet black hair and a dark complexion; she spoke in broken French and was a real good looking lady. Hubert was very jealous over his wife and some of the other men in the mines would give him a hard time about that," he chuckled.

"Any chance he could, Hubert would make jokes about me in front of the other men, trying to get me to fight back. Of course, I wasn't about to do that, as he was almost a foot taller than me and about a hundred pounds heavier. Whenever we worked nightshift, the miners would get off an hour before the maintenance crowd. Rumours were starting to service that during nightshift, certain miners from dayshift were paying Hubert's pretty wife a visit, late at night while Hubert was working. Hubert would become irate at even the mention of this, which made him even nastier and more difficult to work with." Pop remembered.

"Hubert kept on digging at me and kept it up to the point where it was now a daily occurrence and I could no longer take it.

So, one November morning, just before daybreak, I was walking home from work and marveling over the fact that sometime throughout the night, we had our first snow fall. Everything was clean and beautiful and white and as I walked out Main Street to get home, I passed right along Hubert's house. I looked in Hubert's yard and noticed the 2 inches of fresh snow that blanketed everything. I looked around to make sure no one else was coming, then I opened Hubert's gate and I slowly walked backwards right up to his front porch. Then I carefully retraced my steps back to his gate and onto Mainstreet," he said with a mischievous grin.

"Now there was a perfect set of footprints in the snow, leading from Hubert's house, looking like maybe last night the Missus had a visitor. Well Buddy, I don't know what happened after that, but Hubert never showed up for work the next night and a day or two later, I heard that he packed up the Missus and moved back to the West Coast of the Province!" Pop sat there killing himself laughing as Dad just shook his head in disapproval.

Later that night after we returned home, we usually got the first wave of visitors. Friends of Mom and Dad's would come in with their guitars and accordions and no sooner were the drinks being poured that the live music was blasting and feet were stomping. Paul and I would watch all of this from our bedroom door and I would stand at the ready, anticipating my call. Before long, I would hear Dad yell, "Brian, get in here."

I knew I was up as I ran eagerly to the living room in my new Christmas pyjamas. I knew what Dad was looking for; he wanted the same thing every Christmas. As I entered the living room I could see that everyone was feeling no pain and Dad ordered me to give the boys a few Elvis tunes. As soon as I started belting out a few lines of *All Shook Up,* one of the men accompanied me on the guitar and before I knew it, I was performing a live concert.

I could see Mom was clapping and enjoying herself and that only made me try harder. She never participated in the drinking, but she loved to see her boy singing Elvis. Mom was the one who got me into Elvis, as we would spend hours listening to her old Elvis records. Before I knew it, Mom handed me a white bath towel and I wrapped it around my shoulders like a cape and suddenly I was Elvis, live from Hawaii.

In true Elvis fashion, I ended my show with *Can't help falling in love with you,* then I tossed my towel out to my adoring Mother, took a final bow and ran back off to my bedroom. Everyone clapped and cheered as I left the living-room and Paul would be waiting for me in the bedroom, shaking his head and saying, "There's something wrong with you buddy, you're not all there."

That's pretty much how it went for the next couple of nights over Christmas. People dropping in with musical instruments and the music, booze and laughter filling the air. For the entire 12 days of Christmas, people partied and celebrated, right up until old Christmas Day. It wasn't uncommon for at least one person to get drunk and fall in on the Christmas tree or trip in the bathroom and end up in the bathtub. Last Christmas after a night of drinking and music, one of my Uncles, in a drunken stupor, thought it would be funny to show Paul and I how he can catch one of his farts on fire.

He dropped his pants and sat back on the couch and you could see the shit stains in his underwear, which was funny enough. But when he held a lighter to his ass and farted, he set his graffiti underwear on fire. For the rest of the night the whole house smelled like scorched dingle-berries and arse-juice.

My Mom and Dad always looked forward to going to a New Year's Eve Ball every year. This was really the only time that my Mom would go to a bar. They would get all dressed up that evening and leave us with a bunch of instructions. Paul would be in charge and as soon as they would leave for the evening, they would tell Paul to lock the door behind them and not to let anyone in throughout the night. Dad would call home several times that night to make sure everything was ok and, in particular, that I was behaving.

Last New Year's Eve, I convinced Paul to get into Dad's homemade wine and before midnight, Paul was passed out on the couch, drunk as a skunk. Jason and Jennifer were already long asleep, so I stayed up and watched TV. Suddenly the phone rang, and when I answered it, I could hear a lot of noise and loud music in the background. "Hello," I could hear Dad shouting on the line, "Is that you Paul?" "Yes it's me," I said and Dad shouted, "Happy New Year!"

I could tell by the sound of his voice that he was having a few beers and laughed to myself. "Did Brian give you any trouble tonight?" Dad shouted.

"No, he was pretty good," I answered. "That's good," Dad responded, "Anyway, me and your Mother will be home in a couple of hours, don't let the woodstove go out and I'll see you when we get home."

I hung up the phone and again laughed at Dad's mix up, as I looked over at Paul on the other couch, still sleeping. I managed to get him off the couch and into his bed and I stayed up and watched TV and kept an eye on the woodstove. Later that night, Mom and Dad walked into the house with streamers and wearing Happy New Year's hats and horns...

"Eat your supper and stop daydreaming!" Dad's voice yelled at me as I was startled from my fantasy world. My mind had once again drifted off and I had just spent the last 15 minutes, sitting at the dinner table, day-dreaming about Christmas.

"I don't know what I'm going to do with you my Son," Dad complained. "Why is it that you can't focus on what's going on in front of you? Where do you drift off to?"

I just shrugged and continued eating my supper as I glanced over at Mom who was still looking through her brochure that had come with her new Vanity.

After supper, Paul and I walked down to Lahey's field where the crowd was already starting to gather. It was the end of August and you already needed a light jacket on in the evenings. We all knew that summer was nearly over and that next week we would be on our way back to school.

Lenny built a little fire and as usual, we all sat around it, talking, telling jokes and sharing stories. Suddenly a car pulled up to the field and out walked David Brazil and his good friend Charlie Bown. Both these guys were good East End boys and they had just finished their 3rd year at Memorial University. They were both in their early 20's and regulars to Lahey's field; although they hadn't been around too much this summer because they were both enrolled in the summer semester at MUN.

Everyone was happy to see the boys as they greeted us all with handshakes and pats on the back. They only stayed for a short visit because they had a couple of University textbooks that they were dropping off to Lenny. I wished the boys could stay for a longer visit but sadly I guess they had outgrown us and they were busy preparing for their futures.

David was an aspiring lawyer who lived and breathed politics. Although only a young man; he already served on over a dozen committees throughout Bell Island. In past summers,

David would assign us different Political Cabinet Portfolios. The evening fires would serve as our caucus table and "Premier Brazil," as he liked to call himself, would hold caucus meetings right here on Lahey's field.

"Ok Randy," David would say, "Since you like to drink and party so much, I'm making you Minister of Tourism and Recreation. Now do what you can to bring more tourists to our Province. Morris, since you are always out on the water fishing and down on the wharf illegally hand-potting, we are going to make you the Minister of Fisheries. Now get on the ball Morris and do what you can about all the foreign overfishing. Paul, since you spend so much time over in the barn shovelling shit, I'm making you Minister of Agriculture. We need to bring agriculture more to the forefront, so make something happen. Consider partnering with someone in the private sector and initiating a giant green house, perhaps in the Mt. Pearl area!"

Pointing at Snots, he said, "Since you are enrolled in the Special Ed program in school, you can be Minister of Education. Now I know you can hardly read or even tie your own shoes for that matter, but Snots do what you can to ensure all Newfoundlanders and Labradorians are getting the best education possible. Andy, since you are the only one of us who drives his own car, you can be my Minister of Transportation. I want you to deliver an analysis on the cost of putting a bridge or tunnel from Bell Island to St. John's." David said this as seriously as any desperate leader in a crisis.

"And Brian," David continued, "Since your father is a janitor in the hospital, I'm making you my Minister of Health. Now do what you can to keep the costs of healthcare down while attracting more doctors and nurses to the province. Rod, Greg and Snaggletooth, I am going to keep you three in my back-benches for the time being, although your roles are equally important as my Ministers. You will be known as my back-bench dream-team and I will refer to you as the Trinity........."

He paused at Snaggletooth and crinkled his nose as he caught a whiff, "The Father, the Son and the Holy Shit your breath stinks!"

We all got a great kick out of David's antics and we would actually sit around the fire on summer nights of past and hold political debates and caucus meetings. Of course everything that was being said was not so much a comment on the current political landscape, as it was getting a jab at one of your buddies.

Usually Lenny would be named as Speaker of the House and the heated debates would incite. Snaggletooth, who thought he was being smart, would start off by saying,

"Mr. Speaker, I would like to stand before this Honourable House and congratulate my friend and colleague Mr. Brian Hickey for being named the Minister of Health. However, Mr. Speaker, it is common knowledge that his father is the head janitor at the Bell Island hospital and therefore his appointment to the Department of Health reeks of scandal and political patronage".

Everyone started clapping loudly and shouting "Shame, Shame."

Naturally, I felt an overwhelming sense of obligation to defend my Dad's good name, so I yell, "Point of order, Mr. Speaker?"

Lenny then silenced the other Members and said, "The Chair recognizes the Minister of Health on a point of order." So I rise and say, "Thank you Mr. Speaker for the point of order, and I just wanted to point out to my honourable colleague the fact that my Dad works as a janitor at a hospital has absolutely nothing to do with my promotion as the new Minister of Health and the only thing here that reeks, is the Honourable Members breath."

"Furthermore, I take great exception to his comment, in fact, if we as elected Members were given Cabinet Portfolios based solely upon what professions our parents have chosen; then I submit the honourable Member, Snaggletooth, would have been sworn in as the Minister of Social Services, since his Dad never worked a day in his life!"

Everyone laughed and cheered and shouted, "Hear Hear" as

Snaggletooth turned blood red, knowing all too well that on this particular occasion he was outsmarted by a much younger political adversary. I sat back down by the fire, folded my arms, soaked in all the laughs and cheers and needless to say, no further comments were made concerning this Minister of Health!

These types of lively debates, which were really a battle of wits, were a lot of fun and thanks to David Brazil; a lot of us younger kids were well versed in the proceedings of our Provincial House of Assembly and really had our thumb on the political pulse of what was happening around our Province. *David Brazil currently serves as our Provincial Member of the House of Assembly for the proud District of Conception Bay East – Bell Island.*

Charlie Bown was David's good buddy and he was enrolled in the MUN school of Music and academically, he was nothing short of a genius. He was extremely polite and friendly and it was rare to see him without a book in his hand. He was always smiling and his positive attitude, amazing outlook on life and jovial way, were very contagious. He had just successfully completed his 3rd year of MUN with a perfect 4.0 Grade Point Average and was well on his way to becoming something great. He sang every weekend in the church choir and had the voice of an angel. It seemed like every challenge that was put in front of Charlie; he would happily take on and surpass everyone's expectations.

He was a hero to many of us younger kids, as he had taught many of us how to swim down at Freshwater. There was never any doubt that Charlie Bown would do something great with his life.

No Sir, there simply weren't enough fine individuals in this world with the same character, charisma and heart as that outstanding young man.

In October, 2000 my Mom called me on the phone at my apartment in St. John's and informed me that Charlie Bown had passed away at age 37 after a courageous battle with cancer. He had touched the lives of everyone that he met and he was a symbol of everything that was good and pure in people. I was honored to have known him and I personally believe that this world wasn't good enough for such remarkable human being.

We all waved goodbye as David and Charlie drove away and the jokes and insults resumed. The mood got a little more serious however, once the discussion turned towards school reopening next week. This year we will be losing Lenny, Gerald, Randy and Morris who all just graduated from St. Michael's High. Lenny and Gerald were moving on to university, whereas Morris and Randy are contemplating moving to Ontario to find work. As for the rest of us, we were discussing who we will have teaching us this year and what we could expect.

I would never say it out loud but I was looking forward to school reopening. I had thoroughly enjoyed my summer holidays, but I enjoyed school as well. Who knows, this year may be the big year that I finally get a girlfriend. At the very least, I am planning on kissing a girl this year. I will be 13 years old in November and as soon as I become a teenager I have made a promise to myself that I will once again, take the puck-in-the-head for the team and finally ask a girl out on a date. The thought of it is both frightening and exhilarating but I felt in my heart that I was ready to take that massive step and transition into immortality.

My thoughts of school and girls were suddenly interrupted by the site of someone coming staggering across the meadow. It was Randy walking home from the Skin-Hut, which was odd because it was barely getting dark and this was very early for him to be leaving. He walked up to our fire, with an open beer in his hand and struggled to sit next to Lenny.

"What's up Randy," Lenny said, "Early for you to be leaving the Skin-Hut."

Randy, who was visibly intoxicated, took a mouthful of beer and said, "Yeah, early night for sure. Hey guys, do any of you know Broad-Back Betty?"

Of course, we all knew who Randy was talking about. She was a regular to the Skin-Hut and like most of the girls who frequented that shed, her reputation preceded her. She was a chain smoker and a heavy set lady. She would get drunk every Friday night at the local Legion and brag to all the men how she was a triple threat; she was a dancer, a model and a singer. I always thought that by triple threat she meant that at any moment, she was likely to have a heart attack, take a stroke or shit her pants!

"Well," Randy continued, "Morris called me at home tonight and said, 'Dust off your elephant gun Buddy, we are going on the hunt.' So I grabbed a shower, picked up a dozen of beer and head on over to the Skin-Hut. Morris and I had old Broad-Back Betty over there tonight for a couple of beers and a game of strip poker." Sadly, this came to as no shock to anyone.

"Anyway," Randy continued, "Morris and I had Broad-back down to her bra and panties, when all of a sudden, there was a loud knock on the door. We didn't answer it until we heard a man's voice yelling 'Betty, are you in there?' Betty's jaw dropped and she quickly got dressed. She was panicking and crying as she told us that it was her husband knocking. We all got dressed and when we finally opened the door, there was Broad-Back's husband standing there crying like a baby, begging her to come home to him and their children. He came into the shed and sat down, still crying and bawling. I grabbed my smokes and my last two beers and got the hell out of there."

We all just sat there dumbfounded; I couldn't believe what I was hearing.

"So this guy caught you and Morris in a locked shed with his wife?" Al asked. "He must have been pretty pissed off."

Randy lit up a cigarette and responded, "I don't think he was as mad as he was upset. He was really crying and begging old Broad-Back to come home with him."

Again, I was shocked. I couldn't even imagine my Dad having to go out during the night, looking for my Mom to come back home. Then again, if your wife is out, doing who knows what, with two other guys, is she really worth even going after? What has to happen in a marriage, for a husband to have to knock on the shed door of a couple of teenagers, who are playing strip poker with his wife, and beg her to come back home to him and their kids?

I shuttered at the thought of either Mom or Dad being like that and as I stared off into the fire, I began to realize how grateful I was for coming from a somewhat 'NORMAL' family. Sure, there were too many chores in my opinion, but at least we were together and we weren't in want for anything. Admittedly, I can recall times when I wished we had more money, a cooler car, a bigger house, nicer clothes and more expensive bikes but who knows what sort of trouble that could lead to.

I had this friend named Jesse in my class whose Dad was a dentist and his Mom was a nurse, so their family was extremely financially well off. Two years ago, I went to Jesse's house after school and I thought I was visiting Graceland. You could fit our whole house into this guy's living room. He had his own bedroom equipped with his own T.V., telephone and stereo system. We were looking through his hockey card collection in his room and he had his stereo turned up really loud. Three different times, his Dad walked into the bedroom and politely asked Jesse if he could please turn down his stereo.

When his father walked in the fourth time and asked to turn it down, Jesse snapped and threw his hockey cards on the floor and shouted, "No Dad, I'm not turning it down, can you stop coming into my room and acting so stupid?"

I sat there in total disbelief at what I had just witnessed. What was even more unbelievable was the fact that Jesse's Dad just walked away without doing anything. When he left the bedroom, all he said was, "I think you need a time-out Jesse."

I couldn't believe it; Jesse just called his Dad stupid to his face and now his Dad is talking about taking a time-out. I shuddered as I imagined what Georgio would do if I ever called him stupid. I'm pretty sure he would kill me and bury my body in the manure pile behind his barn. I didn't even know what a time-out was.

The last time I experienced a time-out was when Dad took a time-out from kicking my arse! I have to tell you that when I first walked into Jesse's room and saw all his prized possessions, I thought that he had to be the luckiest kid in the world. However, when I heard the way he spoke to his Dad, I lost a lot of respect for him.

A few months later, Jesse was rushed to the hospital after he overdosed on pills, trying to kill himself. Thank God he didn't die and shortly afterwards, his family moved to St. John's so that he could avail of some kind of substance abuse treatment. Although he is the same age as me, his life was already messed up with drugs. I remember at that time asking Dad, "Why would a kid who has everything possibly want or try to commit suicide?"

He was popular and well liked, he was great at sports, he got good grades and all the girls adored him.

Dad looked at me and said, "There's more to life than money my Son. Those parents were working so hard to give their son all these expensive material things, but they forgot to give them what is really important - their time and attention. Kids today get too much and do very little to earn it." He paused as he said this.

"I know that you and Paul don't get everything you want, but everything you do get, you damn well work for and deserve it. This makes you appreciate it more and learn the value of an earned dollar. When that young fellow overdosed on drugs, I don't believe he was trying to kill himself, he was crying out to his mother and father. Please God, his parents can get him on the right path now and give the boy what he needs."

I sat there watching the fire dance over the embers and listened to my friends talk and laugh. I thought to myself, thank

God that Dad cares enough about us to give us a curfew and a set bedtime on school nights. I thought about how grateful I was that neither Dad nor Mom was out getting drunk at bars every night or working 10 to 12 hours every day so that we would never get to see them. Yes, I was grateful that there was a hot supper on the table every evening and we had a Dad who cared about us enough to ground us or give you a pat on the shoulder or a swift kick in the arse when we needed it.

All the little antics and harmless pranks we were getting away with under Dad's watchful eye, only begged the question, what kind of trouble would I have gotten into if Dad wasn't there to keep me on the straight and narrow? I'd probably be in jail by now or maybe even worse. If I've learned anything from Dad it was that a little bit of fear can go a long ways. At the end of the day, I may complain about my chores and my hand-me-down clothes and my weak-ass teabags, but I was happy, healthy and loved

Throughout the last couple of days before school reopened, I spent the days riding my bike all around Bell Island, trying to find my beautiful brown-haired girl. I searched high and low looking for any signs of her or her bike or even the gentleman who was with her on the wharf at the beach that day. I rode passed the post office and the library and even the supermarket, hoping to catch a glimpse of her. Of course, I spent most of my time riding back and forth Long Harry, where I originally spotted her but alas, she was gone forever.

This was a lesson that I would surely carry with me for the rest of my life. In the future, if I ever encounter someone as lovely again, I will boldly tell her how I feel and let the chips fall as they may. Besides, life is far too short to worry about rejection, so from now on, if I see something that I want; I am going to go after it.

The first day of school was here and as Mom was getting everybody's breakfast ready, Dad was busy yelling what chores he expected to be done when we get home from school today.

I think everyone was sad that we are all going back to school except for Mom and me. Dad is going to miss having us do his morning chores for him. Paul never did like school and was going to miss being outside all day. Jason and Jennifer are going to miss sleeping in and staying up late playing and watching T.V.

Mom however, is very excited that we are going back to school. She had her hands full all summer, God love her, watching out for us and now she can get a much deserved break from her four little nuisances. I too am looking forward to school and am relishing the idea of a possible first date, followed by a first kiss followed by whatever else might happen.

I've learned a lot about myself this past summer. For the first time in my life, I really took the time to listen to both my Grandfathers and was lucky enough for them to pass on a little bit of history and wisdom to me. I managed to deal with my first heartbreak as Rod and Karen are still a happy couple and I'm ok with that. I dealt with the passing of a familiar face who had sadly drowned.

I still have many unanswered questions, but I have plenty of time to try and figure out things for myself. I was keen enough to once again elude a shit-load of backbreaking chores and physical labour and yet still managed to be part of the celebrations and accolades associated with it all. I learned a very valuable lesson about the importance of taking the initiative, seizing the moment and reaching for that brass ring. I may have let that pretty brown-haired girl pass me by, but by God I will never let that happen again.

I learned the importance and value of teamwork and friendship. It's true, if you have a solid group of trustworthy companions; you can pretty well accomplish anything. Perhaps most important, I realized the value and tremendous strength of our family. Just three short months ago, I thought our family was from another planet with all its oddities and seemly backwardness. However this past summer has taught me just how lucky I really am, to be part of such a loving, caring family and for that, I will always be grateful. All and all this summer has been a wonderful, eye-opening and memorable experience. Not bad, I'd say for a scraggly, 12 year old boy from Bell Island, Newfoundland!

9

The Next Morning

The next morning, I looked over at Zachary, Cole and my nephew Spencer and they were all dead asleep in their sleeping bags. The sun was coming up and I could hear the familiar sound of the crows and seagulls squawking on the tree tops and telephone poles. I checked my watch and it read 6:15 A.M. I couldn't believe that I had talked though the entire night. There were two empty wine bottles lying at my feet and the small fire that we had going outside the tent, had been extinguished for several hours.

I looked at Marilee, who was snuggled in the sleeping bag next to me and she was strangely quiet. I knew she wasn't sleeping, but she just lay there very subdued, almost as if she was upset with me. I kissed her on the cheek and said, "Are you okay, Babe"?

She just nodded in an affirmative matter and left the sleeping bag saying, "I'm going to grab a quick shower and then I'll put breakfast on for everyone."

I watched her leave the tent and knew immediately that something wasn't right. I wondered if I had said something too inappropriate, or perhaps some of my stories were forcing her to look at me a little differently. I decided that I would try to cheer her up and I left the tent and went inside the house to cook breakfast for everyone while Marilee was in the shower.

I had the bacon and eggs and toast all going and the aroma quickly filled the house. I looked out the window at the beaming sun and I could tell that today was going to be another beautiful day. Just as the kettle starting whistling, in walked Zachary, Cole and Spencer, still tired from their late night adventure.

I asked, "Did you guys have fun last night?"

The boys immediately started talking over each other, as they all excitingly described in great detail, what their favourite story was from last night.

"I liked the story that your Grandfather told you about working in the mines, it was very cool," Zachary said.

"Me too," Cole added, "Although I preferred the funny story of how you pooped in your pants so that you didn't have to help your Dad plant potatoes". All the boys started laughing.

"Hey Uncle Brian," Spencer said, "I liked the story about you and your friends sleeping out in a tent and drinking wine and talking about girls."

The boys again started laughing and I thought to myself; 'Oh God, over the next couple of years, I'm going to have to keep an eye on my nephew for sure!'

I told the boys to wash up in the kitchen sink as I poured them all a cup of hot chocolate. As I began taking up breakfast, I couldn't help smile and listen in as they reminisced and talked about the stories that I had told them last night. Then as Cole went to fridge to get the milk, I watched as Spencer snuck up behind him and dropped his pants and said, "Look Zach, Cole got dingle-berries hanging from his butt."

All four of us burst out laughing as Cole struggled to pull his pants up. Although it was funny, I made a George Hickey–like roar at the boys and told them never to repeat to anyone outside this house, any of the stories that I told them last night. You know the ways kids are; monkey see, monkey do and the next thing you know the boys are in school trying to drop one of their friend's pants. My God, all I needed was for Child Services to come knocking on my door.

"Listen up," I yelled, "Most of those stories I told you were all made-up and pretend. I better not hear you telling anyone those stories, or worst, acting out any of those stories. Remember, it was all for fun, so we will keep it between us."

The boys all agreed and I laid a plate of breakfast in front of each of them. I yelled out to Marilee and told her that her breakfast was ready.

"Thanks," she yelled back, "Just put it in the oven for me please, I'll be downstairs in a few minutes." So I put her food in the oven and sat down to eat with the boys.

"Hey Uncle Brian," Spencer said, "I have a friend and one time I was over to his house and he showed me his Dad's Skin books."

All the boys starting sniggering and I told Spencer that he was too young to being looking at things like that.

"I know Uncle Brian," he said, "But one girl had gigantic boobies!"

We all laughed out loud until finally I said, "Ok, that's enough about that; eat your breakfast." We continued to eat and I constantly had to make a yell at the boys who continued to recollect things that they had heard last night. Something told me that I was going to regret telling the boys these stories.

Perhaps that's what was wrong with Marilee this morning. Maybe she didn't feel that my stories were age-appropriate for the boys. If that is the case, it's strange she didn't say anything about it last night.

"Hey Uncle Brian", Spencer said, "Can we all sleep out in the tent again tonight"?

"Yeah," Cole pleaded, "That would be awesome."

I finished my breakfast and stood up from the table.

"I don't know boys; I don't have any stories left."

"That's ok," Zach responded, "You can tell us the same stories that you told us last night. Besides, we fell asleep half ways through, so we only got to hear about half your stories."

"I don't know," I said, "We'll see. First of all, I need the yard mowed and raked today and I also need some help cleaning out the basement."

"We'll all help", Cole said, "And maybe when we're finished, we can take a walk up to Long Harry?"

"Good enough," I answered, "After breakfast we will mow the lawn and rake up and clean out the basement. Then we will have lunch and take a walk up through Long Harry. We will have to see about sleeping out in tent again tonight; perhaps the three of you guys would like to sleep out alone?"

The boys all looked at each other and agreed excitingly.

"Ok," Zach said, "we will sleep out by ourselves."

After breakfast, I sent the boys outside to get started on the lawn, while I took care of the dishes. I couldn't help but be a little worried about Marilee, who still hadn't come downstairs for breakfast yet. Maybe she was tired from being up all night and decided to take a nap. But I had a sinking feeling that for some reason she was upset with me. I thought, I'd better check on her and walked upstairs. I walked in the bedroom and I could see Marilee sitting there on our bed, going through some old photo albums, while she stroked our cat, who was purring next to her.

"Everything alright?" I asked as I sat next to her.

"Yeah, I'm fine," she sighed, "I just looking through some old photos of Mom and Dad. A lot of those stories you told last night, brought back a lot of memories of Mom and Dad. Dad used to have his own potato garden and Mom used to bake homemade bread just like your parents did."

I gave her a big hug. I felt awful about telling all these stories about my own Mom and Dad, forgetting that Marilee's parents had passed away. I apologized for being so insensitive, as I wiped away a tear that was streaming down her cheek.

"No worries," she said, "I loved your stories. They just brought back a flood of memories and emotions, is all. I'll be fine, I'm just a little tired from being up all night."

I kissed her on the cheek, pushed her back on the bed and pulled her comforter up over her.

"Here you go," I said, "Have a little nap this morning while the boys and I do some yard work. After lunch, the boys and I are going for a walk up Long Harry and maybe you would like to join us."

Marilee just smiled and nodded yes, as I pulled down the

shades in the bedroom window, closed the bedroom door and headed back down stairs.

The boys and I spent the rest of the morning mowing the lawn and cleaning out the basement. We managed to round up four large bags of old trash from the basement, so I threw it in the back of my truck and the boys and I took it to the dump. On the way back, I bought the boys an ice-cream each and when we returned home, I instructed them to stay outside and play while I prepared something for lunch.

"Can we bring our I-Pods outside to play?" Cole asked. I automatically felt my blood pressure rise as I looked at him and yelled, "No, it's a beautiful day, grab your bikes or soccer ball or Frisbee and go play."

Damn video games, I thought to myself as I went inside the house. There is nothing that pissed me off more than to see a kid with a video game stuck in his face on a beautiful summer day. I quickly prepared a couple of hotdogs for the boys and called them in to lunch. They washed up and while they were eating, I prepared a little snack for us to take on our hike up to Long Harry. I could hear water running in the bathroom upstairs, so I knew Marilee was awake. I went upstairs to greet her and I could see that she looked a whole lot better than she did this morning.

"How was your nap?" I asked as I gave her a big hug.

"It was wonderful," she exclaimed. "Sorry I was acting so sensitive this morning," she added.

"Don't worry about it," I responded, "Your sensitivity is one of the biggest things I love about you."

We both headed downstairs and she heated up her breakfast left over from earlier this morning.

After lunch, we all got ready to head out on our hike to Long Harry. Marilee greased up the three boys with sun-screen and I packed a knapsack with snacks and plenty of water for our trip. Marilee grabbed her camera and we all headed on up the road. Along the way, we walked by the house where Marilee lived and grew up. We paused in front of it for a few minutes and she asked Zach, "Do you remember when Nanny and Poppy White used to live there?"

Zach thought about it for a minute and he answered, "I can remember Poppy White, but I can't remember Nanny White very well."

"That's ok," Marilee said, "You were only a small boy when Nanny passed away."

I took Marilee by the hand and we all continued on our journey.

Once we hit Long Harry path and we were surrounded by trees, the smell of all the flowering trees and bushes automatically transformed me back to my youth. I took in a deep sniff and let it out slowly and I told the boys, "You may not know it boys, but you are all living in the greatest place in the world. Just smell that fresh open air and wild flowers."

The boys all paused for a minute and made some sniffing sounds, but I knew they had no idea what I was talking about.

"You see boys; before I started dating your Mom 5 years ago, I lived in St. John's for about 20 years. I swore that I would never move back to Bell Island because I loved the City so much. However, once your Mom and Dad decided to divorce, I dedicated the rest of my life to winning over your Mom's heart. I've chased your Mom for the past 20 years and I was even a guest at her wedding," I said.

"In fact, I danced with your Mom on her wedding day and I told her that, although I'm happy for her, I loved her and I will always be waiting for her." Zach and Cole just looked at me in disbelief.

"Is that true Aunt Marilee?" Spencer questioned.

Marilee just cracked a smile and responded, "Yes, I made your uncle wait an awful long time before I gave him a date. When we attended University together in 1990, Brian used to ask me out on a daily basis; sometimes 2 or 3 times a day in fact. But I couldn't date him because I was with the same boyfriend that I had since I was 15 years old."

"Did you and Brian know each other when you were kids?"

Zach asked.

"No," Marilee responded, "Although we are both the same age, Brian went to St. Michael's School and I went to St. Boniface. It's funny though, because had we gone to the same school, we would have been in the same class because we both graduated from High School in 1990. So, we were both born in 1972, we grew up on this small Island less than 2 miles away from each other, we graduated from High School the same year, but we didn't meet until we both moved to St. John's and started University in 1990. Now how funny is that?"

Marilee let out a little laugh as she pondered the irony of the whole thing.

"Yes," I added, as I kissed Marilee on the cheek. "She made me wait a very long time, but now she's mine and she was well worth the wait!"

We all continued up Long Harry path, stopping from time to time, just long enough for Marilee to get a couple of photos of me and the boys.

"Is this the same Long Harry you told us about last night in your story Uncle Brian?' Spencer asked. "You remember; the story about the pretty girl and her bike."

I couldn't stop myself from grinning ear to ear as I answered, "Yes little Buddy, it was right along this same path, that I saw that pretty little girl and to be honest, I can still picture her in my mind 30 years later."

Marilee pulled away from me playfully and said, "OH, is that right?"

The boys and I got a big laugh out of this as we all stopped for a snack and a bottle of water.

Once we finished out snack, we left the path on Long Harry and followed the cliff side in an easterly direction - which led us right to the lighthouse. We posed for several photos by the lighthouse and then we continued following the cliffs until we reached Fresh water; my favourite swimming area on Bell Island.

Unfortunately, the cliffs are so eroded and caved in that you can no longer get down to the beach area from the top of the cliffs. But we just stood there, looking over the cliffside as I pointed out to the boys where we used to swim. After a while, we left Freshwater and headed up Freshwater path. The boys and I stopped along the way and picked some wild strawberries, just as I used to do 30 years ago. As we left Freshwater path, we hit Quigley's Line and decided to drop into Mom and Dad's house for a visit.

When we arrived, Mom was sitting out on her deck, enjoying the sun and Dad was hosing down his potato garden. It still amazes me how small Dad's Garden had gotten over the years, for now it was only 12 feet long by 12 feet wide. He doesn't even own a horse anymore; he simply ploughs up his garden with his Quad. He says he doesn't need to grow his own vegetables anymore; he only does it because he likes it and it gives him something to do.

Marilee walked over to the deck to chat with Mom, while the Boys and I followed Dad to his tool shed to help him put away his hose. We all made our way over to the deck with Mom and Marilee while Dad ran into the house to bring out a cold beer for us and an ice cream for the three boys. He made another trip for a glass of ice water for Mom and Marilee.

We were all sitting around chatting until Spencer speaks up and said, "Poppy, we all slept out in a tent last night and Uncle Brian told us about all the work you used to make him do."

Dad just let out a loud laugh and said, "Spencer my Son, if our family had gotten paid, based on the work that Brian did when he was kid, we would have been better off on the Welfare!"

Everyone laughed at Dad's joke and I couldn't say anything to defend myself because it was all too true.

After our visit at my Parents house, we all decided to head home. We had been gone for nearly 4 hours and I needed to sit down and take a break. I had forgotten that I had stayed awake all night telling stories and now it was starting to catch up on me.

When we finally made it home, I kicked off my sandals, and sat on Marilee's porch swing. It was still a beautiful evening but all I wanted to do was sit down. I told the boys that they could take their I-Pods out in the tent for a short while, just so I could have some peace and quiet. When I think about it, I guess that why parents allow their kids to play so many video games today because it sort of acts as their babysitter. What a sad concept, I thought to myself. As I was enjoying my little swing on our deck, Marilee came out of the house with a beer for me and a glass of water for herself.

"Thank you so much," I said, as I gulped down the ice cold, refreshing beer. She sat in the swing next to me and rested her head on my shoulder.

"Can you believe it?" She said, "We lived that close together when we were growing up and yet we didn't meet until we were 18 years old?"

I just shook my head and downed another mouthful of beer and said, "Yeah I know, kind of crazy for sure."

Marilee gave me a little kiss on the cheek and said, "Hold my water for me; I have a surprise for you inside. I was going to wait until tonight to give it to you, but I can't wait." She handed me her glass and ran back in the house. I just sat there drinking my beer, wondering what she could possibly have for me. She returned a minute later with something behind her back. I handed her back her water, but she wouldn't let me see what she had concealed behind her back.

"What do you have?" I asked with great curiosity.

"Well," she said, "Remember this morning when I was looking through my old photo albums?"

"Yes," I responded, "What about it?"

She was wearing a smile from ear to ear, so I knew that it had to be something big. From behind her back, she pulled out a photo of a pretty little brown-haired girl standing next to her bike. I was speechless; I couldn't believe what I was seeing.

The amazing thing was that the photo looked exactly like the picture I still carried with me in my mind.

"But......who.......how?" This was the only thing I could manage to stutter.

"It's me," she said, "It's a picture of me standing next to my older sister's bike on my 13th birthday, July 21st, 1985."

Once again, I was flabbergasted. You quite literally could have knocked me over with a feather. After all these years of wondering, the beautiful little girl with the gorgeous brown hair and brown eyes was Marilee.

"As soon as you told that story last night about Long Harry, I knew you were talking about me."

She said, "I remember a skinny, polite boy tying up my front fender with his shoelace and then rushing out of there like his pants were on fire. The truth is, I returned to Long Harry, several times that summer, hoping to see my knight in shining armour again; but you never returned."

I still couldn't find any words and I just took the photo from her hand to stare at it. I'm normally not an emotional guy, but I couldn't stop the tears from streaming down my face as I tried hard to swallow a lump in my throat that just wouldn't stay down. I mean, what are the odds that I ended up with the same lovely girl that I met over 30 years ago? How is it that we have been together for these past 5 years and neither of us has ever mentioned that fateful day in Long Harry? Marilee just grabbed me and gave me a big hug and we just sat there holding each other until we floated away into space.

Then Marilee pulled away from me, stood up and said, "I have one more surprise for you." She reached into her pocket and pulled out on old red shoelace.

Again, my jaw dropped as she handed it to me. I recognised it immediately; it was my red lace that I had taken from my sneaker and used to tie up the front fender on her bike!

Tears streamed down my face; I couldn't believe that she kept that lace all this time.

Today, we have that red shoelace framed and proudly displayed in our home as a constant reminder of just how amazing life can be. I continue to share stories with Marilee and the boys about growing up on Bell Island and spending time with them has truly become My Happy Place....

Manufactured by Amazon.ca
Bolton, ON

34022236R00122